SPIRIT TALKER

SPECIAL EDITION Book 1 of The Seers Series

Theresa Dale

Paper Doll Publishing

ISBN-13: 978-1-989897-10-2
ISBN: 978-1-989897-11-9 (eBook)

For the gifted ones, and for those who've forgotten.

CONTENTS

CHAPTER 1 – FEAR

"But, *why?*"

At four, she knew enough to tense when she said it, because the result could be only one of two things: her mother would sigh and get a faraway look in her eyes while she crafted the perfect answer, or she'd reached her limit and her mother would roll her eyes, muttering something about her "answer well" having dried up for the day. Or worse, giving Shya that look – the one that meant *stop.*

Thankfully, this time her mother took her onto her lap and wrapped her arms around her, and Shya nearly swooned in the warmth of her embrace. But then came to attention, remembering to search for that faraway look in her mother's eyes and straining to see it. It made her mother laugh. She kissed the top of Shya's head.

"Daddy believes in what he can see," she said.

"But -"

Her mother shook her head, her lips on Shya's crown so that she would sense the movement. "It's just how some people are, sweetheart."

"But I *know* there's someone in here," Shya whispered, her eyes flicking to the dark corner, the closet door, the foot of the bed.

Her mother was quiet for a time. Shya moved against her chest as she inhaled and exhaled rhythmically. She perceived her mother's heartbeat against the back of her head and her eyes drooped, some past, pervasive sense of comfort threatening to overtake her completely.

"I know," her mother finally said, her tone as hushed as Shya's had been and the words tangling in her hair like extensions of the faint moonlight that filtered through her bedroom curtains.

Shya twisted around, needing to meet her eyes, and her mother loosened her arms, straining, too. Connecting. Understanding her need. "You do?" Shya asked and then held her breath, already having experienced enough interaction with people to know that they teased and sometimes even lied in order to smooth the truth. Mommy hadn't ever done that – it was why she trusted her so completely! – but she needed reassurance, anyway.

This was important.

Her mother nodded. "I do," she said. Her eyes were luminous in the darkened room, somehow picking up the glow of the night sky and gathering it there, so her gaze was very nearly magical.

"How?"

Her mother smiled. "My mother knew, too. And my grandmother. There is a long line of ancestors that knew, Shya. But we know something else, too: you don't have to be scared."

Shya hiccoughed suddenly as her eyes filled with tears. Her chest had filled so quickly that it shocked her, and the sound escaped her on its own, making her mother giggle. Shya didn't mind; it *was* a funny sound. Besides, the fullness of her chest was what mattered. The fact that others knew. Others like her.

"I believe there are many things that exist outside of our perception most of the time," her mother said, her eyes going to the window dreamily. Shya would remember that statement for the remainder of her life, repeating it in the early years until she understood it fully, and then coming back to it when she needed the solidity of it.

Shya frowned.

"What?"

"I hear them, but I don't see them."

Her mother pursed her lips, nodding.

"Is - was it like that for you and Grandma, too?"

"It was," she tucked a lock of hair behind Shya's ear, her face unreadable, "but then it changed, and we could see them, too."

Shya gasped, but her mother shook her head again.

"I was afraid too, at first, but then it became part of who I was and it stopped being scary."

"Really?"

Her mother nodded solemnly.

"So, will I see them, too?" Shya felt her eyes widen at the thought and shivered a little.

Her mother paused again, rubbing Shya's upper arm with an absently-moving thumb.

"Mommy?"

Her mother met her eyes again. "Probably, darling. But hopefully, it won't be for a long while, and we can talk about it before then, so you'll be ready."

It was so simple, but so fulsome. So perfect. Her mother had a way with words.

"OK?"

Shya relaxed into the warmth of her again, confident enough to let go of the nagging sense of urgency that had nipped at her earlier.

Her mother kissed her forehead, the scent of her lingering in Shya's nostrils intoxicatingly as she lay her down and tucked her in. Whispered, "I love you, sweet girl" into her hair and kissed her again.

Sweet orange, lavender and rosemary. Her mother's nighttime oils were as much a part of her as her voice. Her touch.

Shya would catch them on the air long after her mother stopped gathering her into her lap. And remember her words – the ones that ended up being a lie, after all – "You'll be ready."

CHAPTER 2 – SOLACE

A darkened night
An unlit stair
She left her bed
And found her there

Led by her whispers
Murmurs, fissures
Desperate tones
Spells and wishes

And the voice
That answered back
Was cold and dark
A filtered trap

She stopped inside
The door, ajar
Her mother there
But her eyes far

Affixed on something
Left unseen
Frosting the air
Window glass a sheen

More careful mutters
From Mother's lips
Warm breath a cloud
A sinking ship

And then a gasp
Escaped her, lost
A whoosh of movement
Rough seas toss

A cry escaped
The tiny girl
Mother cried out
Shocked, she whirled

"Shya!" she gasped
Extended arms
Soft, spirit faded
With threat of harm

CHAPTER 3 – CONFESSION

"When did you write that?" Rory's Adam's apple bobbed as he talked, then swallowed.

Shya crossed her arms as she sat back against one of the many hard-backed chairs in the coffee house. Intended, certainly, to cause discomfort and encourage shorter visits, but judging by the constant din of voices, could not stifle dedicated coffee drinkers and laptop starers.

Rory looked up from the page, expectant.

"Uh -" she shook herself lightly, trying to remember. "I don't know. University?"

He laughed. "Which time?"

It set her teeth on edge instantly. Her step-brother could get to her with barely an effort.

She rolled her eyes, grabbing the well-worn notebook.

He laughed again, grabbing her hand in both of his own and forcing her to meet his eyes. "I don't mean to pick, sis. Come on." His eyes twinkled.

She shook her head. Tried to retrieve her hand from his grasp and failed. He raised his eyebrows, giving her puppy-dog eyes. "You don't need to take things so hard, Shy."

She observed him critically, aware all over again of his impossible charm – he was a jogging-pants-wearing, stubble-sporting, bed-headed thirty-year-old, refusing to conform to anyone's idea of "normal," and yet he was entirely handsome. Endlessly captivating. She'd watched others of her sex fall victim to the sway of his very presence, and many of his own, as well.

It was maddening.

He pulled her fingers to his lips and kissed them, successfully disarming her. "You know I'm only joking."

She pulled her hand back and resumed her position, arms folded over her chest as if in an effort to shut out his freakish charm. "Don't treat me like one of your *followers,* Rory."

His face transformed into a mask of mock surprise. "I'm not a cult leader, sis. I just have a lot of frien – oh!" he checked his watch, then stood. "Gotta go. Nice poem, by the way."

She raised her hands in frustration.

He paused after slinging a very metrosexual-looking brown leather satchel that should have been ridiculous with his sweat suit over his shoulder. Shya hated that it only seemed to enhance his inherent intrigue. "What? It's not a date."

She made a face.

"I swear!"

She waved him off. "Whatever."

"We'll talk more about this later, OK?"

"What if," she paused, eyeing neighboring tables and then fixing her green-eyed gaze on him intently, "what if, by the time you have a second for me, it's too late?"

He scrunched up his features in a scowl. "Regardless of what's been," he lowered his voice "*going on,* you can't be in real danger, can you? Physically, I mean?"

She shook her head. "Just consider that whether you believe me or not, Rory, this is happening. And it's changing, and I'm scared."

He sighed, his eyes flicking to the door and then back to her.

His obvious annoyance isn't so charming, she thought with an odd sense of satisfaction. They were very different, both in their degrees of ease with others (in that he was easy with others, and Shya was most definitely not), and in their priorities. Rory's were as plain as the flecks of gold in his brown

15

eyes, but although he was quicker to dismiss those who sought his attention, he remained far more popular. Shya had always thought it was because he demanded it. *Expected* it, really.

She'd never met his father, but was convinced he'd inherited his sense of entitlement from him, for his mother (and her now ex-stepmother) was nothing like her son. She and Shya were far more similar than she and her own flesh and blood! Not that it had made things between them any easier.

Rory adjusted his shoulder strap. "I'm playing basketball with work friends," he reasoned, his eyes pleading with her to let him go. "If we don't have a full team, we forfeit, and... "

"Ugh. Just *go*," she cast her gaze to the window, refusing to watch his face change as he smiled. He was most beautiful when he smiled.

"I'll call you later?" He asked, rather than stated, as though he was asking permission, but Shya knew the question was really about whether he'd be bothered to follow through.

"Sure," she shrugged, her eyes resolutely on the people walking by.

He was gone before she could soften, and she was glad. There was nothing more infuriating than forgiving him just to make sure he would still be around – still be on her side – if she *really* needed him. God knew her father was useless when it came to heart-to-hearts, and though she wished it weren't so as fervently now as she had when her mother had died, her mother remained... gone.

She pulled her agenda out of her bag to check when her shift would start and longed as she always did for something better. Independence, money, relationships. But as Rory was so quick to point out, Shya had seemed to be unable to break up with post-secondary education for far longer than she'd originally intended, even though she'd reached a point where it no longer served her. And to add insult to injury, she'd never even applied for a job she was qualified for, choosing instead to shun commitment – shun acceptance of a *career* – in favor of waiting for the perfect opportunity to knock on her door.

Five o'clock. Good. At least it would be busy, and she could mix and serve drinks until she was ready to fall into bed and sleep until noon.

And that was good, because when she slept, they stayed away.

CHAPTER 4 – LOSS

The weather didn't make sense.

At ten years old, Shya had only witnessed funerals on screens and in stories, but she felt she knew enough to declare the day all wrong. The sun shone bright, but soft, through wispy clouds of pulled cotton, and the sky was a resolute shade of cornflower blue. Not a dark or heavy cloud in sight. Birds sung from every tree, creating a symphony at once chaotic and beautiful, and the large group of gathered mourners chatted animatedly in groups as they awaited the officiator.

Even her father was strange – he greeted folks with a sandwich handshake and a sincere smile that reached his eyes and engaged in conversation. How a man whose usual outlook seemed dull and unexpectant be transformed into a welcoming source of comfort at his own wife's funeral escaped Shya, but she couldn't complain; he had been so attentive to her since her mother died.

Relatives and strangers alike fussed over her as they had at the wake, touching her hair and frowning. Muttering unhelpful things like, "You and your father need to take good care of each other, now," and "Your mother would want you to be happy, Shya." As though a person could manufacture happiness. She watched as her father smiled and knew it wasn't real. The face you showed to others didn't always reflect what was going on inside. She knew that, too. But she'd never separated the two as successfully as others appeared to.

"You never wonder what Shya's feeling," her father had remarked to her mother, more than once.

"It's what she's *thinking* that I wonder about," her mother had laughed in reply.

It was a strange thing to observe others' puzzlement

over her. She felt anything but mysterious! Regardless, she must be different, for she never seemed to slide comfortably into any notch. Her school friends were a mashup of similarly-defined characters: different, but refusing to belong to the established groups of gamers, bullies, cool kids or nerds. The one thing they all seemed to have in common was the refusal – or outright dismissal of the idea – to act a certain way in order to fit in. Instead, they seemed to slump together to watch the other kids as they worked to be the coolest or the smartest... and always, always, to be liked and accepted.

Bethie was who she was closest to, and so she was at the funeral with her parents. Shya raised a hand to her and Bethie returned the wave, her eyes sad, but piercing, even across the casket adorned with a spectacular arrangement of starburst lilies and purple allium. She stuck her lower lip out and Shya fought the sudden urge to sob, her eyes hot and swimming in tears at the mere acknowledgement of how she felt. Bethie's own face crumpled slightly, but then she gave herself a shake and blew Shya a kiss, smiling.

Grateful, Shya smiled, too. Her eyes were already sore from crying. But there was something else that came along with the sadness, and she thought it might help to explain her father's uncharacteristic ease. It was relief.

Watching her mother die had been overwhelmingly sad, but watching her suffer in the weeks and months before her death had been worse. "Agonizing," her father had called it, and she thought he was right. To watch a loved one suffer, helpless to ease their pain, was surely the cruellest torture that one could be subject to. And Shya felt it keenly, for her mother was her best friend as well as her parent. A safe harbour in a world that felt ceaselessly stormy to a little girl tormented by sights and sounds that simply did not exist for others.

Her mother had promised a change upon her death, but lamented the early and impending arrival of that time. She'd talked endlessly about what was to come for her young daughter. Not to her husband, but to Shya herself. And Shya's anticipation was a mix of dread and uncertainty – compounded, of course, by the spectre of her mother's absence.

She'd asked why so many times. Why couldn't it happen

while her mother was still there to guide her – the materialization of those persistent presences. The faces to match the voices. And her mother ever had only one, disappointing answer. It had always been that way, passed to daughters in part until the mother's passing, and then blooming in their wake like a lingering debt and gift, simultaneous.

But now, with her mother's body encased in a casket and soon to return to the earth, Shya's thoughts were on her misery rather than what was to come of her strange endowment. She was ten years old; too young to worry over consequence, but too old to be oblivious to the state of her reality.

Her mother was dead.

Her mother was dead and the crowd had finally arranged itself as a group around the coffin, the officiator solemn-faced at the head and already beginning to speak. Words of reason were short, but those on comfort were long and delivered skillfully, though Shya paid less attention to the details of them than to how they washed over her as she stared at the contrast of lacquered black cherry wood and bursts of colorful flowers. Lost in the weight of it. Comforted by the words. And entirely untethered, having lost the only sense of grounding she'd known.

Suddenly the flowers were garish against the shining wood, and the colors could not make up for the bleak reality of their purpose: a forever-bed for a body that wasted in decay even now, where only a short time ago it radiated life... joy! Solace.

She felt her knees go out as an observer might. Became aware only peripherally of the cool grass against her tights when she fell. The slight sharpness of the blades of it against her palms. Thought to look up at her father, but her neck was too tight from the ball of emotion that had gathered there, so a sob was forced out as she did, and he bent to her, silhouetted against the impossible blue of the sky and mumbling anecdotes of comfort already, his hands beneath her arms. Raising her up. Holding her on his hip as he had when she was smaller, warm lips at her ear mumbling sweetheart and darling and *I know, baby, I know.*

She buried her face in his neck for a while, and when she finally looked up, it was to look over his shoulder and through the rows of attendees – those who'd loved the dead person, too – just to disallow her eyes to land again on the place that held the body and screamed the reality too clearly. *You are alone, Shya. She is gone.* But her eyes landed on something equally shocking.

A little girl stood twenty feet back, beside a tree. She was alone, which was odd at such an event, and perhaps even odder than that, she was smiling. And beckoning Shya closer.

Shya caught her breath and frowned deeply, perplexed. The girl wanted her to leave the gathering, that much was clear, but she couldn't begin to fathom *why*. And there was something vaguely familiar about her – was she a classmate? That didn't seem right. A sibling of one, then, or a cousin who'd grown so Shya couldn't recognize her. She just couldn't place her. And as separate as the girl was from the crowd, she wore mourning clothes, too, but her dress drooped and pooled in the grass at the hem.

At once too curious to stay, Shya found herself wriggling out of her father's arms, which let her go easily, as distracted as the rest of him was, and then she wove herself through the crowd – they were nothing but obstacles now – her eyes pinned on the small figure.

She hesitated as she approached and the girl dropped her hand. Observed the dress again, and knew why it was strange. Obviously, it was much too big for the pixie of a creature that smiled in her direction, but there was something else.

It was the dress her mother was to be buried in.

"Come on!" the girl urged, smiling still and bending at the waist a little in anticipation.

Shya went to her as though mesmerized, and perhaps she was.

And when she stood in front of the girl, who was Shya's height exactly, she saw something else of her mother's. It was *her* eyes that looked out from the little girl's face. Her smile that greeted her. Her heart that fluttered frantically against Shya's chest as she pulled her in for a hug.

"I wanted to be the first," her mother's voice said quietly through the girl's lips. "I don't want you to be afraid."

Shya cried in her mother's childish embrace until the tears dried up. And when her father called her name, the girl-mother was gone, but Shya never questioned the experience, for the warmth of her mother's touch still lingered on her skin as she ran back to her father.

CHAPTER 5 – THE ABSENCE OF RAIN

It should've rained that day
It would've been an expected presence
But like you, it stayed away

You – your body - that was there
The shell that had held your effervescence
All frigid skin and strange, dull hair

And then you were there, too
Shrunk to my size and drenched in heaven
The wispy, lighter shade of you

Ghost of my mother, eyes alight
An introduction to life's new lessons
A gentle transition to my towering plight

Full, softly then came your embrace
Impossible cocoon, singular impression
Full grown behind your childish face

What monumental task to come
To traverse the boundaries, get through the fris-

sion

For an embrace beneath unlikely sun

It should've rained that day

Sky black and pendulous to threaten

But the sun brought you, sweet relief, solid joy, in the most magnificent of ways

CHAPTER 6 – FIRST

The first – besides her mother - was a very angry man. Her mother had warned her, but she couldn't have prepared, really.

Her mother had taught her that when a spirit was particularly passionate about something – regardless of whether it was romance or retribution or somewhere in between – their ability to communicate was boosted. She knew that, sort of. Many of the voices that whispered in the corners and just beside her ear were upset. Most, in fact. The calm ones only spoke if she was near someone they needed to get a message to. But *appearing* to a live person was a whole different effort. Monumentally harder.

It was the night of her mother's funeral and Shya lay awake, waiting, because of course it would be soon. Her mother was there, though she said she wouldn't be again for some time after that, their second bodily visit since her death. She had work to do. Shya was devastated by that; it hurt as though her mother was dying all over again, but the fact that the spirits would start appearing to her at any moment proved a ready distraction, if not rather frightening in and of itself.

"Will you stay the whole time?" Shya whispered from her bed, clutching her comforter to her chin and searching the dark corner opposite for the little girl that was the ghost of her mother. Her voice had been fading in and out since their embrace at the funeral, and she openly informed her daughter of the increasing difficulty. A warning. A preparation.

But there she was, wisping into the darkness like a creeping fog, then answering first with an echoing call that materialized as her form did, finally ending with, "I'll try, darling."

Shya's throat squeezed against the emotion that filled it. "I love you," she tried to whisper, but the constriction turned it to a high-pitched whimper.

There was a warmth upon her instantly, infused with her mother's unmistakable scent. She closed her eyes against it, breathless in her grief, but just as relief begun to fill her, it all changed. A blast of chilled air banished the warmth and her eyes flew open, quick enough to see her mother's retreat and then witness the black mass that replaced her.

Her lungs ached in the sudden cold such that she held her breath unconsciously. The darkness came together above her – a massive face, all encompassing, menacing and mad.

Shya's skin burned. The being radiated heat like an open furnace and she saw that there were flames in the coal-dark sockets where his eyes should be, and at last her breath was let out on the wings of a shriek that ripped from her throat. The disembodied head recoiled, shrinking as it went to the ceiling, then hardened and came at her, growing and charging like a speeding truck. She screamed again, pulling her comforter over her head and bracing herself for what might come. But it was just a breeze; he went through her as though her flesh was nothing, permeating her with a blast that was sucked through her front and pulled just as quickly out her back, and the searing heat was gone with it, leaving her trembling in its wake and sobbing against her covers.

Her father's footfalls sounded in the hallway. She pulled her comforter away from her face and saw him, then, a full-bodied mass of charred flesh standing at the foot of her bed, eyes simmering like glowing embers. *I burned,* he said, and then he was gone and her father burst in. She reached for him and he ran to her and gathered her up and sat with her on the edge of the bed, rocking, rocking and whispering "It'll be OK, baby girl. I'm here. Daddy's here."

CHAPTER 7 – JUST

Breathing, just
And listen
Just mist gath'ring in air

Just waiting
To be christened
With my protector fair

Just breath
And fear and whispers
Will you stay? I ask, and tarry

Just love
Cover and glisten
Lavender, sweet orange, rosemary

Just a blast
Dark against light
Menacing, blows her away

Just terror
Denial vanquished

Forever changed in night and day

Just death
Crossing the boundaries
Tortured with answers long unknown

Just passing
On the story
Of the thing that made him gone

Just embers
For his eyes
Flowing lava 'neath charred flesh

Just words
I burned - two words
To tell the story of his death

CHAPTER 8 – HOLD ON, GIRL

"You keep saying 'different' without explaining what that means," Dawn cut in, frustration saturating each word. It was rarely a difficult thing to puzzle over how the fiery woman was feeling. Her face bore all like a movie screen.

Shya sighed, frustrated as well.

"Look, I'm sorry for bringing us back to that point over and over again, but how do you expect us to help you if you don't even know what you need help with?" Dawn cocked her head, her eyes steadfast on Shya. Her dark skin pinked at her cheekbones as their gaze elongated, the atmosphere charging palpably.

Finally, Mel, who was the group's dependable voice of reason, inched forward on his seat, which was one of Dawn's green plastic dining chairs – vintage style, modern-made, and genuinely as uncomfortable as a true antique from the fifties would be. Which was why Shya was stuffed between Big Ed (whose nickname was well-deserved) and Sheila, a deceptively frail-looking woman who had the perpetual look of a spooked horse about to take flight.

"We *do* want to help, Shya. We just don't understand how." Mel gestured hopelessly with his hands, which landed heavily on his knees.

Shya shook her head, regretting her repeated efforts to make the close-knit group – Dawn had dubbed them "The Seers" – understand her mounting discomfort over a gift she'd thought to have become comfortable with nearly two decades before. But they were right. How could they understand when she so obviously did not?

"Shy?" Mel leaned over the coffee table and placed a hand on Shya's own. It immediately imparted a sense of calm, which was his gift, and Shya pulled her hand away reflexively. "I see how distressed you are, Shy. I'm just trying to help."

Shya softened. "I know. I'm sorry, Mel." She looked at Dawn, whose stern expression aged her beyond her forty-odd years considerably. "And you're right! I *can't* expect feedback if I'm not able to describe the problem!"

Dawn rested back into the La-Z-Boy that was unquestionably *her* chair. The couch was the next best seat, so those who managed a spot suffered the consequence of being pressed against other comfort-seekers, as Shya did in that moment. "Don't stop trying, girl," Dawn said on an outbreath, her hand going to the bowl of honey-roasted peanuts on the end table between her and the couch.

Shya shook her head. "I don't think I can. You guys are the only thing in my life that makes me feel sane, sometimes."

Jane, one of the inseparable psychic medium twins, inhaled audibly, sitting up straighter, and the group hushed. Neither she nor Anna, her identical other half, ever said anything unless it was either completely off the wall, or entirely enlightening, but regardless of which, they gained attention easily. In addition to being identical, and seemingly unable to leave each other's sides, they were albino, with striking long white hair and strange eyes that shivered now and then in their sockets – a common accompanying condition to albinism called *nystagmus*, they'd explained. In typical form, Anna spoke after Jane had their attention, achieving the discombobulating effect of acting as one, as always.

"Why don't you stop trying to explain it and just say

what's happening?"

Sheila tittered, high-pitched in Shya's left ear. "Sorry," she muttered when Shya jumped. "Just – what's the difference?"

"Don't try and make sense of it before saying it," Jane answered, her pale eyes on Shya, "just… " the twins finished together, "*say* it."

Shya swallowed as if to digest their words, but even Mel, who sat nearest the twins, had clearly put their statement into the "off the wall" category rather than the "enlightening" one. He chuckled quietly, but Dawn put a hand up.

"Wait, now. Maybe they're onto something." She met Shya's eyes again. "Tell us one thing that's got you unnerved lately, without trying to frame it, you know?"

Shya searched her thoughts, and nodded. "OK. But – that's the thing. It's a lot of the same. I've been dreaming of them a lot, and having visions…"

"Anyone stick out?" Dawn was trying, she really was. Shya clenched her jaw as she thought.

"Don't *try*, Shya," Anna pushed.

"One sticks out. A boy. I've been dreaming of him a lot."

"You see him when you're awake, too?" Dawn was leaning forward in her chair with some effort; the footrest was known to stick.

Shya shook her head.

"Well, *that's* different," Dawn raised her eyebrows at the members. "What else?"

Shya shook her head. "It's not related, but the dark stuff – it's more persistent. Harder to shut out."

"You've mentioned having ups and downs with that,

too," Mel frowned.

"Ebbs and flows," Big Ed mumbled, and Shya nodded.

"This feels different," she grimaced, feeling the circle turning back again, to something she couldn't articulate. "Ugh! I'm sorry," she rested her head against the back of the couch, frustrated.

Sheila patted her knee lightly. "How do you know it's not related?" she asked, her voice high and wavery.

Shya turned to observe the woman, frowning. Frowning both because the question annoyed her, and because she had no answer. "I don't know, actually," she finally answered.

"That's because they *are* related," the twins said, in perfect sync.

Shya shook her head. Though the twins' gift was difficult to deny, having known them for some years, and seen their intuition prove accurate countless times, "How?" was all she could think to say as a counter.

The women only looked at each other soberly.

"What are the dreams about? The ones about the boy?" Dawn asked.

Shya shrugged. "He's sick. He doesn't say much of anything, but when he does, I don't understand it. Most times, children don't leave because they have someone here they need to get a message to, or who is in danger. I figure he doesn't know how to get it through to me. He keeps trying, though."

Nobody spoke. The twins seemed to have retreated back into silence, and Dawn had sat back in her cushy chair again, eyes distant.

"The twins say they're related," Big Ed started, easily referring to Jane and Anna as though they weren't there, and nobody protested, because the twins never did, "so why not start there? Are the darker things only in dreams, too?"

Shya shook her head.

"Do you find it's worse when you've dreamt about the boy?"

Shya frowned. "I don't know. I've told you – I don't acknowledge the darkness. That means I don't think about it. I don't try and connect it or track it. That way, it can't… "

Mel leaned forward. "What?"

Shya's skin broke out in gooseflesh such that she had to consciously stop herself from shuddering. Her mother had taught her about the dark energies early, but though she was experienced at recognizing it, it hadn't always been easy to shut it out. "Get… *hold*," she finished, and then she did shudder, and Big Ed nudged her gently with his left shoulder.

Dawn had been watching the twins, but now she turned back to Shya. "Maybe in order to shake it, you *need* to pay attention now," she broached, and Shya could see the guarded look in her eyes. "As an observer, you know?"

The twins nodded in unison, sending a chill up Shya's back, and likely through the others, too, for Sheila shivered on her left, and Big Ed chuckled on her right, but it was a decidedly nervous laugh.

Dawn threw her hands up, then brought them down on her thighs. "Well! You know our numbers, sweetheart. Call us if you need anything between now and the next meeting. But now, y'all got to get out because my show's coming on!" She rubbed her hands together excitedly, then reached for her remote.

It was the usual end to their meetings, but Shya was still at loose ends. Dismayed, she watched as the group started moving, standing and stretching, confirming rides and grabbing an extra cookie or piece of fruit for the road.

"I know you ain't interested in my shows," Dawn smiled kindly at Shya.

She was right. The dramatic true crime stuff that Dawn seemed to live for had never held her attention. She saw enough crime through what the spirits showed her. Dawn, however, was an empath, and seemed obsessed with the victim's stories as well as the perpetrator's. She felt everything – got lost in it, and thrived on it because it wasn't close. It was someone else's trauma. She'd said she could almost pretend her commiseration with the subjects' feelings was part of the show.

"Sorry." Shya rose, a bit unsteady.

Dawn stood, too, and reached for Shya's arm. Shya steeled herself, let the woman touch her. It was how she related in a more meaningful way, after all, and Shya had spent years learning that having friends who truly understood her was a lifeline she couldn't afford to turn away. "You're scared," Dawn nodded as if to confirm her own statement.

"Paying attention to them?" Shya laughed breathlessly, but couldn't sustain her smile. "It goes against everything I've ever learned about handling... *everything*." A heat begun behind her eyes. The old feelings rose up in her: the missing of her mother, the fear, the *why me* of it all, all over again.

Dawn gathered her into a hug, and Shya rested her chin on the shorter, stouter woman's head of frizzled curls. She'd learned to relax into the embraces of her friends. To draw from them, as much as she could. When they pulled apart, it was only so Dawn could hold her at arm's length, her gaze steady. "Don't think of it as breaking the rules. Think of it as opening the doors a crack, just to get a hint at what's inside."

Shya knew she was right, but her long-established rules still balked. "Maybe I'll just peek in a window," she tried to joke, but her lips trembled rather than smiled.

"We got you, Shy, always. You need us, you call."

Shya became aware of Big Ed, who was nodding his agreement from behind Dawn. His jacket was draped awkwardly over his forearm. A hand landed on her shoulder and she knew it was Mel's, and he was nodding, too, beside her. And Sheila was behind him. She was well supported. A tear escaped, then, and she laughed for real. "Thanks, guys."

"Right!" Dawn released Shya's shoulders and clapped her hands with gusto. "Now y'all get out!"

A rumble of laughter went through what remained of the group as they filed out. Shya found herself smiling and joining in, even accepting a ride from Big Ed, who offered every week, to her and anyone else who was without one.

It was all very comfortable. All warm, all friendly.

Far too cozy for the prelude of what was to come.

CHAPTER 9 – THE DARK

Do you feel them creeping there?
Beyond the door, under the stair
Roiling belly, whisper, glare
Dark energy dwells there

You're right to shun the musty rooms
Forgotten casket, eternal tombs
Headache pulsing, thick dread looms
Heavy heart, impending doom

They reach with twisted fingers, limbs
Hot, bubbling beneath the skin
Incite the boiling fear within
Paint canvasses of chain-linked sin

Once tethered, they will grasp and hold
With frost-lined tendrils, veins of cold
Infused with thoughts and dreams so bold
To terrify, sicken and drain when told

So do not let them hang from you

Dripping menace, sticky dew
Hell's honey clinging endless to
The secret danker spots in you

Turn body and mind's eye away
T'ward lighter thoughts, dwell in the day
Let paths of good lead you and sway
Your tendency to joyful play

Turn, child, be safe! Build solid home
Between sinew and blood and bone
Hold strength and comfort, lessons shown
Your beating heart is not alone

CHAPTER 10 – STRUGGLE

Bethie took another drag of the stolen cigarette – it was actually the *butt* of one of her father's cigarettes, a fact which was not lost on Shya as they passed it back and forth, their mouths not only on the spot where Bethie's dad's had been, but where it had touched the filthy ashtray of his work truck – and giggled, then broke out into a fit of coughing. Shya observed as her friend bent forward, then jumped from the cement half-wall they were sitting on.

"Not there!" Shya hissed, laughing too as Bethie dramatically collapsed onto one of the gravesites.

Bethie rolled to her back and put a hand to her chest. "Smoking's gross," she sighed, then coughed some more.

"Bethie, you shouldn't lay there," Shya whispered, then glanced around the graveyard, which was bathed almost romantically in moonlight and, thank God, deserted.

"It's beautiful," Bethie replied. "Come down."

Shya pushed herself off the wall, but paused beside her friend. "I won't lay there."

"Why not? Didn't you say they don't hang out in graveyards, anyway?" Bethie's eyes were still on the sky, but she patted the grass beside her.

"It's disrespectful," Shya muttered, stretching her head back to take in the expanse of the night sky. Bethie was right; it was breathtaking. With no cloud to hide behind, the stars winked down at the earth in a rare and spectacular demonstration of their infinite number. "Wow," Shya breathed, "they go on forever."

Bethie sighed. "Come down here."

Shya did. There *were* spirits there that night, but they paid her and her friend no heed, and whomever shared their resting place with the girls had neglected to appear, either to chastise or to welcome them. The grass was cool and damp on her palms as she sank to all-fours. She touched the stone at the head delicately in thanks, then lay beside Bethie. She could do things like that openly with Bethie and depend on acceptance. They'd always been honest with each other, and Bethie had known about Shya's abilities since before Shya had known to keep quiet about it. She was grateful for that, for after her mother had died, her best friend became the only person she could talk to about what she saw that nobody else could.

"Whose grave is this?" Bethie asked then. Casually.

Shya shrugged. "He's not here. The stone says 'Franklin Rosco,' though."

"Frank," Bethie whispered, and when Shya turned to see her expression, she was smiling.

"What?"

"It's just cool to know." Bethie flung what was left of the cigarette into the air and a spark fell, orange and blinking between them.

Shya looked to the sky again. She let it overwhelm her in its glory, millions of glittering gems in an endless skyscape of darkness. After a while of laying in silence, the grass tickling the back of her neck, she begun to feel weightless beneath it all. Had to squint to see just one pinprick of light within the multitudes. And then she saw the duller stars around it – those further celestial bodies just hinting at their existence. Always there, but dwarfed by their brighter counterparts. "Like ghosts," she wondered out loud, and Bethie jumped a little beside her. Shya giggled. "Sorry. I didn't even mean to say that out loud."

"Pfft, I forgot you were even there!" Bethie giggled. "I think I nearly fell asleep."

Shya found her friend's hand and squeezed it. Bethie held on tight when Shya went to pull away, murmuring, "Tell me about them."

Shya held her breath, remembering her comparison of the distant stars to spirits. "Why?"

Bethie let her hand go but rolled into Shya's side rather than opening the space between them. She wrapped herself around Shya's arm and let her head rest on her shoulder, yawning. "I like to hear," was all she finally said.

Shya tried to settle into the new warmth of her friend, who'd always been a snuggler. Searched her mind for something new to tell her.

"Any dark spirits lately?" Bethie asked before Shya could settle on a story.

Shya shrugged. "Nothing that's bothered me." She remembered walking past the gap between the junior and senior campuses the day before. "Oh. Actually, there was something outside at school," she frowned. "I ignored it, of course, but it felt heavy. Made me walk faster."

Bethie raised her head to look at Shya. "Smoker's alley, right?"

Shya gave her friend a puzzled look. "How'd you know?"

The gap between the senior and junior campuses had long been known to shelter the smokers at lunch, though Shya had never understood the choice of hiding places – getting caught was all too common, and one really only had a single choice as far as an escape route, and it led to the fenced edge of the yard, where there were no entrances into either building.

Bethie grinned, her eyes twinkling in the starlight. "I heard the boys talking."

Shya couldn't help but smile, too. "The boys" meant Drake and Connor, the former of whom was Shya's crush, and the latter that of her best friend, though she wondered if it was a bit forced on Bethie's part, for convenience. "What'd they say?"

"They were saying they needed to find a new spot; that they always felt like they were being watched in there."

"Huh." Shya frowned up at the stars.

"Connor said Pudge thinks the school installed cameras in there," Bethie giggled, then snuggled back into Shya's shoulder. "He's an idiot, though."

"That alleyway's too narrow for the likes of Pudge," Shya commented absently, making Bethie giggle again. "I don't mean it like that," Shya laughed, too. "I mean he's not the sharpest tool in the shed, and he's been caught in there more times than even he can count."

Bethie laughed some more, then sighed. "Ah, but it works the way I thought you meant it, too."

Shya couldn't help but grin at the heavens. "True."

They lay in silence another long while, until Shya wondered if Bethie had dozed off again. But it was she who jumped that time, when Bethie began to speak.

"Sorry!" her friend laughed. "I was just going to say I'm cold." Bethie sat up, wrapping her arms around herself.

"Should we go?"

Bethie nodded, looking thoughtful. "You know it's time to do something about our crushes," she said, smiling.

Shya shook her head, then pushed herself to sitting. "Nah."

"Why not?"

Shya gave her friend a look. "He thinks I'm weird, just like everyone else."

"You are!" Bethie laughed.

"Hey!" Shya punched her friend's arm lightly.

"You're different, Shy. But that makes you cool as well as weird."

Shya pressed her lips together, then reached for Bethie's hands. They pulled themselves up, then brushed at their jeans as though it would rid them of the damp. "Not everyone sees it the way you do," Shya said, finally.

Bethie linked her arm through Shya's and they started out of the graveyard, their progress through the grass the only sound in the chill air. "The right guy will, too, Shy. I know it. And Drake's cool." She looked sideways at Shya. "We could at least hang out with them a bit? See if they're smart as well as cute?"

Drake's dark features filled Shya's thoughts. She shivered a bit.

"What?"

"He *is* hot."

Bethie laughed. "They *both* are! I can't believe I never noticed Connor before! We've been going to school with him since we were kids!"

A flash of the scene that Shya hoped nobody from elementary school remembered filtered into her thoughts. "Oh, God," she lamented. "Do you think he remembers... "

Bethie laughed. "That little scene you made when your

ghost friend fell off the monkey bars?"

"I didn't know she was a ghost!" Shya protested, but without gusto. It was an old story and her defenses were tired.

Still, Bethie shook her head. "How the heck did you not realize she was a ghost when you were the only one who talked to her?"

Shya scoffed. "You know how confusing it was at first. I was only ten!"

Bethie squeezed her arm. "I know, Shy. I'm sorry."

Shya peered upward again as Bethie scaled the wrought-iron fencing. The trees at the entrance blocked the view somewhat, but the moon was still spectacularly bright.

"Come on," Bethie danced a little on the spot just outside the fence. "I'm freezing!"

Shya took a deep breath and made the climb.

"Can we talk to them, then?" Bethie was looking expectantly at her.

Shya shrugged. "We can try."

Bethie punched the air before linking arms with Shya again. "Yes!"

Shya laughed quietly. "Just don't expect much. And – I'm sorry in advance if my reputation ruins your chances."

"*Our* chances, silly," Bethie skipped a little as they walked, jostling Shya.

She laughed, because Bethie made it impossible not to. But inside she was wary, disappointment already wriggling into the anticipation over Drake that had been so pure until then. It was always like that. Always the excitement, then the same obstacles over and over. It seemed it didn't matter where she turned – they were always waiting. And though she knew enough to identify them, she still hadn't mastered the art of shutting them out.

Except the dark ones. Her mother had made sure she was good at that.

It was the good that took her focus, though. The ones who needed her. The never-ending line of them, needing, needing. Needing her so much they buried her own sense of need until she barely recognized it anymore.

CHAPTER 11 – A FORK
IN THE TRAIL

It was nearly twilight, and Shya was on her way to meet Bethie at the park, where they'd played when they were younger. Now it was just a place to sit and giggle, a place to imagine their futures and sometimes swing, their eyes on the endless sky as they dreamt of freedom. It was what all teenagers longed for, but perhaps felt more keenly by the girls, one having lost her mother, and the other having carried her through it.

Shya's thoughts were on nothing in particular. She was lost in the rhythm of her sneakered feet against asphalt and charmed by the changing sky. Birdsong still floated on the air, as did the sounds of neighborhood kids at play. Just trying to squeeze a few more minutes of daylight in before succumbing to the drowsy dwindling of the evening, from TV to snacks to warm baths and bed time. She loved this time of day, when the bustle and brightness faded into the quieter, calmer hours of night.

The grass was already dampening when she veered off into the soccer field. She inhaled deeply as she meandered through it, toward the sudden closing in of the trees and the dark mouth of the forested trail that would lead her to the park. Bethie would be waiting, for sure. Her family was small and tightly knit, and by now existed in their house more like amicable roommates than parents and child. Bethie said the freedom was strange, though, in that the loss of formal mealtimes and a stricter routine felt more like giving up than the imagined letting go process as she matured. And that her parents' relationship had evolved, too – though they got along at least as well as the best of friends, they seemed less tethered, too. Like roommates, again.

In the end, what it meant was that Bethie came and went as she pleased, but let her parents know her plans as a courtesy, while Shya observed from the outside, envious and longing for her mother. *Two* parents to balance each other out. A *family* rather than an awkward father forcing the routine they'd kept up since her mother died. She knew it was out of love and good intentions, but longed for just a taste of what Bethie's family shared. That trust.

She wondered whether her father would ever lose the guilt that had gripped him during his wife's long decline into disease and death, when he was hit with the realization that he didn't know how to father Shya. Didn't *know* her at all, really, except to say that she was his and that she was like her mother and that he loved them both.

And now it was stranger, still, because he'd found someone – a woman. A fellow epidemiologist at the hospital campus. Someone who seemed to have inspired the light in his eyes to resurface. Shya resented her for that before she even met her, and then she resented her more afterward because she was so unlike her mother. She'd probably have hated her if she *had* been like her mother, though. There was no replacement for the woman she and her father lost. So, in her differences, the woman who was doomed to be scrutinized by her boyfriend's offspring either way at least fell on the easier side of Shya's disaffection.

Still, her animosity toward the woman – Louise – was very real. And not helped by her father's excitement over an upcoming dinner with both Louise and her son, Rory, who was a year older than Shya.

The trees closed in on her as if in response to her

thoughts. She didn't want or need someone new in her life – not a woman who seemed determined to become her step-mother, and not a potential step-brother, either.

Shya pressed her arms against wayward branches as she progressed through the woods, her thoughts turning to Bethie. She thought of spilling everything to Bethie – not that she hadn't before, but Bethie didn't mind – and felt immediate relief. But as she spotted the narrow opening into the park, her relief dissolved. She stopped in her tracks, her eyes on the little group at the picnic table. It was Bethie, alright, but it was the boys, too. Drake and Connor. And Bethie was giggling.

They'd come.

They'd been tagging along at lunchtime when the boys would go for a smoke, Bethie gluing them together with her bubbly ways and Shya even finding her place as the sarcastic, funny one. She still had no idea if the boys ever thought of either of them as more than groupies, but at least their little group seemed to be solidifying, with the boys seeking them out now before going outside.

Bethie had been enthusiastic over the developments, but Shya realized something else, too. Her friend had stopped talking about Connor as the object of her affections, and never encouraged Shya where Drake was concerned, anymore. It was subtle, but undeniable, and it made Shya's stomach tighten every time she thought about it. And watching them now, she saw it – a closeness between Drake and Bethie as they leaned over whatever he was carving into the picnic table, and a distinct separation between them and the quieter Connor. Shya pushed onward and Connor saw her. He raised a hand to wave.

"You guys came," Shya said, a bit breathless as she approached her friends.

Bethie was up and running to hug Shya instantly. Shya met Drake's eyes over Bethie's shoulder, pierced by the way his attention made her stomach twist.

Drake gestured toward Bethie. "We had to, just so she'd stop bugging us about it." He smiled at Bethie as the girls withdrew from their embrace and Shya saw it again: a teasing admiration in the look he gave her. Suddenly feeling overwarm and a bit sick, she sat across from Connor.

"You OK?" Connor turned to face her, concern etching his features, which were the polar opposite to Drake's. Light where Drake was dark, easy where Drake was intense.

Shya swiped imaginary sweat from her brow, self-conscious. "Huh? Yeah! I – I ran through the woods," she lied, wanting to change the subject but coming up empty.

"Oh, did you see a ghost?" Bethie smiled, but it faded as quickly as it had come. She glanced at Drake, then Connor, then back to Drake again.

Shya sighed. It wasn't the strangest thing for a person to say, but Bethie's reaction to her own words made the boys lean in.

"Why are you always saying shit like that?" Drake grinned in the lopsided way that Shya had grown to love. "You scared of the dark?"

Bethie grinned. "No."

"You scared some cold, dead hand will reach for you from the trees or from underneath your bed?" Drake continued, obviously teasing, but Shya's relief paled in the ache she felt as Drake reached across the table to tickle Bethie, saying "wooo, oooooh!" in a poorly-executed falsetto.

"Stop!" Bethie cried, any unease forgotten as she playfully shoved Drake's fingers away.

"What? You think *I'm* a ghost?" Drake stood, wiggling his fingers menacingly until Bethie was rising and then running from the table, squealing as Drake chased her.

Shya focused on breathing. It was real, then. And not just one-sided.

"He really likes her," Connor mumbled as he folded his hands on the table, his fingers interlacing with a slight rasping sound.

"He said that?" Shya couldn't help but ask. She'd never liked not knowing. There was enough of that with the spirits she saw. She held Connor's gaze, unafraid of what he might think. Needing to know.

Connor pressed his lips together, nodding.

Shya watched the two as Drake caught Bethie and they tumbled into the first fallen leaves of the season, laughing. She looked back at Connor, who seemed to be studying her with questioning green eyes. Searched her mind for the right words, but got lost in his gaze, embarrassed. She knew it was obvious that she was disappointed. No use trying to cover it up. And facing Connor, she couldn't blame Bethie. As kind as the boy was, he shrank in the presence of his best friend. Drake was gorgeous, gregarious and fun. It occurred to Shya that she didn't know much about Connor at all.

"Seems like she likes him, too," the boy said, and it was a bit wistful. Shya watched as he turned his gaze to the two, just as she had, and knew he understood her pain.

"Sorry," she muttered, and Connor waved it off, but said nothing.

"*Did* you see a ghost in the trees?" he asked, after what had seemed like a very long time as they watched Bethie bury Drake's lower body in leaves - both of them laughing, oblivious to their audience.

Shya jumped a bit, then looked at the boy whose presence she'd forgotten. "Not tonight," she answered, and tried for a smile.

But Connor's eyes were serious. "I believe in that stuff," he said, eyebrows raised as if to challenge her.

Shya's stomach clenched again, though she wasn't sure she could explain why. "You do?" was all she could think to say.

Connor nodded. "I saw one once."

Shya followed his gaze to their friends, who seemed only to be chatting, now. Bethie smiled into the boy's eyes as if enchanted. Maybe she was.

"It was the day my uncle died," Connor went on, and Shya found it easier to watch Bethie and Drake than to look back at Connor as he told his story.

She'd been fooled by stories before, and disappointed in the end.

"I hadn't been asleep very long," he continued, gesturing mildly with his hands and then folding them again, "and then suddenly, I was awake. I knew something was off; I could feel it in the air, like -"

Shya looked at him, waiting.

"- like electricity, almost." His face was so open and sincere that Shya had to nod. "And – it didn't feel *scary,* really. Just different."

Shya nodded again.

"When I made myself look, there he was! Uncle John was at the window! Just looking out. He had his hand on the windowsill, as though he was thinking about leaving that way. I really thought he would. I was confused – half my thoughts were saying it was a dream, and the other half were saying Uncle John was really there, but he was different."

"Did any part of you think he was there visiting? And just came in to check on you?"

Connor shook his head. "I knew before I opened my eyes

that whatever was there was *not* anything I'd ever seen."

Shya bit her lip. Thought of the years before her mother's death when they were just voices. How she felt them there before she heard them.

"You probably think I'm crazy," Connor laughed quietly.

"No," Shya said, and then he was asking her questions with his eyes, and just as quickly it was all forgotten as Bethie and Drake returned.

They were holding hands.

Bethie frowned when she saw her friend again, and took her hand away from the tall boy's as though it was hot, then sat beside Shya, throwing her arms around her as she always had, but leaving them there. She rested her chin on Shya's shoulder and trembled a bit against her, like she was trying not to cry.

Shya forgave her in that instant. Bethie was sweet, and lovable, and well-intentioned, if not scatterbrained and rash. Shya had watched it happen between the two; had seen it just as clearly as she could feel her best friend's arms around her now. She ducked her head a bit, so Bethie's smooth hair pressed against her cheek. Whispered, "It's OK" into her ear.

"I'm so sorry, Shya," Bethie whispered back, but she hadn't needed to. Bethie had loved Shya – and made sure she knew it – since they were little girls. As far as Shya was concerned, Bethie deserved anything her heart desired, even if it meant Shya didn't get what she yearned for.

She was used to that, anyway.

CHAPTER 12 – DREAM

It started out as something beautiful, as nightmares tend to do, both in the states of sleep and wakefulness.

She found herself in a vast expanse of color: ombre blues and pinks and purples stretching out in all directions and mesmerizing as they shifted, fading in and out of one another. She wondered how she came to be in such a place, and upon discovering she couldn't remember, felt the tides of color shift, and as the strips of pastels deepened into greys her stomach dropped.

It was all wrong.

She cast her eyes in each direction and now instead of endless gorgeous blends of light and color, there was nothing. Deep and dark and motionless, yet somehow sucking at the very air like a vacuum, the depths of darkness stealing her breath and faltering her steps. She tumbled to her knees, finding an odd, cool plane against her fingertips. An invisible sort of ground, hard and smooth and thusly unlike anything she'd ever encountered in nature and it struck another note of dread in her.

Before standing again she realized the ache in her lungs and gasped at the air. It tasted stale and barely filled her lungs, was thin and much too empty here. Wherever she was. In the nothing.

"Hello?" she tried to call but her voice was a weak reed in shallow waters, listing in a burble from her lips and falling flat onto the ground. But she *was* answered by a single sound behind her, at some distance: a hitching rasp of breath against a desert of throat and dusty lungs.

She whirled, nearly falling as a dizziness took hold first in her head, then twisting down into her stomach where it twirled and lurched. She held har breath, bending slightly at the waist and willing herself to be steel against the nauseating tide that gripped her with metal fingers, hot and vibrating with every throb of pulse and blood.

But she was immediately distracted when she saw a spot where the blackness had lightened into varying shades of grey and within that space her eyes fell upon the source of rasping breath: the boy. The one she'd seen so many times in dreams but never in her wakeful hours, and her recognition of him fuelled a final outbreath on which flowed some of the roiling terror from her gut and she was lighter.

But relief could not grip her where terror had fled, because she was travelling effortlessly toward him now and knew she was powerless to stop it. "Wake up," she whispered to herself, but she barely heard her own words in the vacuum that was this dream. It sucked the words away. As she slowed, nearing the boy, she saw that though he'd appeared to be standing, the originally puzzling position of his arms – which were stretched tautly to either side as though he was being pulled in both directions – made sense, for he was stood against a bed, upright, and tethered to its headboard with filthy linens. A king bed for a diminutive prince.

His dark eyes were on her, but his hollow-cheeked face was slack as if he was sleeping, and judging by the drape of him, hung bare-chested from the standing bed, he was.

Shya felt her face twist in confusion as she took in his state – each blade of rib a pronounced line, his tethered arms nothing but bone and sinew, and his pyjama pants draped across protrusions of pelvic bone. And for all of that, he couldn't have been more than six or seven years old.

Her hand flew to her mouth. She struggled to breath all the more as her heart went out to the boy, whose feet dangled several feet above the edge of the mattress. And taking in his face again, she wondered at the eyes, which did observe her, still, and saw they were indeed dark, but much too black and without relief of white or circles of blue or green or even brown, but black throughout, pure black and glittering and watching her from the motionless form until it tilted backward away from her and fell, unknowing that she reached for him, fingers fumbling in the air.

And when the bed made contact it emitted such a solid thud that Shya, too, fell down, and watched a spotlight flicker on to illuminate a cloud of buzzing insects that rose from it and from the boy with buzzing fervor, then come for her.

She woke with a shriek, bolting up in bed and swatting at the air until she knew she was alone. And then she put her face into her hands and sobbed 'til she was empty, and lay down again, asking herself why – why, when she hadn't consciously opened herself, had he come again? And why only in her dreams?

The questions came, circling and repeating, until she sat up again, her hands pressing in on either side of her head. And then she did something she never had before, despite being on the receiving end several times for members of The Seers: she picked up her phone and looked for a name that encouraged her. For one that would be understanding instead of put out, and for one that had done the same to her during a sleepless night, full of questions.

And, fingers shaking, she dialled Big Ed.

CHAPTER 13 – TOUCH

They were meeting at the park again, but later that night because it was Halloween and the boys thought going out later would be more fun. Shya suspected they also wanted to trick or treat, despite the fact that they were much to old to go around collecting candy by teenager standards. Bethie said they were showing their slower maturation – they'd learned in Health that girls were typically a year or two ahead by their age. It got laughs around the lunch table, and Connor had the decency to blush, but Drake had only scoffed as he slung his arm around Bethie.

As she approached the dark mouth of the woods that night, Shya wondered again why she and Connor continued to subject themselves to their friends' make out sessions. For Shya it was partly her undying loyalty to her best friend and partly out of a lack of options. Watching Drake and Bethie snuggle and paw at each other was better than hanging out at home, where her father either made himself scarce in the garage, or most recently, was absent entirely, having gone out with Louise again. Which, she had to admit, was better than when Louise was home with her father.

The dinner with Louise and her son had been...odd. Rory's arrogance had been the most obvious trait about him aside from his inherent good looks, and Shya had found herself struggling to deal with her conflicting reactions. Unwilling to ruminate on it, she'd reported relief that the event was short and left it at that.

Completely ignored, in fact, Drake's questions about the

possibilities for the future, which had earned a sharp jab in the side from Bethie.

In any case, she found herself regretting the choice to take the wooded path that Halloween night as the trees closed in on the trail. The air had a bite to it, signalling the oncoming season that, where she lived, meant minus forty weather on the coldest, most lung-freezing of days, and ice storms in between. She'd experienced winter in only two provinces, and Québec won hands-down where slippery conditions were concerned.

But it wasn't just the darker-than-usual forest or the chill in the air; Shya was on edge. She assumed it was the distant sounds of trick-or-treaters at first. Childish screams and whoops of laughter clearly signalled the special circumstances. But as she progressed toward the park and emerged from her thoughts, she was forced to realize a different reason for her jitters.

She was being watched.

Her mother had taught her to recognize how the atmosphere changed when a spirit was around. It was as though the air around her – as though all the focus of her surroundings was on her. And it wasn't that it was surprising! When she deigned to open herself to it, the energies around her would often make themselves known. But that night, it felt off.

Her mother had said that fear made her vulnerable – gave the darker energies a chance to get in. But she couldn't be on her guard all the time – it blocked the neutral ghosts out, too.

But the realization she was not alone stopped her in her tracks that night. She wouldn't have stopped if she'd thought about it, but the combination of her already spooky surroundings and her sudden realization of a darker-feeling visitor made the decision for her. The shadow that stepped behind a tree trunk just off the path ahead of her did not help.

She felt her heart gallop to a sprint in her chest as she froze. Her fingers tingled with adrenaline as she pondered her next move. She saw herself turning to run back to the mouth of the trail, but knew the resulting chase, once she acknowledged the presence and ran, would be challenging.

So, she walked forward.

She'd picked up the pace, her eyes resolutely on the trail ahead – what was visible in the encroaching gloom, anyway. But the sickening heat on her right when she passed the tree the dark energy had hidden behind was undeniable. And before she even pondered it, she ran.

And there it was: a distinct blast of satisfaction from the spirit at being recognized, followed by a determination to elicit more from the teenager who fled in fear. And there was inevitably something else: the recognition that she was different, and a spark of curiosity.

Underlined with malintent.

Shya flew. She was gasping by the time the trail's end was in sight, and working to bite back the scream that had lodged in her throat. And just at the spot where the trees opened up again and Connor came into view, a hot gust of putrid breath blasted against the side of her face, with the words *What can you do, little girl?* burning in her ears.

A shriek escaped her then. Of course it did, and Connor whirled to look at her, a look of confusion marring his features.

She'd come to like his looks. He wasn't so striking as Drake, but there was something else that etched itself around his eyes and in the corners of his lips: Connor was mild-mannered and easy-going, yes, but mostly, he was *kind.*

Cursing herself as soon as the presence pulled away from her and back into the trees, she became overwhelmed that

Connor had heard her scream, and only moderately relieved that Bethie and Drake had not yet arrived. Bethie understood, at least. Shya stumbled as much because of her dismay as the tree root her toe struck, and fell to her hands and knees.

Connor was by her side in seconds, his hands on her shoulders as he knelt.

"You OK? What happened?"

She peered up at his face to gauge his reaction. He was trying to smile, bless him. Shya tried a laugh, intending on joking about her clumsiness, but his face changed when it came out high-pitched and shaky.

"Did someone scare you in there?" he looked behind her, toward the trees, his jaw hardening, and she saw something – a hint of the look he'd sent toward Drake and Bethie that first night they got together.

She struggled to relax. Told herself she was being ridiculous. "I – sorry," was all that came out, but at least the words were clear.

He regarded her again. "Come on." He helped her up and led her to their picnic table.

"It's dark," she laughed successfully, that time. "Of course you can count on me to trip over a root I've avoided a hundred times before!"

He was quiet as they sat.

"Where are they?" Shya asked, still shaky but making an effort to gaze toward the road to find their friends.

"You screamed," Connor replied.

She met his eyes. The smile she'd pasted on felt tight. "Like I said, it was dark!"

He reached across the table, totally surprising her as he took her hands inside the warmth of his own.

"You're warm," she said, her voice barely audible.

He rubbed her chilled flesh gently. "You can tell me," he said.

Something in her shifted. There was no hint of humour in his words. Rather, he sounded – *knowing.* She frowned.

"Don't worry," he squeezed her hands then, but still gently. As though he was pre-emptively preventing her from pulling away. "I won't laugh."

She did try and pull back, then. Had Bethie said something? *No,* she reasoned inwardly. Bethie had always held her secret. Shya trusted her explicitly.

Connor held her hands more tightly. "*Did* you see something?" he smiled. "Are there more on Halloween?" his eyes twinkled, and she couldn't comfort herself completely at his look of eager curiosity; she'd trusted that look before, only to be slapped by the doubt and teasing that tended to follow.

Shya shook her head. "She told you?"

Connor's smile faltered. "No. I mean – *shit.* Don't tell her I said anything, OK? It was Drake she told." Connor laughed, giving her hands another squeeze. "He's not the most subtle of guys, but he'd kill me if he knew I said anything." He glanced back toward the trail. "I just thought – it seemed like you were afraid, and I wanted to -"

Shya pulled her hands away and balled them in her lap. She'd told Drake. *Why?* Wasn't the fact that she was with Shya's own crush enough? And the fact of Shya's unspoken acceptance. She'd been counting on a heart to heart with her best friend since it had all started, but the boys seemed always present, now. There hadn't been the chance to hash it all out, and Shya was left feeling it was an unfinished thing – her best friend's sudden relationship with the boy Shya had admired.

It helped a bit that her feelings for Drake had downgraded as the four of them had started hanging out. He was a moderately annoying handsome guy, now, and a change of heart on his end at that point would be refused, anyway. But the slight by her best friend still hurt.

"Shy?" Connor was reaching across the table, still, but his hands were flat in front of her, palms down.

She shook her head. "I can't believe she said anything."

"Shit. *I* shouldn't have said anything!" he pulled away. His eyes went to the road. "Please don't tell them."

Shya followed his gaze to find Bethie and Drake approaching under the streetlight's glare. Feeling entirely beyond the ability to act as though everything was OK, she stood and headed, without thinking, toward the trees.

"Shya, wait!" Connor called. She heard him greet the other two, but refused to turn.

She did stop when she reached the trailhead, though. It was darker, still, and the air was thick with that same energy as before. Tears welled in her eyes.

"Hey!" Connor ran up and stood beside her. "I messed up. I'm sorry... please don't leave."

Shya looked sideways at him, but his features were difficult to read by then. "I need to go."

He was quiet for a moment. "You really want to go back in there?"

She laughed.

"What're you guys doing over there?" Drake called from behind them.

Shya glanced back to see the two had reached the picnic table and were sitting, but Drake was motioning them back while Bethie sat, uncharacteristically quiet.

"I don't want to go in there, no," Shya said quietly as she turned back to the woods. "But I can't stay here and be quiet." It wasn't a perfect articulation of how she was feeling, but it would have to do; any more words she'd planned on saying had lodged uncomfortably against the lump in her throat.

"I'll walk you," Connor said, and to her surprise – again – he went toward the trees to prove his intent.

She gasped. As sweet as it was that Connor wanted to come with her, she knew she was not in the frame of mind to deal with the dark energy in the trees while fielding further questions about the fact that she saw ghosts. "No!" she cried, then covered her mouth with her fingers. She sounded crazy.

Connor looked back at her and, to her dismay, the shadow that had chased her only minutes earlier loomed up behind him.

"Please," she begged, but to whom, she couldn't have said.

"It's alright," Connor laughed half-heartedly. "I ain't afraid of no ghosts!"

The Ghostbusters theme should have made her laugh, but she was backing away, instead. Her ability to ignore the shadow was completely gone and she was trapped between it and the friend who'd betrayed her trust in the worst of ways.

And then Bethie was approaching, saying "Hey, what's going on?" with a bit of apprehension in her voice, and it was too much. Shya was running then, but toward the road, that time not thinking. Not even trying to keep it together.

"Where you going, weirdo?" Drake called after her, but his teasing hit harder than even Shya knew he'd intended.

And she just kept running. Changing everything. Thinking about it later, she was able to place some of the blame on Bethie. It didn't matter by then, though. Everything was too different.

There was no going back.

CHAPTER 14 – CREEP

There are those nights when darkness comes and eats up daylight without pause

When sunlight dips and takes the day and brilliant sunset fades to grey

When creatures slow, forget their work, hide in their homes while spirits lurk

They're always there, but in the dark, they need not hide neath ruse and hark

Silence pulls the mindless hoards, lost energies from times of lords

And ladies lost to tragedy, ne'er satisfied nor drawn to flee

Untethered souls with forgotten purpose seek out the living and entreat us

To connect with warmth and kindness, learn the tales of how they left us

And sometimes they delight to find those gifted few who cannot hide

Who hear them, see them and abide the unreal tales from unseen sides

And if they've found one of the sought out few who have some skill in what they do

There is a path revealed to them to end their torturous suffering and

They can let go, ungrounded, soar where earthy
sorrows are no more

CHAPTER 15 – AGAINST THE CURRENT

The Seers met outside of Dawn's condo every couple months for a change of scenery. A lot of them leaned - some heavily - toward introversion in their regular lives and appreciated the time out with friends who understood. The aquarium was a popular choice; it tended to be very quiet on weeknights, and somehow the low lights and meandering ways of the creatures on display felt, in a word, safe.

Big Ed was sticking close to Shya that night. He'd been eager to come to her aid the night of the dream, and not only for the opportunity to pay back some of Shya's past support of him in times of need. Shya was, in addition to being an incredibly gifted medium, beautiful. And kind. And unassuming, too.

He'd been in love with her since they'd met at the first Seers group meeting. It had only been himself, Dawn and Mel at first. Or so they thought. Shya was a surprise late arrival, and a reluctant one, at that. But she was quickly accepted, and the four had formed a quick bond.

But Shya was unusually withdrawn that night. She peered into the waters behind the glass as if mesmerized, biting her nails absently. Ed had tried to engage her, but though she seemed happy enough to stay beside him, her mind was elsewhere. The rest of the group seemed glad to relax and enjoy the sights. The twins were especially animated, exclaiming to each other, one grabbing the other's hand to draw her attention to something she found exciting. Animated, yes, but somehow still in their own private bubble, on the periphery of the group.

Dawn stepped in beside them at the stingray tank. She elbowed him lightly in the side. He frowned downward at her; she must've been a foot and a half shorter than him. "She OK?" she mouthed, pointing subtly in Shya's direction.

Big Ed shrugged, the movement of his massive shoulders anything but subtle.

Shya barely perceived Dawn, though it was obvious she and Ed were talking about her. Her mind was on other things – emaciated little boys, black eyes and falling beds. Clouds of insects that had seemed to emerge from sleep with her, for every now and then she heard a buzzing and had to look up quickly just to make sure she was awake.

Her mind was on her shift that night, too. She hated the nine to close shift, especially on weeknights when it was slow and mostly regulars winding down their day in the company of others like them. Drinking beer after beer or repeated mixed drinks – their favorites. The drinks they counted on to take them down into oblivion every night, until sleep – or other form of unconsciousness – took them.

To Shya, it was sad. It was predictable, too, and left too much room for introspection, unlike the weekend nights, which were filled with a younger crowd and live music.

Big Ed's voice was suddenly rousing her from her thoughts. "I was going to suggest she tell everyone about her dream…"

"Maybe this isn't the right place," Dawn answered quietly. "But has she been -"

"Hey!" Shya made them both jump. "I *am* here, guys."

"That's a matter of opinion," Dawn retorted, her eyes on the rays as they flew majestically by.

Big Ed looked regretfully at her. "Sorry. We're just worried about you."

Shya recalled how sleepy Big Ed had looked when he showed up at her apartment that night. Then she remembered how comforting it was to have him on her couch while she fell back to sleep in her fully lit bedroom. How just knowing she could call him if she needed had let her sleep each night since then. She sighed and patted his arm. "I know."

Dawn met her eyes then. "You been letting them in during the day at all?"

Shya clenched her jaw. She'd intended to... well, she'd been seriously considering intending to, anyway, but then there'd been the dream. It had felt like enough darkness, sleeping or waking states notwithstanding.

Dawn made a disapproving noise. "How you gonna figure this out if you won't even look at it?"

Big Ed put a quieting hand on Dawn's forearm, and suddenly Mel was there, too, his hands on Dawn's shoulders as he rested his chin on the top of her head with a smile.

"They got you talking, did they?" he aimed his smile at Shya, but she only bristled further.

"Apparently I'm not hanging out with dark spirits enough," Shya said, coldly. Now her mind was on Bethie, somehow. On betrayal, she guessed. She shook her head, suddenly regretful. Realizing she shouldn't make others pay for the distrust she'd fostered after her childhood best friend's disloyalty. But Dawn spoke before Shya could smooth it over.

"I never wanted you to make friends with the darkness, girl, and you know that."

She and Shya shared a long look, and Shya was the one to break it with a nod. "I know, Dawn. I'm sorry. I guess I already feel shitty for not knowing how to handle all this, and that makes me defensive."

Dawn looked mildly contrite. "I suppose I could word things differently, too," she said, eyes on the floor.

"How *have* things been going?" Mel spoke up from behind Dawn again. His hands were still on the woman's shoulders, and Dawn showed no signs of brushing them away. Mel really did have a comforting way about him.

Shya shrugged. "I had a dream. It sucked."

"Why didn't you call us?" the twins chorused suddenly from behind Shya and she whirled, hand on her heart.

"Good Lord!" she managed a nervous laugh.

"Sorry," they both said.

Shya glanced at Big Ed. "I called Ed, actually," she gestured to him, making sure to give him a grateful smile. She knew he cared for her, but didn't think on it too hard. She couldn't take on the responsibility for his feelings; it was too much.

"That's good," Dawn seemed genuinely satisfied.

Big Ed shuffled his feet. "God knows I've called on her before," he said dismissively.

Dawn smiled thinly, making Shya realize she knew Ed had feelings for Shya, too.

I'll need to nip this in the bud after all, Shya pondered.

"Anything happen since the dream?" Sheila spoke, seemingly dissatisfied with standing just outside the group any longer.

Shya tensed. "Not really. I mean, it could've, I think..." she though of the heat on her skin when she walked past dark alleyways, and how it felt to meet her own eyes in the mirror – as though she had to work to recognize herself. As though her eyes would blacken and shine as the boy's had in her dream. Of how hard it had been *not* to see them – to feel them there but refuse to see. To look past them as though they were shadows, only. Shadows where shadow shouldn't be. "I guess I haven't been able to fully -" she paused as she looked to her friends, "- I've been too afraid."

"We can help," Anna interjected.

Shya frowned.

"Let *us* look at them, through you," Jane explained.

Shya was dubious. The twins were truly gifted, but that was all the more reason they shouldn't go looking in the dark for something less savoury than the ghosts they were used to communicating with. "No. It's too dangerous."

"We know what they're like," Jane replied soberly.

"And besides, we have each other for support," Anna added, as though she'd read Shya's thoughts.

"Don't you have a shift at nine?" Big Ed cut in, and just in time – Shya had been about to clam up again.

She looked at her phone. Eight forty. "Yep!" she replied, relief obvious in her voice.

"You should consider letting them see, Shya," Dawn did brush Mel's hands from her shoulders then. "We could do it next week, together."

Shya turned back to the group and shrugged. "Fine. But *I* decide when we're done!"

Dawn nodded, satisfied. The twins were, of course, unsurprised.

CHAPTER 16 – SELFLESS, SELFISH

The shift passed more quickly than she could have hoped. The boss was in, which always made the staff quicker on their feet and readier with a smile. And he'd brought a group of friends – Shya and the others joked that he never gave them a heads-up because he assumed they were the same with everyone as they were with him: professional. Eager to please. It mattered little in the end. What the unplanned crowd did for Shya was keep her busy. Distracted.

Just what she needed.

She'd barely had a moment to think by the time the place was closing down and she was wiping the bar down a final time. Inventory was taken, tips were split with the kitchen and the cash was balanced. And she was *tired.* She was smiling as she left, grateful for the whole-body urge to sleep that promised to overtake her. So, she jumped when a voice greeted her from the darkness of the parking lot. She and the others were relegated to the far corner by the metal garbage bins, and though the light for that section of the lot had been vandalized months earlier, the boss was as slow as he was thoughtless when it came to the big crowds he showed up with.

"Hey," came a casual-sounding male voice from the dark expanse of the parking lot, and Shya stopped, squinting into the darkness and making out the outline of a figure leaning against her car. Relief flooded her instantly. If his voice hadn't tipped her off at first, the posture of him did. Nobody did effortless cool like her step-brother did.

"What the hell, Rory? You scared the shit out of me," she mumbled, not surprised to find herself annoyed at his presence.

"Sorry, sis. I locked myself out of the house again," he pressed himself off the car and spread his arms as she approached, but she avoided the embrace gracefully.

"You know it's two in the morning, right?"

He laughed. "Yeah. A few of us closed the Chuckwagon down after work," he said, a hint of humour in his voice.

"Why didn't you just go home with one of them? God knows your co-workers have offered you a bed before." Shya was in no way eager to deal with Rory's irresponsible ways that night, and it felt good to let it show. She was certain the fact that his face was in shadow helped; he couldn't plead with his eyes.

"Hey, come on," he said instead, the trace of humour still alive and well.

"Rory, something confuses me," she stopped before unlocking the driver's side door and looked at his outline in the dark, "and it's this: how can you be a successful criminal attorney while juggling an impressive – some would even puzzle at the reasoning, but let's keep focused, here – crowd of friends and admirers, and yet lock yourself out of your townhouse at least once a month?"

He raised his arms, laughing, then sighed. "Maybe I forget my keys *because* I have so much going on. Seems obvious to me."

She rolled her eyes – an impotent gesture in the dark, but one which occurred without giving her time to consider. "Always the lawyer."

"You have a bad night, Shy?" There was a twinge of impatience in his voice, now, and it was satisfying to hear it.

"Not at all!" she retorted lightly as she opened the door and gestured him toward the passenger side. "Until now, that is!"

He paused while she sat and did up her seatbelt. She eyed him casually in the side mirror, then started the car. That got him moving.

"I can always just go to a hotel," he muttered as he got in.

She sighed. "No, I'm sorry, Ror. It just feels sometimes like -" she chuckled, "- like neither of us has ever grown up all the way."

He was quiet for a moment. Just long enough to let her hear her words again and tense up. "We got past some childish things," he murmured, finally, and she had to clench her teeth to hold her words back.

He knew it bothered her to bring it up, and yet he did whenever there was tension between them. As if what happened was all on her, somehow. She put the car in reverse, breathing slowly. Giving herself time like her University therapist had taught her. When they were on the road and she felt steadier, she managed a light laugh. "I guess the fact that I still believe in ghosts makes it hard to leave childhood behind completely." She flicked the radio on.

Rory mumbled something but she ignored it. She sung to the music, instead, amping it up when he groaned and pulled his hood low over his face as if to hide.

She found herself feeling surprisingly light when they went into the apartment. Rory's presence wasn't always solicited – and somehow he managed to be scarce when she did need him – but that night she was glad for the company as she went to bed. So much so that she began to think about the twins – about the next Seers meeting and how her friends would tease the information she was purposefully blind to out into the open. To help.

And she thought maybe she should try – just open up a crack to the dark energy that had been plaguing her.

The thought made her squirm beneath her covers. Even with Rory there, it felt wrong to invite that presence in.

But the boy...

She sucked in a breath, remembering the nightmare with tremendous discomfort. But she couldn't deny the logic. If she had to deny the worst of it, that left the boy, and no matter how he puzzled her – no matter how he frightened her – she knew he needed her, too.

They all did, one way or another.

So, she went to sleep with an invitation on a stream of prayer-like thought.

Come. I'm ready.

CHAPTER 17 – SLEEP

Shya opened herself up, reaching out for the guidance of the one spirit that could be counted on as a guardian. The resulting emptiness wouldn't have bothered her – sometimes her mother was unavailable, and that was alright, but Shya realized as sleep took her down into unconsciousness that she hadn't been able to connect with her mother the last time she'd tried, either. Nor had she shown up on her own. Combined, the circumstances *were* strange. But her puzzlement floated away; just a wisp of thought that remained in the realm of wakefulness.

And she was asleep. And even without her mother's steady support, she found herself indeed in the presence of the boy, but it was different. She was discombobulated immediately, for she felt the boy, but could not see him. It was only when she began to move that she realized the reason. It was because they were one. She had landed behind his eyes and it was *he* that moved now. He that gazed toward the crashing waves with a feeling of unease. He whose bare feet crunched painfully on the sharp points and crevices of a rocky shore. A glance to the right revealed a steep cliff wall, dark and towering tall above them as the tide bore the waves in, slowly, inch by inch closer as the boy travelled further away from higher ground.

It was getting dark, too. She could feel him realize it with another look to the water, and then to the horizon where it touched a sky whose sunset pallet only clung weakly as inkblot shades of grey and blue and black seemed to press in from above, chasing the sun beneath the rolling waves. A fear took hold within the chest of the small boy she inhabited, such that each intake of breath pained them both. But she could not comfort him; despite efforts to make herself known, it was quickly clear that she was an observer, only.

And then his vision changed as the darkness deepened. It twinned slightly, so that everything was shaded by an overlapping double of itself, crimson-colored doppelgangers to usher each object into night – the silhouetted trees atop the cliff, the waves that tossed and plunged into the shore, a small hand that was held up for examination. Each observation driving home the metaphor of the red wine stain of it's double, as though everything was seen through a twisted lens of blood. And finally, she saw the rocks beneath the boy's feet as his focus moved from his hand to the ground beneath him.

The double-vision made Shya and her host dizzy, especially as his eyes struggled to focus on the uneven ground, but soon he did see, and the dizziness ceased to matter... for what solidified just before the darkness was complete was a landscape of whitewashed bones and dead creatures – lifeless bodies of broken birds and crushed kittens between skulls of all shapes and sizes. The boys's horror was palpable. Shya thought to call for her mother again, but the boy was kneeling, his eyes on one figure as all light was extinguished: a baby bird, featherless and too young to even have opened its eyes just yet.

He sobbed; she felt it in her own throat like a lump of smoldering coal. And then it was in his hands. She felt the thing's racing heartbeat beneath a delicate ribcage. Felt how its naked flesh moved over each bone.

The sound of the waves intensified and the boy stood, the tiny bird in his palms like a cherished treasure, and peered desperately into the darkness behind him. But there was nothing – just endless night beneath a moonless sky. Panic gripped at his chest again and as if in response, the crashing of the waves became a deafening onslaught as his feet were covered in spray.

The tide.

In a blast of determination, Shya screamed, producing an echoed anguish inside the boy's head, and before he could think, he raised his hands to cover his ears, which sent the bird to plummet and when he realized he screamed, too, and the world was bathed with blinding light and from the sky came a thunderclap so powerful, it knocked the boy to his knees.

Which landed, thankfully, not on the bones and bodies of dead and dying creatures but in cool grass. And suddenly, it was silent.

He bent forward instinctively, his hands moving again, but this time to protect his eyes.

Shya needed out. Needed distance. Needed comfort. But she remained trapped inside the vessel of a boy to whom she had no known connection. She'd reached him when she screamed, but it had failed to dislodge her. The terror she perceived now had no borders – no distinction between her and the boy, and it was too much.

She felt she might explode.

He opened his eyes in that moment, blinking against the sun as his pupils worked to adjust, and Shya felt his fear wane. She worked to quiet her own desperation and peered through his eyes, needing the thing that had calmed him, too. And it was familiar... but not to her. Nonetheless, when she saw it, she knew it was his back yard.

And she knew why his heart began to thud when he looked toward the house. That the thing struggling in the grass just beneath a corner soffit was a baby bird, fallen from its nest.

And that it would be featherless and frail.

And as he walked toward it, she knew it was a memory – a true one from which had borne the nightmare they'd started in. She knew, too, as he picked it up with a lump of compassion in his throat and a surge of determination filled him that he would beg his father to let him take it in. Take care of it.

And that the bird would die, and to a little boy who'd already lost too much, it was a failure whose weight he couldn't begin to shake. She saw bits and pieces of it happening, as if she were watching it on a screen inside her mind, and longed to save him from it all. Longed to tell him it wasn't his fault; that he'd tried and that made him a hero, even if the little bird was likely pushed out of the nest in the first place, already destined not to live. Not this time.

She awoke so quickly she felt as if she'd been forcefully ejected from it all – the boy's body and her state of unconsciousness, alike – and she shot up in bed with a wail of fright.

She reached for the phone and dialled Big Ed before she could ponder it, and was just hanging up when she heard footsteps rushing to her door.

Rory, she remembered, and a wave of relief washed over her.

Rory was there to rescue her once again.

CHAPTER 18 – AN UNLIKELY SAVIOUR

Shya's purposeful avoidance of her best friend as well as Conner and Drake coincided quite painfully with a sudden intensification of her father's relationship with Louise. She and Rory were at the dinner table more nights than not, and it felt like being kicked while she was down – to be suddenly uncomfortable in her own home, and yet have nobody to run to for commiseration was a doubly fierce blow.

Bethie hadn't tried to mend things; it seemed to Shya that her friend had found more valuable rewards in her relationship with Drake than Shya could offer, and Shya never questioned it aloud. She'd always felt like Bethie's friendship was too good to be true – certainly no one else that took the time to know her accepted her so readily. But now Bethie was gone and Shya was forced to look back on their friendship with a critical eye, questioning her worth again.

Now and then, in class or on the bus, she'd catch Bethie studying her, but she dared not try to read her features. She'd sooner accept that she'd lost out to the boys than face whatever could darken her lost friend's eyes that way. At the time, it felt easier to lose than to justify her worth.

So, when Rory, who was two years older and monumentally more self-assured than Shya had ever been, came into her life and home, it was natural that he filled Bethie's spot in some ways. Not all – Rory was leagues less sensitive than Bethie, and just as much more self-confident. But despite what he lacked, he won the vacant spot in Shya's heart largely due to circumstances. Unlike Bethie, he was *there.*

Rory was the new kid, and while he was unphased by the tasks of meeting new friends and fitting in, he came to Shya for familiarity. For advice on local hangouts, and the little information she could glean about the pretty girls in her grade. And also because she was there, too. Besides the weekends he spent with his father (it started with every second weekend, but dwindled quickly over the first year), his home was with his mother, Shya, and her father. And it was funny: she expected him to fade from her life as quickly as he'd entered it, but he never seemed to consider it.

That's not to say she was high on his list of priorities, though. He gained popularity mind-bogglingly quickly. Even with his undeniable good looks and charm, Shya eyed the ever-present group of kids that surrounded him in awe and not a little confusion. For she knew that underneath all that glamour, her would-be step-brother was pissed about his parent's divorce. Was mystified, most of the time, by what made folks tick, and perhaps most importantly, had a bit of an entitlement complex.

Which meant that when Rory was being real, he was quite often annoying and almost as frequently kind of a dick.

Over the years, Shya came to realize that she was one of the precious few in Rory's life that he opened up to. She imagined him being more "real" with his dad, but never got to see it in action. If nothing else, it explained why she was always his fallback when plans fell through or he was feeling moody and wanted to stay home. He relaxed with her.

In any case, because of both Shya and Rory's immediate needs, they became close very quickly. And somehow, over time together spent exploring the woods or sitting at the marina, Shya found herself opening up to him, too. And though he did laugh, he never questioned the validity of her claims of possessing odd talents. He even seemed interested in them for a time, asking questions and demanding to know the story of her mother's experiences before she died, but then it got to be old news and Shya's differences became just part of who she was. It was, in a word, freeing.

He mostly talked about dreams of the future; conquests for a high-paying career and a beautiful family – but not before he'd travelled the world and had a myriad of amazing experiences. He would talk for hours about how he envisioned his life playing out, and Shya would get lost in it, closing her eyes as they lay in the grass and watching his stories unfold in her mind as he narrated them. Sometimes, she fell asleep in the grass, taken on the wings of Rory's imaginings beneath calm, cornflower blue skies.

One time, it was not the sky above her when she reopened her eyes. It was Rory's own eyes, staring down at her in a frown.

"What?" she demanded breathlessly, already squirming to get away, but he stopped her with a hand on the arm furthest from him. "Rory!" she objected, but her voice was quiet. His eyes held unspoken questions and his upper lip revealed the beginnings of manly growth. They hadn't been children when they'd met, but the unexpected proximity of him proved that they'd both matured in leaps and bounds in the eight-ish months since they had.

"You were sleeping," he said, rather dreamily. His hand warm on her bicep and the length of his arm hovering almost palpably over her budding chest.

"So?" Shya struggled to talk without breathing too heavily into his face. She wondered absently what she'd eaten for lunch that day and whether she'd brushed her teeth at all since the night before.

He released her arm and the coolness of the air against her skin was almost an insult. But then he ran the back of his index finger down the side of her face and she was warm again, but all over, and surprised to have to struggle to keep her eyelids from drooping. When was the last time she'd been touched? Since before her mother had died? *At the funeral, maybe,* her mind chattered dumbly as if to excuse her from trying to get out from beneath this boy who confounded her with his opposing charm and arrogance. "I just," he paused and let his eyes rove over her face. She tingled beneath his stare, but seemed at a loss to do anything to escape it. "I just never noticed how pretty you are," he finished, and she felt her jaw drop just a little. And that was when he kissed her, soft but firm, and all thoughts were banished for four overwhelming seconds when his mouth and hers were the only things that existed.

But then she was pushing him away and scrambling backward, dizzy and angry to boot, at being kissed for the first time in her life by the son of the woman her father was hinting at marrying in short order. She swiped self-consciously at her lips even as Rory sat up, a lazy smile stretching his still-moist lips. Shya inwardly cursed the strange heat that snaked in her lower abdomen. Outwardly, she yelled, "How could you *do* that?"

Rory laughed. "What? Wasn't it nice, sis?"

"Oh, *God!*" she wailed. Missing Bethie. Glad her mother would never know – and then worried that maybe she would. She appeared now and then, after all. "You're practically my *brother!*" She exclaimed with her eyes wide, as much to the field around them and the water trickling nearby as to Rory himself.

Rory studied his fingernails, then went to work biting at one of them. He eyed her through his eyelashes coolly, seemingly unimpressed by her theatrics. "I'm not though, Shya. I won't be after the wedding, either." He spit out a shred of fingernail, then casually lay backward, lacing his fingers behind his head and sighing as Shya fumed.

"That was my first kiss!" She bit her lip as soon as the words were out.

He didn't laugh, though. Only looked at her sideways, eyebrows raised. "Huh."

Something he'd said resurfaced. "Wait. After the wedding? What do you mean?"

Rory grimaced, then covered his face. "Oh, shit."

Shya crawled through the tall grass to him, her heart pounding. "Dad didn't say anything about a wedding!" she pulled his arms away from his face and held them in the grass on either side of his head. The sun shone in his eyes and they were different – tawny, the golden flecks glittering hypnotically.

"I'm sorry," he whispered. A slow smile stole over his features again. "Mom made me promise not to say anything. They're thinking about doing it in the fall."

Shya shook her head, tears brimming in her eyes.

"It's not that bad," he said, and she let him go, falling onto her butt and peering through tears at the river. Rory sat up, too, and took her hands. "What?" he tried to catch her eyes, making her laugh as he bobbed his head. "You hate me that much?"

She swiped at her tears with her free hand.

"It won't make her any more gone," he said quietly, and she knew he meant her mother.

She hiccoughed loudly and he kissed her again, taking her breath away. It was sweet, and it felt right, because in that moment, she needed it, somehow.

He pulled away to meet her eyes. "There," he said, looking a little smug. "I don't think I'd be able to live with myself if I didn't know what that felt like before I could never do it again."

He smiled and released her hands.

Her fingers went straight to her lips. They sat in silence, watching the water, until Rory stood and stretched. "Pot roast time, sis," he announced, offering his hand to her.

She frowned up at him and stood, avoiding his hand. "You shouldn't have done that," she said, but she felt like smiling. She felt like hugging herself just to keep that warm feeling in a little longer. And when he'd called her "sis" again, it stung.

"It's no big deal. We didn't break any laws." He shoved his hands into his pockets and glanced toward the trail back home. Bored already.

More like perpetually hungry, she reasoned, and had to bite her cheeks to stop herself from laughing.

"If it's no big deal, why do you say you can't ever do it again?" she challenged, petulantly crossing her arms over her chest.

"Ah," he smiled, his eyes twinkling. "Why? Do you want to?" He took a step toward her and she made a sound of frustration as she punched his shoulder.

"Quit it!"

He did laugh, then. "Come on," he nodded toward the trail and they got moving.

The trail was cool after lying in the sun, the floor dancing with shadows of maple trees and pine moving in the breeze. Shya peered up into the leaves, grateful for the lush green of the canopy. No red or yellow in sight. There was still some time before autumn. *Before the wedding.* She shivered.

Rory looked back as if on cue. "You OK?"

She shrugged.

He stopped suddenly, and faced her. "I'm sorry. It wasn't all bad though, was it?"

Tears sprung again and she had to press her lips together.

"What? Is it the wedding?"

She nodded, looking up at him. The sun glinted off of the highlights in his hair and she hated herself for noticing.

"It'll be OK," he smiled, and then hugged her. "And I promise not to kiss you again," he chuckled into her hair and she couldn't help it; she laughed, too.

He did, though. Kiss her, that is. Rory was never one for keeping promises.

CHAPTER 19 – AHA!

Rory's arms were around her before she could even sit up fully.

"What is it? You were screaming," his lips were at her ear.

She immediately relaxed and then hated herself for having such a low threshold against his charms. She pressed him back and sat up, then turned the side-table lamp on. Rory repositioned himself on the bed and gazed at her, both expectant and concerned. His hair was perfectly mussed up. She softened. Despite his usual self-centred ways, he truly cared for her. Always had.

She rubbed at her eyes as images from her dream filled her head. "Oh, God."

Rory took one of her hands in his. "A nightmare?"

She chuckled sardonically and met his eyes. "That's putting it mildly, but I guess it's the closest descriptor of it."

He frowned. "Tell me."

She shook her head immediately. "You don't want to know."

He squeezed her hand. "Have I been so distant that you really believe that?"

She studied his face for a moment, then flushed with guilt. She couldn't blame their distance on Rory completely. "No," she answered, finally. "But – well, I don't even know how to describe it." She paused, her eyes going to the window and then the corners as if to confirm they were alone. "I told you things were strange these days."

He nodded. "You didn't tell me how, though."

She snickered and took her hand back, rubbing it as if to banish the way his touch still made her feel. "You had plans, remember?"

He looked confused for a moment, then his face cleared. "I'm sorry I didn't call."

She looked into her lap, nodding.

"I *do* care, Shy."

She smiled. "I know."

He moved to the middle of the bed and crossed his legs and Shya followed suit, wanting to giggle as he folded his hands and fixed his eyes intently on her. "So, tell me."

She sighed. How was it that he could make her feel invisible one moment and then so special the next? She briefly recalled past psych classes and the "aha!" moments she'd experienced as they discussed sociopathy and narcissistic tendencies. But any relief had been fleeting – Rory refused to fit neatly into any one category, despite her efforts.

"What?"

She snapped back to the present. "I was just pondering your disposition," she smiled.

He rolled his eyes. "How many times have I warned you not to try and figure me out?"

She laughed.

"Hey," he gave her a little wave. "I'm here. Tell me what's been going on."

She inhaled deeply, then sighed the breath out. "It's like – it's like I'm being shown something, but for the life of me I can't figure out *what*."

He nodded.

"There's a boy – I only see him in dreams. But there's something else, too...something dark. Something like what I've refused to acknowledge all my life."

"And...what? The two are connected somehow?"

She frowned, her eyes going to the quilt as she considered the question, following the patterns in their neat and tidy rows with gratitude for their predictability. "I don't know," she whispered, finally. She met his eyes again. "It feels different than anything I've ever experienced."

"Well, what was the dream about?"

She shuddered. "Nightmare."

Rory nodded.

"It was like – I *was* the boy. Inside his body, this time, and we were at the shore." Her eyes lit up. "Like the one Mom and I used to spend hours exploring in Port Williams!"

He shrugged. He'd heard the stories, but hadn't seen it. Those visits to Nova Scotia took place long before Rory and Louise had joined the family. They were, after all, trips to visit her mother's family.

"Anyway – it only reminded me of that place because of how rocky it was, and how it felt to know the tide was coming in and it was a long way back to higher ground."

"OK," Rory motioned her on, his eyes clouding slightly in that telltale way his body language let her know he was getting impatient.

"Well, it was getting dark and it *wasn't* rocks on the shore. It was bones and the bodies of animals," she said quickly, then grimaced at the harshness of her words. Even Rory made a face.

"Jesus. Sounds like a nightmare, alright. How do you even know that wasn't all it was?"

She cast a questioning look his way. "What do you mean?"

"Everyone has nightmares, Shy. Why do you assume this dream was anything more than that? I mean, you haven't seen the boy in daylight, right?"

It felt good to consider it as an option, despite her certainty that it was wrong. "No," she shook her head sadly. "The darkness – the presence." She worked to compose her thoughts. "The nightmare changed; I saw the true memory of the boy, and knew the dark entity had twisted it into something terrible. The little boy had found a dying baby bird on the ground, tried to nurse it back to health. When the bird died, it was almost like a little piece of him died, too. These evil energies…that's what they do. They distort the things that affect you most into something ugly and terrifying."

"Sounds like that – energy – is bothering the boy, not just you," Rory said quietly, and something clicked in Shya.

Her eyes widened as she peered into his, but any response was cut off by a knock at the door. She peered into the hallway, remembering Big Ed. "Oh! I forgot," she looked at Rory, "I called a friend right after -"

"Why?" he accused, his brow darkening.

"I forgot you were here!" she exclaimed, standing already and rooting around for her housecoat. "I called him after the last one and I guess it felt like the thing to do!" She threw the robe on and looked back at Rory, who was frowning at her bare legs by that point. "Sorry."

He lay down on the bed, positioning his head on her pillow and pulling the covers up to his chin.

"What are you doing?"

He opened one eye. "Seems you'll be busy with your *friend* for a while, so you don't mind if I take the bed, do you?"

She sighed.

"This one of your freaky friends from that group?" he teased, but it was half-hearted; his face was already going slack as he burrowed into Shya's pillow.

"You're a pain in the ass," she muttered, then went to greet Big Ed.

CHAPTER 20 –
MIDNIGHT COFFEE

Big Ed hugged her as soon as the door opened enough to allow it. Shya remembered how wonderful it had been to have him there – to feel his strong, solid arms around her – the last time she'd called him. But it was different this time. Despite how he annoyed her, Rory had taken the edge off her terror.

She pulled away from her friend, whose eyes were tired, but concerned. "Hey. I'm sorry to have gotten you up again."

He shook his head, one hand raised against her apologies as he slipped his shoes off. "Come on, let's go sit."

She grinned as he led her to the kitchen, fingers gentle on her elbow, as though it were *she* who was visiting her modest apartment. She was nearly giggling when he gestured her toward the vintage linoleum table she'd scored at an estate sale, then got to work making tea.

"It's just occurred to me that this has happened far too often," she sighed as he sent her a questioning look. "You know your way around my kitchen as well as I do."

He chuckled quietly. Shya watched as he moved comfortably between the fridge and cupboards, observed as he squirted a bit of honey in her cup, then a splash of milk. Just as she liked it.

"You're good to come," she muttered.

He placed the cups on the table and sat, grunting quietly as he pushed the seat out in order to accommodate his girth.

Shya found herself wishing, not for the first time, that she felt something more than friendly toward him. He was a kind man.

"So?" He sipped his tea, pursing his lips a little afterward. "Hot," he explained with one word. He studied her for a few moments. "You don't seem as bad as last time."

She busied herself stirring her tea so she wouldn't have to look at him. "I – my step-brother is here. I'm so sorry, Ed; I dialled you before I even remembered he was out on the couch."

He ducked his head, then leaned out to look toward the living room.

"He's stolen my bed," she rolled her eyes. "Guess that's my punishment for waking him." She smiled, hoping she sounded light. Hoping he wouldn't be upset.

She needn't have worried. He smiled. "Did you tell him about it?"

She nodded.

"You said – he knows about your gift, right?"

She nodded again. "He was sort of the only friend I had for a while," she answered, feeling the need to explain but resenting it, too. She'd always felt that if she and Rory had had a normal blended family-type relationship, she'd never bristle at friends' curiosity about him.

Ed nodded, then sipped at his tea. "Do you still want to talk about it? If you want to get some more sleep, I'll go…"

She patted his hand. "No, don't go." She gestured toward her room. "He's asleep now and I could use the company."

He seemed to be put at ease. "Well then, tell me about it."

She pressed her lips together, then started talking. Ed listened as he had the time before. The way he listened to everyone: with sincere interest and boundless compassion. She did feel better once she'd emptied it all out of her mind. She ended with Rory's rather intuitive comment about how the dark presence seemed to be bothering the boy and not just her.

Ed was frowning. "That would make sense of things. You don't see the boy except for in dreams. What if – what if the darkness *is* attached to him? What if the boy isn't a ghost, but in an altered state because of it?"

Shya rubbed her arms as a chill rolled over her.

Ed leaned forward. "I know you don't like to even acknowledge these sorts of energies, Shya, but what if that's the only way to help the boy?"

She threw her hands into the air. "What boy? Where? I dream about him – even see through his eyes, but he's never communicated with me, not really! "

"Maybe that's what the dreams are. Maybe in his – *state* – it's the only way he can reach out to you."

"You're saying he's possessed." She said the words quickly, but they still tasted bad in her mouth.

"You can't say you hadn't considered it."

She looked toward the bedroom again. Wished to be asleep, even if it meant trading places with Rory and having to deal with the hangover he'd surely have in the morning. "Of course it's been in the back of my mind, but that doesn't mean I wanted to acknowledge it," she said, her eyes resolutely on the bedroom door.

Ed leaned back in the metal and vinyl chair, making it creak helplessly under his shifting weight. Shya met his eyes. "Even if it's true, it doesn't help to know it."

"Shya," he paused, clearly struggling to find the words, "with your gifts, you must see the dark as much as you see the light, even if you ignore it. Why are you so opposed to acknowledging it?"

"Because I'm especially vulnerable to it," Shya retorted without pause. "My mother – *I* have ancestors who've succumbed to the darker forces that would take advantage of us because we see them! They delight in terrorizing the most sensitive of us! She said getting involved with those who've been possessed is like an invitation, Ed."

"This little boy – what if he's like you? What if he was vulnerable and didn't know to look away like your mother taught you to do?"

Tears welled in her eyes as guilt – hot and familiar – rose in her. "If that's the case, and I somehow found him, I'd be risking myself." She shook her head and wiped a tear away. "It sounds so selfish, I know."

"I don't understand everything about your family's gift," he said quietly, "God knows you're different from the twins. From any medium I've ever known, truth be told! But shouldn't it mean you're more equipped to fight the evil in addition to being more vulnerable to it?"

Shya focused on her mug. She cupped it gently just to feel the warmth against her palms. Something real. Tangible. Finally, she raised her eyes to Ed's. "I don't know."

"Bet none of your relatives had a group like The Seers to back them up," he said with a smile.

She warmed. Truthfully, she didn't know that, either, but it was reassuring to consider herself so well-armed.

"And," he reached for her hand and she gave one, moving from warm ceramic to warm skin easily. "I think we can find the boy, if you decide it's what you want to do. Together, we can find him."

She knew it was true. She nodded.

He pulled his hand away as he sat back, regarding her. "I

know you hate to hear this, but I wish I knew my own gift as well as you know your own. As well as any of the others do!"

It *was* a frequent complaint of Ed's. His only complaint, really. Besides his troubles in the world of online dating (his stories were always anticipated and received openly by the group as a great source of entertainment), his ill-defined gift was a well-discussed sore point.

"Maybe there's something to what the twins were saying, about your being a sort of... joining element of the different realms of existence?" She wasn't even sure she'd said it right.

Ed's expression echoed her confusion. "It's the only thing I can put into words! I sense energies, but it's more like they're behind curtains, or beneath the ground..." he trailed off.

Shya nodded slowly. She'd heard it before. He'd also described it as "layers" or "levels", and feeling as though people were trying to be heard through water or coming through as a buzzing in his ear. "Dawn is right more than I'd like to admit," she winked. "I'll bet she's right about how everything will be clear."

He rolled his eyes. "When it *needs* to be?"

Shya nodded with a giggle. "What Sheila said about portals was interesting, too." She'd nearly forgotten the quiet woman's input, but now it felt important, somehow.

He gestured in frustration again, his palms landing on his thighs with a clap that had Shya glancing toward the bedroom again. "Sure, it would make sense that I'd be able to sense portals, but so far it hasn't helped," he said. He reached for his tea again. "Ah, I'm sorry," he sighed, then took a swig. "I know I've beaten this subject to death."

She rose, surprising herself as she went to embrace him,

throwing her arms around his hulking shoulders. He made a noise of surprise, then laughed, patting her arms awkwardly. She stood back, meeting his eyes. "Don't forget that *you* have a pretty awesome group of friends willing to help you, too."

He was blushing.

"I know we'll figure it out," she finished, folding her arms over her chest as she stifled a yawn.

"That's my cue," Ed rose before she could protest, and she followed him to the door.

"Thank you," she said as he donned his shoes and felt around in his pockets for his keys.

"Anytime," he replied, purposefully meeting her eyes.

She closed the door with very little apprehension, glad to realize she'd been so hastily rescued by people who cared about her. But though her gratitude was real, it didn't temper her frustration over the fact that she *needed* rescue so often. She couldn't help but to revisit her long list of unanswered questions about how her mother had dealt with these things. She envied the fact that her mother had her own mother – Shya's grandmother – to consult with for so much longer than Shya had, learning everything that had been passed down through the long line of women who'd inherited the strange ability to defy the boundaries between life and death. At least as far as communication – connection, her mother had called it – went.

There'd only been one relative whose gift had not materialized before her own death. Through a combination of circumstances – a mother who'd lived stubbornly to be a hundred and three, a long marriage to an abusive drug addict and a debilitating boating accident in her forty-fourth year that eventually led to her own addiction to pain pills and accidental overdose – she died before it could be passed to her.

But like clockwork, her own daughter picked up where her grandmother left off, armed only with her Nana's journals and her mother's ramblings as she had declined to her death.

But even with a lifetime of knowledge and many more years of preparation Shya had had, she knew, too, that all those who'd come before her had one thing in common when their gift made itself known: they'd lost the one who could guide them as they finally practiced what they'd learned. For while they didn't understand the reasoning, none could deny that the gift seemed limited to one living soul, and was only passed to the next when that soul died. Which meant that no amount of preparation could change the fact that the practicing member – the daughter who'd survived the gifted mother – was utterly alone, whether they had understanding friends and intrusive step-brothers... or not.

CHAPTER 21 – SHAMEFUL

Summer sixteen

And you're new in my life

Friend, boy and brother

Your mom my dad's wife

Gaping hollows, you teach me

When all my friends fly

Fill the gaps with attention

Feed my courage – or try

Summer sixteen

I ponder your caterpillar lip

Rough stubble at your chin

Your hand at my hip

Clouds above

Listless, sailing through oceans of sky

You are not what you seem

What's that light in your eye?

Summer sixteen

You teach me that touch has been missed

But you shouldn't have been

The first boy that I kissed

Summer twenty

I found a replacement for you

Rather, less shameful options

To incite the feelings you do

But I never could look

At your face without feeling

Your lips moving on mine

In that summer of healing

~ *written while Shya was at university, the first time. It should be noted that much of it was stricken through and/or re-written in many places, and that she acknowledged it as "shit" as soon as she was too tired to fix it and called it done. And if asked about it, she would've denied the writing of it entirely, or blamed the whole effort on the fact that she was drunk when she wrote it (which, incidentally, was true). But no one would ask, for it was crumpled up and trashed before anyone else could read it, and lived on only in her memory, like a picture she could read, refusing to fade with time.*

CHAPTER 22 –
CONFRONTATION

"Hey."

Shya woke to her leg being shaken impatiently. She groaned and rolled over, only to find herself squished chest-first against the back of her sofa.

"You awake?" he shook her leg again and she kicked him off. "Fine," he rumbled as he stalked off toward the kitchen.

What woke her completely was the sounds of him cooking. The scent of frying bacon filled the small space, undeniable despite the odds she'd assumed against Rory ever making food for her. She sat up. *Did Ed stay the night?* She rubbed her eyes drowsily, remembering the nightmare and then Ed's visit. She could clearly recall seeing him out the door at the end of it. Still doubtful, she called out. "Rory?"

His head poked around the doorway in seconds, an expectant look on his face.

"What the hell?" she asked, more to herself than in expectance of an answer from him.

He smiled. "I'm scrambling the eggs. I tried to ask you how you like them, but you wouldn't wake up, so I went with the safest bet." He disappeared again, leaving Shya with a look of astonishment on her face.

She pulled her robe on and shuffled to the kitchen, at once aware of a full bladder and the desire to don her beloved slippers to provide a barrier between herself and the cold ceramic tile of the floor. But the desire to see Rory tending to a cooked breakfast was stronger than any of that. She leaned into the kitchen, eyes wide, and found him doing just that. She stifled a giggle when she realized he was wearing an oversized Acadia hoodie from her closet. He dwarfed it. He caught her covering her mouth and turned to give an exaggerated bow, teasing her laughter out, after all.

"I don't think you've ever looked so good," she laughed and shook her head in disbelief as he turned back to the stove, flipper ready in one hand and the other reaching for a pan handle. "Need help?"

He fished a bit of bacon from the pan and popped it in his mouth. "Nope. Go away! It'll be ready in two."

Shya dutifully exited, skip-hopping to fetch her slippers from the bedroom. She observed the fully made bed critically as she stepped into them. *What is* happening? She wondered, but didn't stop to consider the situation further. Nature was yelling rather than calling, by that time.

Rory insisted they sit at the little table in the kitchen, sealing her amazement.

"OK, what is going on?"

He feigned confusion. "What? Can't a brother do something nice to thank his sister for rescuing him?"

She considered his words carefully, eyeing him as he moved her and Ed's teacups to the sink. "Yes," she finally answered, "but I don't think you ever have before!"

He made a show of looking offended.

"I'm not complaining, though!"

"That's a first." He placed two plates on the table, both laden with scrambled eggs and bacon as expected, but also buttered toast and cut-up slices of banana. She watched as he fetched some jam from the fridge.

"This is…" she bit back the words that surfaced first – shocking, incredible, miraculous, and settled on "…really nice, thank you."

He puffed his chest out. "I'm not completely helpless, you know."

She took up her fork and dug in, scooping up a generous amount of eggs. "Mmm."

Rory was pouring coffee at the counter. He sat across from her, cupping his mug as she sipped from the one he'd placed in front of her. "Good?"

"Yeah!" There was no disguising her surprise, that time, but Rory took the compliment at face value.

"Good."

She spread the jam thickly across her toast.

"Work today?"

She shook her head. "Not after a close, thank God." She took another swig of coffee, then raised her eyes. Rory hadn't touched his food. "What's wrong?"

"Huh?" He looked down at his plate, then picked up a piece of toast. "Oh. Hangover," he mumbled through it, but was soon scarfing the eggs and onto the bacon.

"How're you going to get back into your place?"

He shrugged. "The Super's always around."

"If not him, then one of your friends who's earned a key?"

He made a face. "You're the only one who has a key to my place."

"Oh, yeah!" She'd actually forgotten. "You just want to take that one?"

He frowned. "I'd rather you keep it. Don't worry, I'll get

in."

She went back to her food and they sank into an odd silence. He surprised her again when he broke it.

"No big deal, but you didn't have to call that guy over last night."

She studied his expression and found it sincere. "It wasn't meant as a snub, Ror. I told you, I dialled him before I remembered you were here."

He waved her explanation off. "You used to tell me everything."

She laughed. He frowned at her, incredulous. "You're kidding, right?" She drained her coffee in an effort to drown the words that bubbled up.

He was still frowning at her when she put the empty mug down.

"What, Rory?"

"I just miss that."

She fought the laughter down. "I *try* to tell you everything. Remember coffee a week ago? When I was trying to confide in you about these nightmares?"

The puzzlement was clear in his eyes.

"Lemme guess…you didn't connect the two?"

He scoffed. "I'm sorry, Shy. I'm busy! I have a *real* job and *real* friends!"

"There's the Rory I know and barely tolerate." *Shit.* "Sorry," she said immediately, "but I *do* try, Rory, and I try not to complain when you don't have time to hear me, but it's just a bit much when you complain about my talking to someone else besides you!"

His features hardened. Unwilling to entertain a discussion that was quickly going south, she rose and took her dishes to the sink, then turned and did the same with his.

"I don't know how to talk to you anymore," he said, and it struck her, somehow. Made her regretful, though she couldn't have said over what. Everything she'd said to defend herself was true, and she'd done them both a favor by intentionally ignoring his insults to her work and friends.

"Rory..."

He stood, putting a hand up. "Never mind. I have a headache and I'm grumpy over having to go to the Super again for a key."

Shya went to the hallway before he could object and retrieved his spare key from the hook above her purse. "Here," she held it out to him as she re-entered the kitchen. "Just give it back next time you see me."

He shook his head a little, then took it. "Always with the easy way out," he muttered, shaking the key in her direction.

She was done holding back, and knew there was no sense trying as she filled with anger. "What's that supposed to mean?"

He turned, stalking into the living room to retrieve his bag.

"No, really, Rory. What did you mean by that? You think it was 'easy' for me to bring you home and let you spend the night *again*? Easy for me to take the couch? To ignore the comments you make about the people that truly care about me? I'm sorry they don't live up to the calibre of people you like to hang out with, but then maybe that explains why you have no time for me!"

He slung his bag over a shoulder and peered at her, his face unreadable.

"Maybe I'm exactly that type of person, big 'brother,' that

you wouldn't give the time of day to. How many other friends of yours talk to the dead?"

"I'm going," he said coldly, and headed toward the door.

It nearly stymied her. She put a hand on his arm at the last second. "What is going *on* with you?"

He looked down into her eyes and she saw something there. What? Sadness? Regret? The ever-present impatience? "When I said you always looked for the easy way out, I only meant that you never do the thing that requires more of you. It's like you're afraid of anyone relying on you."

"Are you trying to say it was easier for *me* to give your key back than to keep it?"

"Yeah," he said, his face hardening again. "Easier than listening to me complain about having to go to the Super. Or offering to come with me instead of me taking a cab or the bus."

She let her hand drop. She hadn't thought of any of it in that light. She always assumed Rory was the one who wanted things easy. "I thought it would be easier for *you*," she said, but conviction was lacking in her voice.

"Ever think I don't spend as much time with you because I'm scared of disappointing you?"

"What?" She laughed, but he was deadly serious.

"I know your friends know way more about the stuff that's bothering you than I ever could, but that doesn't mean you shouldn't talk to me about it. But maybe you need to realize that it's hard on me not to be able to help you. Not to be able, even, to relate to what you're saying! To see you hurting, but holding back because I just wouldn't get it."

"Rory, I -"

"I've always tried to make time for you, sis. It's always

been you that does the pushing away."

She had no words. She sputtered as she searched for a solid line of defense, giving him just enough time to head to the door and get into his shoes.

"See ya, Shy," he said as he opened the door.

"I had no idea you thought those things!" she cried, but it was weak, and was rewarded with only a wave from Rory as he slipped through the closing door.

Completely knocked off the solid ground she'd built over the years – reliable assumptions, laid one over another, brick by brick, and cemented together by the mortar of her experiences, or her perception of them, anyway, by a single argument with the man who'd grown up beside her, but never was her brother. Not *really.*

And the strange thing was that the argument was far from their first. It just felt, somehow, like a threat to be the last.

CHAPTER 23 – DISCOVERY

It wasn't their first séance-focused meeting. Far from it. The group really shone when it was time to come together and use their talents to help one another, or someone one of them brought.

The latter nearly overwhelmed them in the beginning, so they'd instated some rules around the services they did for others. Most importantly, it wasn't their mandate – they were a support group, primarily there for each other. So, any proposed special meetings for anyone outside the group had to be put through Dawn's rigorous set of questions. And, first and foremost, the group quickly learned not to bring forward requests for parties, curious looky-loos or anything else that could be categorized as a *want* rather than a *need*. That wasn't to say that members of the group didn't engage in such things outside of Seers meetings (in fact, Sheila and Mel both supplemented their income with such appointments, and Dawn herself had in the past run a very successful matchmaking business based on her incredible people-reading skills), but after they agreed it wouldn't be a focus within the group, they all benefitted from a more consistent level of support and understanding. It was something they could count on, most of them for the first time in their life. A place to feel like they belonged.

But when that support was required on a more urgent basis – such as it was for Shya at that time, they had no problem clearing the agenda for a more hands-on session. Most even looked forward to it. And, contrary to the more casual get-togethers, the twins were usually front and center, leading them through the process. And sometimes, including that night, when they gathered to help Shya decipher the dreams and visions she'd been having, they all met at the twins' home – a sprawling Victorian on old family land, inherited and then beautifully maintained by Jane and Anna, whose day job was to run a sought-after decorating business.

To say the house was perfect for a séance would be an understatement. The twins talked about the resident ghosts with ease, and confessed that most meals taken in the massive dining room with its wood paneling and impressive stone fireplace which took up a large portion of the West wall, were séance-like themselves. The women welcomed the dead, with some reservations, of course, and while they were frequently asked to conduct sessions for those who'd heard about their gifts, they never charged. They considered it part of their day-to-day, but qualified the work as a responsibility rather than services rendered. Regardless, the oval cherrywood table in the room had seen many meetings taken by candlelight and crackling fire, and hands joined all around for strength. For connection.

Knowing all of this and more about the twins, Shya took comfort in both the familiarity of the surroundings as well as the vast experience they'd gained over the years. And it wasn't only their own – the women's ancestral tree was riddled with psychics and mediums, empaths and even self-proclaimed witches and healers, not to mention sufferers of albinism, too. As unbelievable as some found their talents, they came by them honestly.

"I love being here," Sheila whispered excitedly over Shya's shoulder as they made their way to the dining room. Shya tingled with shared excitement.

"It's certainly... *active,*" Dawn turned to look at both the women, eyebrows raised.

"I'd love to do some of my appointments here," Sheila replied wistfully.

Shya tried to hear what Mel, Ed and the twins were saying ahead of them. The sisters' hair had been left in attractive French twists from their work day, but their echoed words were indecipherable and by the time they'd reached the dining room their conversation had petered out into laughter. It was quelled quickly as the rest of the group joined them in the high-ceilinged room. They all took it in once more. Sheila rubbed her arms absently, though the space was well-heated by the fire in the stone wall. Shya understood the impulse, though. The room's vaulted wood beams, massive stone wall and vast size *appeared* cold even if it did not feel it. And the twins had, as always, restricted the lighting to dozens of candles and lanterns which dotted the table, mantles and countertops.

Shya shivered. This was it.

"Shall we sit?" Jane had raised her voice so all would hear, but her eyes were on Shya.

The rest of the group turned expectantly toward her, and Shya warmed under the sudden attention. Still, she found herself hesitating. Her eyes went to the shiny surface of the table, where Jane and Anna had been reading tarot cards from a Tree of Life layout. Anna followed her gaze, then peered at her sister with an intake of breath.

"I hope you don't mind, Shya, but we've been trying to get familiar with your situation before making any contact."

Shya gulped, the reality she faced suddenly too much, and reflexively took a step backward, straight onto Mel's toes. "Oh!" she started apologizing immediately.

Mel steadied her, both hands on her shoulders, and a

powerful sense of calm came over her. This time, though, she hadn't the inclination to push it away. "We're all here with you," he said.

She nodded. She *had* been backing away without thinking, but she realized now that the urge to forget the whole thing had been nearly overpowering. "I don't know if I can do this," she confessed, lulled by Mel's magic hands.

She felt her friends gather around her. Some murmured words of encouragement, some added their touch to Mel's without saying anything – but it was Ed whose words made her stay.

"You don't have to do anything you don't want," he stated plainly.

She turned to meet his eyes.

He shrugged. "This is your call. If you're not into it, we leave. Maybe go get a coffee and some pie."

A burble of laughter rolled through the group. Ed was nothing if not perpetually hungry, and pie was his favorite.

"But if you want to go ahead and give it a try, remember you've got the best goddamned group of weirdos around to see you through it."

She nodded, then looked at each of her friends in turn, landing on Jane last. "Let's do this."

They positioned themselves around the table. Anna remained standing as she went to gather the cards up.

Shya stopped her, saying, "Wait."

Anna paused, her hand mid-reach. "We were going to tell you about it." Her eyes revealed something discomforting. A warning, barely veiled.

Shya gazed at the cards. "Lots of swords," she muttered, a wobbly smile failing to reach her eyes. She spotted the death card in the Final Outcome spot and fought not to react.

"You know it could just mean change," Sheila said, looking at the twins for support.

"We see danger, here," Jane said quietly. It wasn't the answer any of them had hoped for.

"No shit," Shya muttered.

"What, exactly, was your question?" Dawn cut in. Shya relaxed at the solidity of the woman's voice. Dawn looked her way. "The cards don't mean anything if we don't know the original question."

All eyes went to Jane and Anna, who were sharing a look. Jane gave an almost imperceptible nod.

"This is our third reading. The first was just to feel out your circumstances in general, Shya."

"And?"

"And we saw you've been troubled, but whatever's been trailing you hasn't taken over. It seems to be... preoccupied with someone else right now," Anna paused to meet eyes with her sister. Shya wished, not for the first time, that she could hear what thoughts they shared in that way.

Jane spoke next. "The boy," she said, leaning across the table to touch the card in the Hopes and Fears spot. It was the Knight of cups.

"He's gifted," Dawn breathed.

"Our second reading was centered on him," Jane continued. She sat back and folded her hands on the table. "He's very young, and more vulnerable than most."

"Like me?" Shya asked, her heart filling painfully in her chest with emotion.

"Not quite, but similar," Anna answered. "But what hurt

him even more was a recent loss."

"His mother, we think." Jane lowered her eyes.

"And *this* reading?" Dawn spoke up again.

Shya followed her gut and flicked the crossing card from the subject. Seeing what she expected, she sat back in her seat. The Empress was always the card to represent her. "Me," she said.

"We asked what was fated," Anna said, "and where there was choice."

"And there's good news," Jane looked up again, her eyes shining. "You will have a choice every step of the way."

"But I will find him?" Shya still couldn't see the answer. Couldn't feel it, and knew her own fear was the reason.

The twins nodded.

"I'm not sure I'm clear on how everyone connects, here," Mel spoke up. "Why is it Shya who needs to find this boy? Why is the dark spirit interested in her?"

"There are old connections," Jane said, and she pointed to other cards in the reading: the Queen of Wands, the Hanged Man, and the Hierophant. She frowned toward Shya. "Something in your past is left unsolved. It comes to find you now, for one reason or for many. We don't know." She sat.

The twins' ability to openly confess a lack of knowing had always been something Shya had admired, but on that night it felt ominous.

"So, what now?" Big Ed folded his hands over his gut.

"We make contact," Jane gave a nod to punctuate her words.

"With the evil presence?" Dawn's voice had raised an octave.

"No!" Anna cried. In Shya's memory, she had never raised her voice as such.

Jane put a hand on her sister's. "Not if we don't have to," she said, her voice level.

Dawn nodded, seemingly satisfied.

"Then, who?" Ed pushed.

Jane looked at Shya. "Do you believe the boy is dead?"

Shya held her breath, contemplating the question she'd been shoving away since the first of her dreams about the tortured child. Finally, she made a gesture of frustration, her hands rising and then slapping her thighs lightly. "I'm connecting with him… up until now, whoever's contacting me has been dead…but this feels different, somehow."

"Go on," Mel leaned forward.

She shook her head, eyes flicking to Ed's breifly. "It feels urgent, like he needs help. And it feels like he's trapped."

"There are circumstances under which a soul does not need to be dead to contact the living in such ways," Jane's gaze was steady on Shya.

Shya knew what the woman referred to. Ed had said as much that night in her kitchen. But Shya hesitated once more. After all, there were options. Those in prolonged, altered states of consciousness could accomplish the same. A coma was one way. Another was an out-of-body experience, whether it was forced (such as by near-death events) or purposefully achieved (such as during acts of abuse or times of great fear), or any sort of crisis that presents with a surreal atmosphere – natural disasters, acts of God. Once the possibility of the unknown becoming known is realized, the human spirit can open itself up. And sometimes, fly.

Whether it returned again was another matter entirely.

But the final way that one could exist outside of oneself was the thing that Shya named that night, because she knew it. It was the only thing that felt right, especially having experienced the energy of the presence that terrorized the boy.

She met their eyes again. Swallowed. And replied, "Possession."

CHAPTER 24 – GROWTH

By the time Shya left home for her first stint at University (at the University of Ottawa, that time, taking business), she was more than ready for a fresh start. Things had been awkward at school since she and Bethie had fallen out. Bethie and Drake had become the couple to watch, which was new territory for Shya's estranged best friend, but she seemed to be enjoying the attention. Drake was used to it, and as always thrived under the scrutiny.

Connor had tried multiple times to talk with her, and while Shya didn't say it in so many words, she'd given him signals not to bother. Sure he was just being his usual, kind self, she convinced herself she was giving him an out. She wasn't up for pity, nor could she tolerate any anguished discussions about Drake and Bethie. She knew he was hurting, too, but his pain was easily dwarfed by her own. In any case, when he stopped trying, she felt relieved as expected, but oddly regretful, too.

Things at home weren't any better. Her father and Louise had established a new, busy routine. Because Shya and Rory were old enough to fend for themselves, their parents took advantage of free time and spent much of it out of the house. Shya had learned to cook and clean quickly – she even took a certain pride in her housework, knowing her mother could see her and would be proud, too. But the days and nights were lonely.

Rory was rarely home, either. He spent time skateboarding or biking with friends, stopping home at mealtimes. Even then he seemed distant, only engaging Shya in conversation if he was bored or needed something from her. Their strange, intimate moments seemed forgotten, at least by Rory. But she was still confused, still curious. And in the face of his indifference, a little hurt.

So, her acceptance letter from the U of O was met with an excitement she hadn't felt in a very long time. Finally, she had something to look forward to, people to meet in the flesh rather than those that waited in the shadows, or visited in that space between wakefulness and sleep.

Rory would head out to the undergrad law program at Dalhousie in Nova Scotia, but his own reaction to the upcoming change was puzzling to Shya and their parents, alike. Just as Shya was pulling away, he seemed to want to hold on tighter. He started hanging out at home, usually wherever Shya happened to be, chattering about anything that crossed his mind while Shya busied herself with her own tasks. Suddenly, after feeling so alone for so long, Shya felt pestered – even annoyed – at Rory's increased presence.

Years later, she would see his sudden interest in a different light. As easy as she'd made it for him to just disappear from her life, Rory seemed determined to hang on. He even followed her to Wolfville after graduating at Dal, and did his graduate degree at Acadia while Shya changed course and studied literature and the arts. He followed back to Québec, too, and then to Toronto where he found a position practicing law while Shya went back to school yet again. But, having grown up feeling isolated and indeed coming to believe that she wasn't worth *anyone's* time and energy, she only wondered what he wanted in the moment. And was puzzled at what he thought she had to offer him.

He complained now and then that she was "standoffish" and "cold," but it was easy to chalk that up to his narcissism. He seemed starved for her attention, yes, but she assumed he was merely starved for any attention he could get, from anyone.

It never crossed her mind that he cared for her, not even considering the times he'd stolen kisses or got caught staring at her, his face unreadable.

Shya had a very easy time of equating such things to his own self-interest rather than an interest in her.

It was a mistake she made repeatedly when approached by other students and new friends. At university, she always had friends, but it puzzled rather than delighted her. She seemed forever stuck on what they must want from her, and for that reason, many of them faded. And she didn't fight for their continued company; their absence seemed right.

And so it was when, at the age of twenty four and halfway through her second degree in Wolfville, Nova Scotia that time, someone showed interest in her in a more persistent and convincing way, and she found herself considering something new. The fact that it was a woman didn't seem as important at the time as the fact that Shya could tell she was truly interested. Convincingly enamoured. And so, she found herself letting her guard down with someone she could never have predicted, and losing her virginity in a way she'd never imagined.

When that ended, Shya wasn't devastated. It had run its course and the two parted amicably, even remaining friends to the current day. But Shya was changed: she'd seen new possibilities and had opened herself to them. So, her next admirer had to work far less to gain her trust and affection. She didn't ponder his gender too much at first. It seemed less significant that she would have guessed in her youth. But by the time she was ready to graduate that second time, she *was* confused, and took herself to the campus clinic to confront it.

It had been the ghost of her mother who gave the extra push she needed to talk to someone. Her ghost, whispering to

Shya when all else was quiet. It had started with *don't fret, darling. You're fine,* but progressed as Shya's anxiety had to *talk to someone, you'll see.*

And she had. Her first clinic visit had resulted in a referral to the on-campus psychologist. Several visits with him had culminated in a referral to an outside psychiatrist, who could prescribe Shya something to ease her troubled mind. The first had labelled her obsessive. Anxious. Even went as far as to blame Shya's general unease on panic attacks. True, she hadn't confessed the main source of her worries (the dead who visited her more commonly than any living person), but the man had glimpsed her underlying fear through what she did say.

The psychiatrist – a woman, known for being openly interested in learning the true contributors of her patients' characters – was somewhat of a friend before Shya moved on. She'd ferreted Shya's secrets from her with good intentions, so that Shya was more comfortable with herself *and* her sexuality by the time their sessions were concluded.

And she learned that her first foray into love and sex, as real as it had been, had not been an attestation to her sexual preferences as much as it had been the first time that Shya allowed herself to be loved. The fact that it was a woman who'd loved her had made her feel safe. Perhaps it was the only way it could have happened. And it had paved the way for relationships that followed.

But even at the end of all the therapy, when Shya was confident she'd jumped an invisible hurdle that had stymied her since the death of her mother, she subconsciously continued down the path that had been forged in many years of solitude and fear, and it manifested into yet another undergraduate degree and the continuation of the bartending profession she'd settled into in her earlier university days.

And Rory unwittingly continued to prove himself an enigma in her eyes, his every move a mystery to her, because she still couldn't see that he loved her, and perhaps never would.

It was after one of those final meetings with her psychiatrist that she left feeling especially buoyant. *There's nothing wrong with me,* she thought again and again, believing it for the first time since she was very small.

She spotted a figure across campus, then, standing in the twilight and facing her. Stock still in a sea of moving bodies. But despite knowing it was a ghost right away, she wasn't afraid. And when the figure turned and started away, moving in that telltale sort of way that separated the dead from the living: skipping a bend of the elbow or a turn of the head as they looked back so that their movement was often halting and jerking. It was something she'd never quite become accustomed to.

But on that night, she felt good. So, with a determination to focus on the positive and make the most of every moment, she followed the figure.

It – he? – led her to the far end of town where there was a small park the town complimented with benches and a small bridge over a man-made pond. The little structure was little more than decoration, but the figure strode upon it, then looked at her as if to tell her to hurry up.

It *was* a man. She could see that now, who'd appeared to her in his youthful state, and further materialized once he stopped moving. He wore tan chinos and a denim bomber jacket, whose sleeves were stuffed at the ends into the pockets. She momentarily pondered how his physical form varied in solidity. His clothes were clear enough, but seemed held up by a body that, in the moment, she could only describe as *wavery.* He smiled, then, and she realized she'd stopped at the foot of the bridge.

Come.

She heard the word in her head, and it made her shudder, suddenly feeling cold herself, but she did go forward. She wasn't afraid the ghost would hurt her; only that he'd want something from her she wasn't equipped to provide... resolution, love, answers.

These things were often more complex than they first appeared.

She stood two feet in front of him, inwardly noting the falling dark, which had chased the sun to the horizon behind her, streaking neon colors over the dykes where the Bay of Fundy swelled and receded like clockwork, unmindful of the restrictions humans put on time and following its own path.

The man's face was an odd shade of watery brown, and moved as water would, too. She was reminded of the cheap packets of hot chocolate powder she and Rory would stir into mugs of boiling water before settling in to watch TV. "Who are you?" she asked, for he seemed unwilling to speak first.

The ghost scanned the park slowly, his face a puzzle, then opened his mouth to answer, but dark water splashed out instead of words, hitting the boards below and making her jump back. The man gurgled and choked, his hands going to his throat. His face darkened and flowed as though it were melting and Shya backed away, gasping, unwilling to be trapped by the woes of a wayward soul who was trapped himself in the final moments of his death.

"I – I'm sorry," she stammered, then turned, sucking in a breath to fuel the sprint that tingled in her legs, and smashed directly into someone, recoiled, then fell, her hip landing painfully on the edge of the bridge. She cried out, half shocked at her fall and half afraid that the ghost had blocked her himself, and she turned to look, but the bridge was empty where the ghost had been, save the darkness.

"I'm so sorry!" the other man cried, already kneeling and grasping her shoulders.

It was too much. His hands felt oppressive rather than helpful, making her stiffen. Pulling a whimper from her throat.

He pulled his hands back quickly, palms outward. "Are you alright? Can I help you up?"

He was young. Her age or a little older, but large. So solid in the wake of a ghost whose body had seemed to flow like liquid. And his features were kind, even in the shadows cast by the flickering street lights. Relieved, she held a hand out.

Her relief was mirrored on his face as he pulled her up, then brushed her off, charmingly awkward and laughing a little.

"Who are you?" she asked, surprising them both.

He put a hand to his chest. "Gary," he replied, and they both laughed. "I – I was walking home," he gestured toward the road, "and I saw you on the bridge and I thought..." he gave his head a little shake, "well, I don't know. You seemed afraid and my first instinct was to make sure you were OK."

There was something about the way he spoke that rendered her defenseless, but there was no accompanying threat. She found herself smiling.

He stuffed his hands in his jeans pockets, making her think of the ghost. She squinted to make out his jacket, which appeared to be more hoodie than jacket, after all. No bomber jacket. No forerunner.

"And so I came and scared you even worse!" he added, smiling. "Sorry about that."

"Gary," she smiled back. Some of her earlier elation returned, making her brave. She linked her arm with his and nodded toward the road. "I'm Shya."

"Pretty name," he breathed, seemingly a little overwhelmed that she'd trusted him enough to take his arm.

Her stomach somersaulted. She wondered at the mysteries the ghosts brought with them. The man on the bridge had been cursed with the anguish of his death – his drowning, if Shya had understood correctly – but he'd also led her to meeting someone new.

"*Are* you alright?" Gary frowned down at her.

She nodded, then glanced behind them toward the bridge again. The rising moon cast its reflection in the still water beneath it, and there the figure's reflection was, upside-down and watching her go, though the bridge itself was empty. She looked back up at Gary. "I thought I saw something."

He nodded as they stopped at the road.

"I just need a little..." hot chocolate came to her mind first, but she pushed it away. "Coffee," she finished.

He pointed over her shoulder. "There's the Merchant."

She nodded. She loved the little café.

He looked down at his feet and then back at her. "Can I escort you?"

His eyebrows raised, he was adorable as well as sincere, and she surprised them both again by nodding. And they walked arm in arm down the pretty main street of Wolfville, already chattering about their programs and courses, already comfortable... already starting something new while the boy who'd fallen for her before she knew she was worthy of love hung out at the bar of the student union building. Drinking. Wondering where she was...and taking a small bit of comfort in that Shya seemed determined to be oblivious to what he longed to give her, and not just from him, but from anyone.

CHAPTER 25 – REVEAL

She met Rory outside the busy New Minas theatre, having settled on it after considering the tiny, but atmospheric vintage theatre in Wolfville and then having Rory veto it on the sole basis of inferior snacks.

He was a little tipsy, she could tell in the looseness of his swagger as he approached after being dropped off by friends. And by the huge, black holes of his pupils as he came in for a hug.

She said nothing, but her features betrayed her, as always.

"What?"

She shook her head and pulled his sleeve as they started toward the door. "We're going to miss the previews."

He laughed.

"I like to be able to get good seats!" she exclaimed, perhaps a bit too loudly.

"Yeesh. Sorry," he mumbled, then bought their tickets, his smile never wavering. He tried holding her hand as they got in line at the counter and she snapped her hand back, sighing. He was always pulling that shit just to get a rise out of her.

They did the routine, getting snacks and flashing their ticket stubs, then finding their way to some decent seats in the already-darkened – and crowded – theatre.

She was irritated. There was always something on these weekly outings with Rory that made her doubt his original enthusiasm. It was his idea to do it – go to a movie every week to carry on their comfortable ritual from the days at home when they'd settle in front of the tv with popcorn and soda to watch whatever movie their parents had rented for them. It had seemed sweet when he'd insisted on it, and he'd appeared to be thrilled when she'd agreed, but whether it was him showing up late or standing her up entirely – or coming as he had that night, a little drunk and a lot oblivious – she questioned her own dedication to the whole thing.

Rory offered her some of his candy and she held a hand up, her eyes on the screen.

"You OK?"

She snickered. "Are *you?*"

He frowned, but said nothing.

She seethed quietly, failing to absorb the activities on the screen as Rory stuffed his face with popcorn, until she could stand it no more. "Why do you have to drink when you know you're meeting me?"

Rory rolled his eyes. "Ah, *that's* what's got your panties in a twist," he whispered, then giggled, amused by himself.

She rolled her eyes and focused on the screen.

"There was a rugby game today," he added, seemingly satisfied with his reasoning, though it made little sense to Shya, as Rory was neither a rugby player, nor an avid spectator.

Regardless, they sat through the rest of the movie in relative silence, and by the time they reached the parking lot, Rory had sobered up completely and was showing signs of exhaustion.

"So, you watched a game, I take it?" Shya asked as they walked toward her car.

He nodded. "And then went to the Axe after with a

bunch of them. Rick knows them."

"Ah," she said as she unlocked the door, still tense. That happened often... she found her irritation with Rory clung to her even after his explanations solved her puzzlement.

"How are things with *Gary?*" He said the name in the same teasing tone he'd used on her when they were young.

She shrugged, refusing to let him get to her any further. "Great!" she answered honestly. Things with Gary *were* great, if not a little... casual. He was kind, generous and seemed totally smitten by her. They both had full schedules, though, which could explain their eagerness each time they met, often falling into bed before finishing their hellos.

Rory gave a wry laugh.

She shot him a look. "What?"

"Just wondering what's so great about the guy."

"Jesus. Not this again." Rory's dislike of her boyfriend since she'd introduced them was consistent, if not ridiculous.

"He's full of himself," Rory offered in explanation, but she held a hand up.

"Let's not talk about Gary, OK?"

He sighed.

"What about you? Who are you dating now?"

He looked out the window silently.

"Don't tell me you and Brenda broke up?" she giggled.

"Brenda?" Now he shot a look of disbelief her way. "I haven't seen her in weeks. I was hanging out with Candace, remember?"

She rolled her eyes. "I can't keep them straight."

He went back to looking out the window. "I really liked

her."

She glanced sideways at him. Rory was nothing if not melodramatic. "I'm sure someone else will come along," she said, lightly, then slowed as she approached his dorm. "Here we are."

He adjusted himself so he was facing her. "Same time next week?" He seemed less than eager to get out of the car.

"If you want," she smiled, then gestured toward the dorm, which towered above the little car. "Go on, sleep it off."

He shook his head. "Come on, Shy."

She sighed, positioning her hands on the wheel and looking toward the road.

"I had a couple beers after the game. You should've seen the players guzzling it!" he laughed, and it hit her that she was being silly. He *had* made it to their weekly meeting, after all. Who cared if he was a little drunk?

She smiled. "Sorry." He nodded, his features awash with relief. "Go! I'm a little tired, and I have a midterm tomorrow."

"You'll ace it."

She shrugged. "You never seem overwhelmed by..." she gestured to the campus around them, "... all this."

He grinned. "It's easy!"

She grimaced. "No way is business law easier than arts!"

He laughed. "You don't see me in the library, sis. I spend hours in there, almost every day."

Shya was dubious.

"It's true. How do you think I get the grades I do? I'm no genius."

She frowned. These rare self-deprecating remarks always confused her. But it was easy to chalk them up to his self interest, as always. His way of getting her on his side. Finally she nodded, deciding on commiseration rather than doubt, which would certainly bring more arguments from him. "That's a relief," she said, laughing quietly.

He reached for the door, then turned back. "Why do I always feel like you don't believe a word I say?"

It struck her so odd that she laughed.

He shook his head. "No, really. You've been like this from the start, and I *always* believed you, even about your ghosts."

She froze, her mind whirring. It was true.

"Did I do something wrong back then?"

She smiled. He *had* to be joking. Famously handsome, popular Rory always came out on top. He'd always been in a different league with people than she could ever dream to be. While she'd floundered socially, and then failed in the wake of her devastation over Bethie, Rory seemed unable to lose on any front. And now he cared how she'd treated him? *Probably can't figure out how I'm not under his spell, like everyone else,* she thought, but for the first time, it felt weak. *Had* he done something wrong? She thought of their stolen kisses, of laying in the tall grass and listening to the sounds of the water flowing by. Of his plans, of how he never doubted that they'd come to fruition. Of how he'd always had a sense of entitlement she couldn't comprehend.

She *had* resented it. Things always seemed easier for Rory, and she'd watched as indeed, everything seemed to fall into his lap while she struggled to figure out what she wanted. Struggled with ghosts as he struggled with his busy schedule full of friends and parties and plans.

A heat rose in her cheeks as Rory maintained his expectant gaze.

Had it all been her? *Her* issues?

No. She shook her head against the possibility. Rory *was* entitled, and selfish, and when he and his mother came into her life and her home, the lingering memories of her mother – and in fact, her mother's ghost, for a time – seemed to disappear.

"Shy?"

She snapped her gaze to his again. "What?"

He shook his head, then. "Never mind." He got out before she could think of what to say, then bent down to say goodbye. "See ya."

She gave a weak wave. "Yeah."

She drove to her tiny apartment in a daze, half mortified at the possibility that *she'd* been wrong all along, and half pissed that he'd even try to manipulate her to feel that way.

And it was the latter that won out. The latter that made sense when she went inside remembering how little time he'd had for her when they were young, and what time he deigned to give her was driven by his wants, his desires, his own ideas in apparent ignorance of hers. And before she could consider that she'd never demanded attention to her own wants and desires, the phone rang and she answered with a jolt of excitement, for it was Gary. And Gary listened to her recount the evening and agreed: Rory was impervious to his own flaws. And why was it that Shya was blamed when he did recognize them?

It felt good to be validated.

It felt almost entirely convincing.

Almost.

CHAPTER 26 – MISSED

The silence of your signals
Or my choice not to hear
Or see them flashing brightly
Or feel them through my fear

The weight of my assumptions
My heavy wall to bear
Knocks all your efforts back
Regardless if it's fair

The ease to misinterpret
Has roots deep in my past
My mother's early gift
Through her own death did pass

And at the same time managing
My sudden empty home
The ghost of my live father
Who, quiet, long atoned

And normal life confused me
Each day past my home's door
My timely hopes and teenaged dreams
Fall flat onto the floor

Resentment built within me
Not only for my fate
But for other's hands in it
Too sad, too strange, too late

So, you were disadvantaged
You entered at the break
Your mother took the last
Of my dad there was to take

A precedent was set, then
With you inside its core
My confusion only mounting
Do you want less, or more?

So, crossed, mixed or warning
With humour, play or dark
Your signals try and fail
To reach their intended mark

I see you struggle onward
As life so fast unfolds
Frustrated in your own right
As I fail to crack the code

CHAPTER 27 – FOUND

A hush fell over the group as Jane placed her hands, palms-up, on the table. The action incited the rest to follow her lead, joining hands as adrenaline coursed through every one.

"Let's begin," Jane focused on the lone candle that had replaced the tarot reading in the center of the oval table, and all eyes went to her and Anna, as singular as they seemed, no matter who had spoken. They closed their eyes.

Shya inhaled deeply, focusing on filling her lungs and warming the air, then holding it as if for comfort before slowly releasing it. Mel, who'd insisted on sitting to her left for obvious reasons, squeezed her hand. She did not fight against the sense of calm that washed over her, as it came with a sense of clarity, too. She squeezed back, grateful.

Big Ed's hand was clammy on the other side. A quick glance at the man proved him sweaty, but his effort to focus clear on his face as his eyes closed. With Jane and Anna heading the table across from Shya, Sheila and Dawn were positioned beside Mel and Big Ed, respectively. The atmosphere fairly buzzed in the quiet, and the candlelight flickered from all around the room. Shya watched the twins. They all waited.

She twitched when Anna opened her eyes and met her own with some intensity, and despite a refreshment of Mel's soothing energy, she twitched again when Anna spoke.

"The room is open."

Those whose eyes had been shut opened them at Anna's steady declaration. The stage was set; now to determine whether the cast was ready.

Sheila eyed the twins. "Can we set a protective barrier?"

Jane nodded as though she'd expected the question, and Sheila straightened, her gaze going to the middle distance as she addressed the unseen presences.

"We gather to commune with the dead and lost! Tonight, we seek the child who haunts Shya's dreams. All others will be held at bay. And all dark energy is refused outright!" Sheila eyed the group, now, and they all met her gaze – even Dawn, who didn't go in for the "witchy" side of such rituals, as she described it. Sheila went on, but addressed the group. "Let us erect a barrier of white light around us."

Shya sucked a breath in as it came - the usual onslaught of arriving souls who gathered just outside their circle, some desperate to be acknowledged, some curious, and some – the ones she'd learned to avoid – hungry for what they loved best: fear. Hopelessness. Vulnerability.

Innocence.

She knew she needed to find the boy, lest the group accomplish the exact opposite of their intentions by subjecting his soul to further darkness when it was already tortured by it.

There was another moment of hushed excitement, during which all were focused on Shya. Among them, she had the clearest sight of spirits themselves.

"Shya, do you feel him?"

Her eyes had closed on their own as she struggled to find him, and now she doubled her efforts. "There are so many..."

Big Ed's meaty hand squeezed hers. She clung to it, a life raft in a sea of spirits.

"Call him," one of the twins' voices broke through as she traversed that unseen space teeming with eager ghosts. Her arms crawled as they pressed in on her. Her ears twitched as they whispered and screamed.

"Calm, Shya," came Mel's voice, which cleared her head as soon as it reached her and she hardened herself, pressing unwanted presences away and calling for him, finally, her voice echoing both in that other place and in the massive room she and her friends occupied bodily.

"Where are you?"

The voices around her quieted and she called again.

"Little boy? I've seen you in my dreams! I want to help, but I need to find you, first!"

She gasped as all traces of souls around her were sucked away and suddenly she was cold. Alone. Existing solely in that other place, her hands empty until she clasped her upper arms with them. Her breath coming in vaporous clouds in the dark. She vaguely heard a voice in the distance, but it faded before she could cling to it. It came again and she heard her name, and seconds later more voices rose, demanding and a bit afraid.

But to her, the dark cold was a more pressing reality. The emptiness. It wasn't wholly unpleasant; she realized it was the first time her own energy was the only one she'd felt at one time since the night of her mother's funeral. And it was lovely. For one, quiet moment, it was bliss.

But then there *was* another, and it pressed in on all sides of her, hot and sickening. She trembled at the shock of it – at the realization that she'd lost focus. She'd dropped her guard.

"Jane!" she cried out, but the word was whipped away as soon as it formed, sucked out of her as the crowds of ghosts had been sucked away. "No," she said, and the sound of the word was flat with her defeat. She collapsed to her knees. Her chest ached as she tried to fill her lungs. She needed to call out again... but to whom? To what? She couldn't remember. And the air was painfully thin.

A voice again, from the distance.

"Shya!"

It was Dawn. She gazed into the endless black and waited, needing more. Needing air. Choking on nothing.

"Fight it, Shya! Find the boy!"

A surge of rage burst through her and she stood, her arms stretched out, her energy blasting from all sides and abolishing the pressure that had been suffocating her. Relieved, she gulped the air. Tears streamed down her face. *Air* was all she could think. Sweet air.

And then it pressed again, but only at her boundaries and she hardened. Breathed. Turned on the spot, arms still outstretched, and protected her space.

"Find the boy!" came the voice again, but she knew she couldn't. One more try – one more attempt to open up and call for him – would let the darkness in again.

"No!" she screamed, pushing against her barrier, making it strong.

And suddenly, a light.

In the distance, like a spotlight, and then tunneling toward her, rushing at a dizzying speed and roaring past her such that her hands flew up to cover her ears on their own accord. She whirled to follow it and saw her friends. Saw herself, slumped at the twin's table as her friends grasped each other's hands and encouraged her back. Back to them. Back to herself.

But something pulled at her from the opposite direction and she turned again. And at the other end of the vast tunnel of light was a figure, heaped in a crumpled ball on the ground and silent. But pulling, pulling. Wanting her to see him.

The boy.

"I see you!" she cried out, and from the other end came sudden silence. She glanced back, afraid she'd somehow made a choice and they'd be gone, but there they were. Quiet. Gazing at one another as though shocked. She turned back to the path, to the distant figure. "Please!" she watched for movement. Became aware of the urge to run to him, held back only by the memory of the destination that awaited her in the other direction. "Please!" she cried again. "Are you alive?" She needed something, anything from him. "Can you hear me?"

He moved.

She began to cry hysterically, relief and horror warring within her.

He pressed himself to sit, arms like twigs. Eyes hollow caves, on her. "Follow the path," he said. The words wafting to her as if on the breath of his remaining hope, weak, strained, but there, still.

It took her a moment to grasp them. And then she was more afraid than ever. "What path?" she called, her voice high, and that was it; the boy was sucked away by some unseen thing, flying backward in the waning light, too weak to scream, and Shya scrambled backward. Back and away. Back, back until she was pulled, too, but toward herself.

But one thing followed her – not that pressure, no, and no attempt by the boy to clarify his message. Not pain or vacuumed lungs. Not that suffocating black hole of nothing. Just two words: *he's mine.*

Two words that ripped through her as she found her shell again, hot and sharp and grating and she felt two hands grasping her own, saw the faces of her friends, snapped into that case she'd been born into for that life, that time, a scream ripping from her as the words sliced her mind in two.

CHAPTER 28 – REVISIT

"His name is Jordan," Anna said quietly.

The group had gathered at Shya's end of the table. Hands soothed her on all sides and she was bent forward, her forehead pressed to Mel's by a gentle hand behind her neck.

"What happened?" Shya asked, and Mel pulled back. She looked around at the group. All focused intently on her. "I mean, what happened *here?*" she added. The events in the place she'd been would remain clear to her for the rest of her days.

"You left," Sheila replied, her voice wavering and her eyes red from crying. "It took you!"

"It's strong," Dawn shook her head, regretful. She looked at the twins. "We shouldn't have done it."

The twins looked at one another, then at Shya. "We didn't know," they said in unison, and Shya waved it away.

"You said his name is Jordan? How do you know that?

Anna looked at Big Ed. All eyes followed. Big Ed, however, looked perplexed.

"What?"

"You spoke with him – the boy!" Jane said, incredulous.

Big Ed laughed. "What?" He peered around the group, and all but Shya nodded. "Why don't I remember that?"

They fell quiet.

"What *do* you remember?" Dawn placed a hand on his forearm.

He thought for a moment. "I remember Shya going limp. I remember her calling for him, and screaming, then acting like she couldn't breathe." He peered at Shya as if to confirm her presence. "I was scared..."

"Then what?" Shya urged him on.

He nodded. "Then, you were breathing again – gasping, really – and then you yelled that you could see him. And then... you were back."

Shya nodded. "You heard everything that happened." She looked at the twins. "I've never been so – detached – before."

Jane shook her head. "Just from this level. Not entirely from your body, which is why some of what you said and did... wherever you were... happened here, too.

Shya frowned.

Dawn made a sound of frustration. "Ed. What's the last thing you remember before Shya came to?"

Ed shrugged. "I just told you. She was trying to talk to him, and then she was back."

Shya pulled away from Mel, who was still holding the back of her neck and her left hand. She leaned toward Ed. "You missed a bit."

Everyone looked at her.

"He was sucked backward. I think it was the evil – whatever it was! But just as the boy was starting to try and tell me something," Shya paused, her brow furrowed. "He told me to follow the path." She fell silent.

"What path?" Sheila said.

"Then what?" the twins chorused.

"Did you hear any of that?" Dawn was still on Big Ed.

Ed nodded slowly. "Not the bit about the path, but I remember that sensation of being pulled…"

"I knew it." Dawn sat down.

"What?" Shya demanded.

Dawn looked around the group. "Nobody else heard the boy say his name?"

Heads shook all around.

Dawn looked back at Ed. "And you heard it after feeling that pull? And before Shya woke up?"

Ed, whose brow was still deeply furrowed, nodded.

"The portal thing," Dawn said, eyes wide.

Everyone stared blankly at her.

She rolled her eyes. "He was the only one who heard it. The only one who *felt* the pull, besides Shya.

Shya straightened. "And I didn't feel the pull toward the boy as he was whisked away; I was pulled back here."

Dawn nodded.

"What?" Ed raised his hands in frustration.

"She could be right," Anna said, but she was looking at Jane as if to speak privately. Shya set her teeth on edge.

"None of this helps me with my situation," she said, her voice steely. The group turned to her and she sat back in her seat, suddenly angry. "No offense, Ed," she gave his forearm a squeeze, "but whether your gift has something to do with portals between levels or dimensions or whatever, I still have no idea what to do next!"

Ed pressed his lips together, nodding.

"I just thought it was an important discovery," Dawn mumbled. Jane touched her shoulder.

"I'm not trying to discount it," Shya continued. "I'm just – I'm sorry. I'm frustrated. That *sucked* for me, you guys."

A nervous laugh went through the group.

Shya shook her head, her eyes filling with tears. "I don't think I can do that again. And he…" she looked at Ed, "Jordan?" Ed nodded. "If Jordan's not dead, he must be, soon. He's wasted away to nothing, guys! He's…" she sobbed, remembering the state of the child, the dark hollows of his eyes.

"He said follow the path," Anna said.

Sheila nodded excitedly. "We just need to figure out what that means!"

Shya buried her face in her hands.

"Maybe there's more to the message," Mel droned to her left. "Maybe more is coming."

"He was overtaken before he could explain," Big Ed's voice came from her right.

Shya peered over damp fingertips. "What if he dies before he tells me the rest?"

Sheila made a wounded sound.

"And – why me?" Shya cried. "Why would he choose me rather than someone closer to him! Someone who could piece the puzzle together? If he can come to *me* in dreams, why not someone else?"

"You know it's easier with you," Sheila muttered, her eyes revealing her puzzlement.

"Maybe it wasn't the boy who chose you," Jane said.

The realization of it washed over Shya like icy water. "The – the demon-thing? The thing that's got Jordan?"

Jane nodded. "I feel this is linked to something from your past. Something left unsolved."

Shya threw her hands in the air. "What, like my mother's untimely death? My father's subsequent ignoring of me and then his marriage to a woman who treated me as though I was a leper when I refused to let her take my mother's place?"

The twins looked doubtful. "Someone who knew your gift. Someone who wished for it."

Rory knew her gift, but he'd never wished for it. Not that she'd known. She folded her arms.

Bethie knew.

And Connor.

"What is it?" Dawn leaned around Ed.

Drake probably knew, too, but Drake didn't care much for things beyond his own immediate interests. At least not back then. Shya frowned, realizing she hadn't a clue what had happened to any of them... except for Connor, who was supposed to have stayed in Aylmer, according to Rory.

"Shya!" Dawn's voice roused her.

"I don't know," she muttered. "I don't know."

The group was momentarily silent.

"That was crazy," Sheila spoke up, laughing, and the rest agreed, and started to rehash the entire evening, so Shya knew what it had looked like from their side of things.

It was only on the way out that Shya felt any sort of renewed hope. The twins held her back at the door just for a moment, while Ed went to warm up the car. "Give it time," Jane said. "Just be open to clues."

Shya shuddered. "I don't know if being 'open' at all is a good idea."

"You resisted it. And you can be open to the boy without allowing his possessor in."

Shya felt the blood drain from her face at the outward acknowledgement of possession. "I guess there's no doubting it, now," she said, her eyes going to Ed's car as it started. "And now, it's harder."

The twins frowned. Shya met their strange eyes. "It's not just 'the boy' anymore, is it?" A look of understanding cleared their faces. "It's Jordan. Something real. Some*one*."

"You're not alone in this," Anna touched her arm lightly.

Shya gave them both a wry smile. "I'd better go."

"Call us," Anna said, and Shya nodded before jogging to the car, knowing the opportunity to call the twins would undoubtedly come, or else Anna wouldn't have said it.

And wanting nothing more than to forget about it for the time being. After all, she'd worked hard to build a strength in ignorance. Her mother had insisted on it, otherwise how could she trust that Shya would have some control over her gift? But it had occurred to Shya more than once that her mother, in her desperation to protect Shya before she herself was taken from her, may have gone overboard, for Shya found that in her ease of withdrawing from the present, she unwittingly missed the good things sometimes, too.

The important things.

CHAPTER 29 – BREAK

Gary shrugged and looked at her, perplexed. They were standing on either side of her bed in her apartment rather than cavorting beneath its sheets, which felt very odd indeed.

"Are you saying you want to break up once we've finished school?" Shya was troubled by the look on his face, which said she should have known this day would come. But she hadn't seen it. She was completely thrown for a loop.

"We don't have to talk about this now," Gary tried a smile, but his impatience was not disguised by the effort.

"Yes, we do!" Shya exclaimed. "I thought – I mean, I didn't think we'd decided *that!*"

He threw his hands up in exasperation. "We've talked about this! What else are we going to do? My job prospects as an engineer will be much better on the West Coast, and you've said more than once that you need to stay and get a few more credits before you can graduate."

That much was true. Stymied, Shya searched her thoughts for the conversation – or conversation*s* – he referred to. She vaguely recalled some talk about him wanting to go to Vancouver for a while, but that hadn't resulted in a solid decision to end their relationship once he was finished – had it?

"Shya," he said her name quietly. Pleadingly. And he looked tired.

"I'm sorry," she mumbled. "I guess I misunderstood. I do remember you wanting to go out West, but I guess I didn't realize that meant we'd be breaking up. I haven't been thinking about that at all." She gave him an apologetic smile. "I guess I've just been enjoying what we have."

His shoulders drooped. "I have, too. And if you were more... if you were ready to move out there with me, I'd love to stay together. But you're not, Shya."

She frowned.

"You've said as much."

Had she? If she had, she certainly hadn't equated that to a breakup. She shook her head. "I do need to finish school, but I can do that anywhere," she voiced aloud as she pondered, but he interrupted her.

"But then there's Rory, and your friends, and, hell, probably a bunch of ghosts holding you back, too!"

His frustration stung. Her mouth snapped shut as she thought of the ghost of her mother; how she'd seen less and less of her as her life had forced her to be independent.

Gary had lowered his head and stood, looking worn out, across from her.

She went around the bed and when he wouldn't look at her, she threw her arms around him, instead. Relief nearly overwhelmed her when he hugged her back. "I guess I don't always think about what could happen in the future," she said quietly, her mouth at his neck. He smelled like soap and spices... something Indian. "Especially if I'm worried about what could happen."

He pulled away, but just enough to meet her eyes. "I get that, babe. I do. You know I don't understand everything you see, but I do believe it, and I can't imagine how you've had to adjust your outlook in order to cope with it all."

Tears sprung to her eyes, not for the hardship he referred to, but for the acknowledgement – the articulation of a thing that she'd been unable to describe so eloquently herself.

"But I'm just a normal guy," he chuckled, then rested his forehead on hers. "I'm ready to get out there and figure out where I fit in the world. What I can do, you know?"

She nodded. Knew as he described his motivation that she wasn't there yet, but the words he said next still hurt.

"And I think maybe you need to figure out how to deal with all your... *stuff*... before embarking on a new life in a new place, you know?"

She couldn't say anything. Moving had never been a problem for her. In fact, the thought of starting fresh somewhere new had always given her hope. But it had always been followed by disappointment when her problems followed her, and the thought of starting over again, without Rory to run to in tough times and with all the pressures of a new role in a new life with Gary, terrified her. She looked up into his eyes. Wanted to apologize again, but banished the urge and held him instead, resting her head against his chest.

"I'll miss you," he murmured into her hair, and she nodded against his chest, now damp with her tears.

Tears of defeat, she thought. *And tears of injustice,* she added, allowing a brief moment of anger toward her mother, who had passed along her gifts too early, too fast. A moment of self-pity, for never having learned the right ways to cope, because when her mother had been alive, there wasn't time, and now that she was dead, priorities were different for the time they did have together.

So much was different.

And that was what jabbed at her the most: the fact that for her, everything was always different, when all she'd ever wanted – or *thought* she wanted, but it would be years before she realized the difference – was the gift of a normal, boring life.

CHAPTER 30 –
THE PATH

It was Halloween.

She knew because she'd been there before, entering the path in the woods later than usual, as was evidenced by the gathering gloom. Distant voices and playful shrieks of trick-or-treaters wound their way into the trees and she was somewhat comforted and a touch melancholy, as one tends to be when reliving a memory.

But as she peered around the trees in the grey of dusk, she realized it was different, now. There was fencing to the right of the path, beyond a recently thinned-out copse of pine, oak and maple. And houses on the other side of it that hadn't been there when she was young, their rooftops silhouetted against the twilit sky.

Shya frowned and stopped in her tracks. She looked down at her feet. The dirty Converse sneakers of her teen years were in place, but the body that filled the shoes felt current – her forearms ached from years of tending bar and her curls, which hadn't come into the extent of their extravagance until she was nineteen or twenty, blew about her head on the breeze.

She got going again, wondering absently who would meet her at the park, given the clashing timelines, but was quickly distracted, skidding in her tracks at the hint of a dark figure slipping behind a tree trunk.

This had happened before, too, and she recalled it was followed by a sudden sprint the rest of the way, that shadow pressing menacingly against her back as she burst from the trees. But this time she was older, perhaps even wiser. Certainly more experienced. This time, she carried on, feet crunching in the leaves at a calculated walking pace, and her eyes on that tree. She noticed the occasional path that jutted to the right and led to a gate in the fence. Backyard escapes. Or entrances. She didn't pry with curious eyes, though. They remained glued to where the figure had disappeared. She recalled the vast height of the thing as she approached. The point to which her gaze was affixed had to be six feet above her. She couldn't remember whether that was the same, too, or if it was different, like the fence. The houses. The new paths. Had the monster changed to match her evolving fears? Regardless, her fear weighed on her at the realization that, despite her gained experience, the dark figure had the advantage as far as her state of mind was concerned.

The characteristics of the tree sharpened as she closed in, the bark separating into fissures and jagged paths, and its branches not only reaching toward the sky, but wrapping oddly about itself, more like thick vines climbing the bark.

Strange, she thought, and slowed, because vines like that didn't grow in those woods. And then halted, because she could see then that they weren't vines. They were made of mottled flesh and twisted sinew, arms too long to be human ending in withered hands that grasped and clawed at bits of the bark and moving like snakes in the fissures as though fuelled by impatience.

For her.

So, she ran, retracing the steps of that Halloween night long ago, a familiar heat against her back once she passed the tree, and an eager mouth at her ear, breathing ragged and laughing deeply. Rumbling like thunder in a rancid gut.

She screamed.

And was answered by another, but behind her, and it shocked her such that she whirled, tripping backward over a root, and screaming again as the thing that chased her filled her vision, all teeth and hollow eyes and hunger before passing right through her. She landed hard, bouncing and skidding on her ass, eyes squeezed shut against the image that would never leave her subconscious – the face of the thing that wanted her. Another scream ripped through the air and her eyes flew open, but saw nothing. The darkness was suddenly complete around her, though her hands still crunched in autumn leaves and the hated presence still thickened the air.

"Where are you?" she called into the darkness, knowing the distant scream had been the boy's. Fearing, also suddenly, that the shadow that had followed her all those years ago was the shadow that held the boy – Jordan – prisoner now.

Another shriek and she was up, but turning toward the park. Running toward what memory that was known, wishing she'd stuck to it in the first place. Regretting what she now knew.

The dark consumed her, but she pressed on, clumsier, arms outstretched, face stretched into a mask of desperation. Salty tears at the corners of her mouth. *Stop,* she thought. *I need this to stop.* But it didn't. Instead, light appeared – a streetlight from beyond the park, and she was running like that night again: a sprint, frenzied and wild. But it wasn't Connor who met her at the end of the trail; it was a woman, on her knees, her face in her hands. Shya skidded again so as not to fall over her, feeling the heat pressing in on her as she stopped abruptly. Stinging heat whispering *I am here.*

Shya focused on the woman. "Who are you?" she demanded, her voice too harsh because of how heavy it was behind her. But she jumped when the woman raised her head, for it was Bethie, older, tears streaking mascara down her cheeks.

"It's my fault!" her estranged friend cried, palms striking

the ground. "I brought it here and it took him! And sad as he was, it took him so *easily*!"

"Bethie?" Shya spoke the name of her old friend, but found herself otherwise speechless.

"But it wants *you* the most, Shya. You could take it from him!" Bethie clenched her fists in the dirt and gestured wildly as she spoke, sand flying from them.

Shya shook her head.

The street light went out and Bethie faded with it, her cries falling distant and another desperate scream echoing into the night from behind her. Closer, now.

Shya turned, well aware she was risking coming face to face with it again – the thing that wanted her – but counting on the darkness to remain complete. And she was relieved when she saw nothing, not even stars in the sky, but she felt it, still. Watching. Waiting. "What do you want from me?" she cried, gooseflesh raising on her arms at the edge of panic in her voice.

Silence. Even the heaviness seemed to draw back, letting a cool breeze touch her cheek. But then he spoke.

"I want to die."

It was the voice of the boy, soft and wavering, melting her resolve and weakening her knees until she crumbled, and it rushed at her in that moment of despair, from all directions crashed through her in palpable exaltation, roaring as it vacuumed up her terror. And it followed her up, that guttural cry, up into wakefulness, harmonized by her own scream as it rendered her awake. She bolted upright as it faded, panting, sweating in the silence, trembling in sudden solitude. Wanting – no, *needing* someone with her. But she didn't dial Big Ed that time. Didn't think to. She dialed the one who had saved her back then.

He came without question or complaint, perhaps remembering the words he'd thrown at her days earlier. *You don't need to call him* and *you used to talk to me.*

CHAPTER 31 – BRIGHT ONE

"I've never seen you like this."

Shya and Rory lay awake in her bed, Rory's arm still around her and her head on his chest, listening to the rhythm there as if it was the answer to the questioning gallop of her own. She raised her head, but regretted it instantly when she saw how the moonlight lit his features. It made her think of when they were young and he'd convince her to crawl out onto the roof from his attic room and they'd lay staring at the stars in silence.

She had ached then, for something more than the life she felt saddled with. For a look from her father, who was absent even when he was there… the potential for a future with the step-brother that felt like something altogether different than a brother should… to be held just once by a flesh and blood mother rather than hoping all the time for her ghost to appear.

To have something she could depend on besides the spirits and the unending list of their needs.

Rory was frowning down at her. "You've always seemed confident, even when it was obvious you were scared, too. What's different?"

She shook her head, placed it back on his chest, then after a few moments sat up.

He did, too, but rested his back on her headboard.

"What?"

"Your heart sounds so... *calm.*"

He chuckled. "You'd think that'd be a good thing."

"It was," she muttered, "but not when you're asking questions that make me nervous."

She saw his eyebrows knit lower in his forehead and sighed.

"It's a possession, Ror."

He said nothing.

"Of a little boy." She thought something cleared on his face. "And he's dying." She rubbed at her face with her palms, then let them drop. "And apparently I could save him if I let it have me instead."

He sat up straight. "No."

She gestured helplessly. "What am I supposed to do?"

"How do you let it have you, even? And why does it want you?"

"Rory, if I knew those things..."

"Do you even know where the boy is? *Who* he is?"

The note of panic in Rory's voice twisted in her belly like a snake. "I have an idea," she replied, weakly.

"Well, your life's not worth less than a stranger's, Shy." Rory folded his arms across his chest in an unconscious move that again reminded her of their younger years together. It had always made him look like a petulant child, and as it turned out, still did.

She giggled.

"How are you laughing right now?"

She shook her head, then let it drop so she could watch

as her fingers picked at the blanket. "Never mind."

"Who is he?"

She looked up at him. "The boy?"

"Of *course,* the boy. Who else?"

"Don't be a dick, Rory."

He closed his mouth. Shya thought she saw his jaw flexing as he gritted his teeth, but recognized that it could just have been an assumption based on past experiences.

"I think he's in Aylmer, near where we used to live."

His frown deepened.

"And I don't know how exactly, but he's linked to Bethie." She shook her head, considering. "Like, it's her fault, somehow."

"Bethie? Your ex-bestie, Bethie?"

"How many other Bethies do you know?"

"Don't be a dick, Shya."

She couldn't help it; she laughed. He smirked, then ran his fingers through hair that was already standing on end.

"You're tired. You don't have to stay." She said it without thinking, then wished she could take it back. Her recent argument with Rory had made her think, and she'd concluded that maybe she needed to be a bit more open with him. Stop basing everything on assumptions, at least.

"Don't just dismiss me, Shya! You called, I came, and now I'm trying to figure out how to help you!"

She shook her head. "I'm sorry. I *am* grateful, but…"

"But, what? I simply couldn't begin to understand? You need to talk to one of your *seer* friends?"

She pressed her lips together to hold back the words that

rose to meet the challenge. Eyed him as she dug for a response that was more forgiving, then sighed, giving up when nothing came to mind.

"What about – does it still help to write about it? Are you still filling notebooks like that therapist taught you?

She nodded. "Yeah, but not as much. I don't seem to *need* to write as much. I just sorta let stuff percolate until it all screams to get out."

He chuckled, but it was not unkind.

"Thing is, Ror... no amount of poetry is going to solve this. It's not just about me!"

"But you can't be the only solution! I mean – how are you supposed to..." He gestured helplessly, then let his hands fall. "We need experts. What about your mother?"

She frowned. "What about her?"

He rested back against the headboard. She saw his effort to relax and resolved to do the same.

It was a nice change, surprisingly.

"You always said she was your guide when you talked about this...stuff," Rory finished.

That feeling rose over her again – that vague, but pervasive feeling she'd forgotten something. Or missed it. "Huh," she mumbled.

"What?"

"Well, as I grew up and sort of got a handle on – things – I saw her less and less. Nowadays it's always a nice surprise when she's around, but honestly, I can't think of the last time she came," Shya shook her head, then met Rory's eyes in the dimness. She wondered passively what time it was. "Don't you have to work in the morning?"

"Stop telling me to go home." He sat up straight again. "Think, Shy. Have you talked to your mom at all about what's been happening over the past few months?"

She resisted without understanding why. "It's not strange for her to stay away for chunks of time. She has other stuff to do, you know." The words should have comforted them both, but Rory looked skeptical and her stomach felt hot and heavy.

Rory raised a finger. "That's a conversation for another day... but for now, I just want you to try and pinpoint exactly how long it's been since you've had a visit from her."

She shook her head. "Why? It's not like she hasn't talked to me about the darker side of all of this! And she always told me to avoid dealing with these types of spirits at all. What could she possibly say now to guide me?"

Rory sighed. "I dunno, sis. Just seems weird that you're going through something so traumatic – and *new*, despite what she taught you about this stuff! – and she's MIA."

She clutched her stomach absently. Let his words settle.

"It's just -" he leaned forward and untangled her arms from her midriff, holding her small hands in his warm ones. "- she's always been your teacher. It seems *off* that she'd stay away on purpose, is all."

She made a face. Half of her wanted to take his sentiments as an insult against the one soul who'd truly loved and understood her, but the other had that niggling feeling again, eating away at her denial.

"What if, even though you haven't directly confronted it yet, this thing is already working to knock you off your guard? Get you as vulnerable as possible?"

Sharp fear shot through her. He held her hands tight as if in anticipation that she'd pull away, run... lose her footing entirely.

"I'm worried about you, Shya."

His eyes backed up his statement. She became distracted by how the moon lit them. How they looked so different in the slowly waning dark – just like everything else did. The tree from her dreams flashed inside her head. How the monster's arms wove around the bark like rotting vines, all twisted sinew, ending in restless, wriggling fingers seemingly unable to stay still enough to disguise themselves as bark. A choking feeling rose up in her throat and she let it materialize: the suspicion that her mother wasn't staying away on purpose. The quiet, but pervasive whisper that said *something is wrong*.

Her breath hitched as she inhaled to say it. Her eyes anchored to his, which watched her as they always had. With curiosity. With something else... uncertainty? No. It was another thing she'd always denied... something like relief. Like comfort. Something like... love. She softened. Grabbed on to that one, positive thing. "You think it's keeping my mother from me?"

He shrugged, gaze wavering, and that time she squeezed his hands. He blew out a breath. "I don't want you to be more frightened than you already are, but if it does want you, like you said, wouldn't it make sense?"

She made a dismissive noise, but her stab at apathy fell flat. "I don't even know if it would make sense for it to want me in the first place!"

He squeezed her hands. Waited until she met his eyes again, then leaned toward her. She felt his breath on her lips before his mouth touched them, but found herself frozen in the realization that he'd kiss her in that moment... or ever again, for that matter. When he pulled away, leaving her lips pulsing and strangely vulnerable in the night air, he whispered, "When we were kids, you told me once that your mom tried to explain that you were *brighter*, both to living souls and those who'd passed on. I see it, Shya. Have always felt it, even though it was clear you didn't want me to. But maybe I'm not the only one. And maybe the dark ones see it most." He looked toward the window and she realized his features were sharpening as the night wore away. "After all," he continued, meeting her eyes again, "it's in the dark that light is easiest to find."

And she nodded slowly, because it was true. Because she'd been reminded of her mother's words, though she hadn't heard them in some time. And because she'd been reminded that kissing Rory felt *right*. Always had. And that the strangeness of loving your own step-brother had been too much when they were younger and she'd already felt as though she didn't belong in this world. But now, the fact that they'd never grown up as siblings was more important. As was the fact that they'd always felt like more than friends – and not in a family sort of context. Easier to grasp, in the wake of a kiss that had fanned a long-lingering desire.

So, instead of answering him, or even thinking more about what would come when she *did* go to confront the monster that sought her out, she kissed the man she'd always colored the villain, when really he was her knight on a white horse all along.

CHAPTER 32 – BETHIE

It felt good to be the one making breakfast; like she was making up for the argument she and Rory had had when he'd done the same for her.

But it felt odd, too. All of it did. The fact that he was asleep in her bed, the fact that she'd given in to what her heart had known all along, finally. The fact that she'd ignored the feelings of guilt and shame that had come along with it all, even when Rory challenged her on it.

The thing was, all of that was nothing compared to her newly-ignored problems. The distraction, in actuality, was a relief. Because as she scrambled eggs and poured coffee, humming tunelessly but humming just the same, the realization that her mother's ghost seemed – gone – was stirring in her subconscious. And knowing that the boy's – Jordan's – whereabouts were clearer, and that somehow Bethie was linked to everything brewed hot in her belly, standing her nerves on edge, teetering between denial and the inevitable leap into action.

That particular bit would be the thing that brought it all down. The sense of helplessness she'd leaned on where Jordan was concerned, the safety of the walls she'd built up around herself - walls blocking the darker spirits. And the comfort she'd always taken in that she was doing it right. She was protecting herself and those she loved. And finally, the ignorance she'd feigned in knowing that one of those dark spirits had found a way around her walls, had conquered the maze of her self-protection, and was nearly to the middle. The prize.

Her own spirit.

She knew it... felt it dangling pendulous above her like an impending storm, and so she determined to hold it at bay for just a few more minutes. For the revelation, brief as it may be, that she'd always loved Rory, too. For the reflection on her assumptions about him, so easily built up and confirmed by his teenaged arrogance. How she'd purposefully been blind to how his parents' divorce had affected him, just as she'd refused to see the hurt of his father's growing disinterest. She needed to realize that. She needed time. So, she settled on just the morning, just for breakfast with Rory.

He was sitting up when she went back into the bedroom. A smile transfixed his features at the sight of her and she let herself know it was for her. Let herself smile back.

"What'd you do?" he asked, his eyes roving to the plate.

She noted how his hair had matted at the back of his head and giggled.

His hand went self-consciously to his wild locks. "What?"

"I don't think I've ever seen your hair look *just* messy," she teased, and handed him a plate. Her own was balanced on her forearm – a waitressing habit that served her habitually rather than consciously. She deftly placed a coffee on the night table, then brought her own breakfast to the other side of the bed.

"What's that mean?" he asked, but his attention was still on his food, making her laugh again.

She reached out to touch his hair, feeling strange again at the new freedom of not holding back. Feeling exalted. "It's usually... I don't know. *Stylishly* messy," she smiled when he met her eyes, and her stomach did a flip when he kissed her, smiling, too.

He shook his head before taking a sip of the coffee. "Yum!" He placed it back on the table and took a deep breath, looking at her again. "I'm kinda feeling like you're seeing me for the first time."

The sadness in his eyes was unmistakable, and it struck a chord in her she couldn't quite name. "I'm sorry," she said, but it felt like a feeble offering when so much more was left unsaid. But time pressed in on her. No; it was the fact that there *was* no time.

He went back to his food and they were quiet for a while, just long enough for her to sense the tension she was barely holding at bay growing, her gnawing thoughts becoming louder. *Time is short. The boy is dying. I have to go.*

"What's wrong?" Rory was getting up, searching for his clothes.

She snapped back to the present. "You're leaving?" Her heart pounded. This was it. Once he was gone, she'd have to call the group, look at her schedule. Plan a trip.

"I have to work," he replied, stuffing his second arm into his pullover before disappearing into it. She watched as he went to the mirror over her bureau and frowned at his hair. "Good God, what did you *do* to me last night?"

She wanted to laugh, but it wouldn't come.

He turned back to her. "You know we didn't do anything wrong, right, Shy?"

She nodded without thinking. Bit her lip when tears pricked in her eyes.

He chuckled, then jumped onto the bed, making her remember her toast, which flew out of her hand when he landed. "Shit!" she exclaimed as it plopped, jam side down, onto the comforter. But then he was tickling her and she was squirming away, begging through her laughter for him to stop, until he was poised above her, the tip of his nose touching hers.

"How can this make you feel anything but *good?*" he asked. Pleaded with his eyes.

Something in her ached. "So much is happening," she started. Her voice sounded small. Scared.

He backed away, nodding.

She retrieved the fallen toast and focused on the jam stain for a few moments, then met his eyes. "I don't regret it."

He frowned. "You say that as if it was a one-off."

"I don't know how to... I've only ever let myself think of you as..." she floundered, desperate to avoid the word "brother".

He shook his head, exasperated. "Our parents are *divorced,* Shya! Anything that connected us in that way has been long dissolved. I didn't even know you until we were well into our teens!"

She couldn't speak.

He stood, his fingers already pulling his collar out of his sweater and making it neat. "I have to go."

"Don't. I'm sorry!"

He didn't slow. "I'm just going to be late for work, Shy. I'm not storming out. But I do wish for once that you could just let *go* already." He stood as he pulled his pants up. "We can talk more later."

Later. She cringed. Later, she'd be busy. The sense of urgency rose in her and she moved to the end of the bed, reaching for him. Her nearly panicked thoughts echoed through her. *If not now, when? Maybe never! Make it right, Shya. Now.* Rory let his hands drop, then squatted to meet her eyes. She touched his face, her opposite hand going behind his neck, and she kissed him, long and slow. He nearly fell backward when they parted, such that she had to grasp his sweater and pull, giggling again.

He rested his forehead against hers when he was steady. "I love you, Shy," he breathed, and the tears were back, but they were good, that time.

She closed her eyes. Finally. Finally he'd said it, on the cusp of something that might take her. "I just need to have some time, you know?" He nodded immediately, making her heart ache for how long she'd refused to see the truth. "I've never let myself hope for you, Rory. I told myself you were off-limits. Convinced myself you could never want me – even convinced myself I couldn't want you, either. I'm so sorry."

He pulled back slightly and moved his hands to her shoulders. "I get it. I never had that sort of resolve, though." When she frowned, he smiled. "I always knew I wanted you. Right from the start."

She threw her arms around his neck, crying, finally. Knowing she loved him but unable to say it because in the face of everything that was coming, it felt cruel.

"I know things are rough for you right now, but I want to help you through it."

She pulled back that time, holding him at arm's length. "No. I don't want you involved! It'll just use you against me."

"I can't let you deal with this possession shit alone, sis."

"You have to stop calling me that!" she smacked his arm half-heartedly.

He shook his head. "Sorry. Habit."

She touched his cheek again. "You're late."

He shrugged. "Don't care."

They sat quietly for some time, his hands warm on her arms, her fingers still caressing the rough stubble of his cheek.

"What are you going to do?" he asked, finally.

She blew out the air in her lungs, then inhaled deeply. "I've got to call The Seers. And then I think I need to go back home; stay with Dad until I can find Jordan. He's not far from Dad's; I know that much." The path through the woods flashed through her thoughts.

"What about work?"

She shrugged. "I can get time off; I've been working there longer than anyone."

"But you shouldn't go alone, Shy."

"I'll see if one of the group can come, or we'll arrange for them to come once I've found the boy."

He looked doubtful, his eyes dark.

"It's just a road trip. It'll take half a day to get there."

"I want to come." Before she could protest again, he added, "And what about Bethie? Shouldn't you talk to her?"

Shya rolled her eyes at the thought of reaching out to someone she'd purposefully avoided for the last half of her life.

"I'll bet you find him quick if you've got her on board," Rory touched her cheek as he said it, melting her resolve.

"I know," she mumbled.

He stood. "I really do have to go. I won't force you to take me with you, but I want you to think about it, OK?"

She nodded, but had to resist cringing as she wondered what they'd tell her father about their relationship. *What I'll tell* anybody! She shuddered, hugging her arms to herself.

Rory kissed her on the cheek, then swept out of the room, briefcase in hand, as though they were an old couple going about their routine. She heard him detour to the bathroom and smiled. *A routine with Rory that doesn't involve con-*

stant bickering, she wondered as she shook her head. *Wouldn't be a bad thing at all.*

She considered laying down again. She had a close shift that night, so it would make sense to sleep some more, but her mind was working already, thinking of going in early to get her shifts covered for the rest of the week. Thinking of dialling Dawn in hopes of calling an emergency meeting for late that afternoon, before work. Thinking of going home, to the Québec side – to Aylmer - with some apprehension. Since she'd left, she'd only made the effort to visit her father on holidays, usually with Rory in tow. After the divorce, it had been less, still. Her father's apparent indifference had made it easy to stretch the time in between.

Her phone rang from somewhere beyond the room and she perked up, hoping for Dawn, one of the twins, or Big Ed checking in on her. She scrambled out of bed, remembering taking it to the kitchen when she got up, but Rory met her on her way there, holding it out, eyebrows raised.

"I thought you were gone!" she reached for the phone, then frowned at his expression. "What?"

"Pitstop," he gestured toward the bathroom in the hall, then nodded toward the phone as she took it. "Speak of the devil."

"Let's not use that particular expression right now..." she trailed off as she saw the name of the caller.

Rory swept in for another kiss on the cheek and squeezed her arm gently. *"Now* I'm going." He backed up a few steps. "This could be a good thing," he called as he turned and disappeared into the hallway.

Shya looked at the name again, her heart racing. *Beth Dorian,* it said. Different last name, but Shya knew it was her, calling just then, when she'd finally admitted she needed to go home. Needed to find Jordan. Needed to confront the thing that held him captive on a dark, rocky shoreline littered with the corpses of tiny animals. A perpetual nightmare for a boy nearly beaten, too small, too young.

"Hi, Bethie," she answered, her voice steely. "Good timing; I was going to call you today."

The sounds of crying came first, and then a voice that hadn't changed, not much, saying, "Oh, Shya! Oh, God, I'm so sorry... for everything! I should've said it so long ago. I've thought of it a million times, but now I need your help, and I *am* sorry, but I'm also terrified." More crying sounds as Bethie's words spun in Shya's head, and then, "It's my fault, Shya. Everything. But I don't know how to fix it. Please. Can you hear me out?"

Shya paused. Swallowed. Then replied, "Of course."

CHAPTER 33 – MEETING

The meeting had a rushed feeling to it, but that only meant it matched the entire day. Only Dawn, Big Ed and Mel made it to Dawn's condo, but Sheila called and they put her on speaker, which meant the harried sounds of a bus ride to a meeting and then her whispered input just before she went into said meeting made the room feel more than full.

The twins had a client consultation they couldn't miss, but told Dawn they'd "go when things were clearer" when Dawn filled them in over the phone. And they asked Dawn to remind Shya to call them as soon as she needed them. Somehow the reminder of their support felt urgent too, though, and as they settled in to start the meeting, Shya was feeling less than calmed by the whole thing.

"Tell us everything about the dream, front to back," Dawn said, leaning forward in her La-Z-Boy and looking intently at Shya.

Shya summed up instead, noting the points that seemed important, but then her friends had questions, and by the time she'd spent all the details, Dawn was tsk-tsking and saying Shya should have told them everything from the start.

Mel placed a hand on both Shya and Dawn's forearms, revealing the purpose behind his strategic seating between them.

Dawn patted Mel's hand and looked apologetically at Shya. "Sorry."

Shya nodded. "You know I'm not the best at…"

"Talking?" Sheila's disembodied voice made them all jump, then burst into laughter. "Sorry, Shy."

"No; I'm sorry," Shya shook her head as she apologized. "But you might be glad to hear that I'm finally realizing that the things I've trained myself to do to deal with this 'gift' I have are sometimes a hinderance, too." She thought of Rory, of her walls of denial, of clamming up instead of sharing freely.

That time Ed patted her arm. "You've done the best you could with crazy circumstances."

Dawn and Mel nodded enthusiastically.

Mel cleared his throat and they all hushed, all hoping for some of the wisdom the man tended to impart. "So, the boy is possessed by a demon most interested in you," he eyed Shya and she nodded.

"Seems so."

"Seems to me you should be the last to confront it, then," he finished, confusing Shya entirely.

But Dawn nodded. "Seems like you'd be doing exactly what it wants you to do."

"But they've already tried exorcisms," Shya replied, her conversation with Bethie playing in her head. "And all they've managed to do is make Jordan weaker." She met their eyes in turn, wishing they could see the shattered boy of her dreams, just for a moment. "He's going to die."

"Can I say something?" Sheila's voice barely won out over a car horn.

"Go ahead," Dawn said, gesturing impotently at the phone.

"If she confronts this thing alone... well, let's just nix that idea right now. Shya, your friend said it followed her through school, ruined a very breif marriage, haunted her dreams - all bent on a fascination for you. I want to hear more about that when this is all said and done, but for now it's enough. We love you, Shya, and as far as I'm concerned – and I'm sure I speak for everyone else, too! – we won't lose you easily."

Shya's chest filled with gratitude as her friends nodded in agreement.

"But I don't exactly agree with Dawn and Mel, either."

Sheila's words met with silence. Shya watched Dawn's face for a reaction, but the woman seemed calm. She raised her eyebrows toward Shya. "What? I'm an empath, remember? How Sheila's feeling makes me want to hear her out."

Big Ed chuckled beside Shya and the perceived tension dissolved.

"No disrespect, but if Shya is what can help this little boy, she needs to confront this thing. Just – not alone."

Mel's face was transfixed with a rare frown. Shya measured the expressions of Dawn and Big Ed, too, and what she saw was that Sheila's words had rung true, though they were reluctant to admit it.

"She's right." Shya said it before anyone else spoke up. "If I don't see this through, I'll hate myself if he dies. But I don't think I can do it alone. That thing is *strong*. And Rory's right, my mother's ghost can't be counted on to guide me."

"The fact that she's not around adds that much more pressure on you as it is," Dawn reasoned, and Shya's stomach dropped when Mel and Big Ed nodded their agreement.

"I have to hang up now," Sheila whispered, "but I'm in, Shya. Whenever, wherever you need me, I'm there.

"Thank you, Sheila," Shya managed.

The room quieted palpably when Sheila hung up.

"The twins said the same," Ed said, echoing Shya's thoughts, and probably the others', too. "And you know I got your back, always."

She leaned gratefully on his shoulder.

Mel and Dawn exchanged a look, and then joined hands with an almost imperceptible nod. "Of course we're in, too," Dawn said, patting Mel's hand.

Shya smiled. The two had always been close, but there was something new there.

"Hmm," Ed chuckled, and Dawn blushed prettily, her dark skin pinking at her cheekbones. She looked more like a girl than ever, and Shya inwardly rejoiced at Dawn's obvious pleasure. The woman, with all her gifts and her matronly leadership to boot, reminded them of her beauty in that small moment.

"Now don't be children, y'all," she chided, but she was still smiling.

Shya hugged Mel enthusiastically, then patted Dawn's hand, which still held Mel's. "I'm very happy for you," she said, and Ed mumbled in agreement. When Shya looked to him, though, he was watching her instead of the happy couple, a wistful look in his eye.

She cleared her throat and straightened.

"That's that, then," Dawn struck the table with her free hand. "You go as soon as possible and we follow, as soon as you find him and get the full story."

Shya nodded, but her stomach was doing somersaults. "I, uh… thank you," she managed.

"Do *not* confront the demon alone. We're doing this together," Dawn said, her voice firm.

A rush of panic filled her. "I might bring Rory, too," she

said, surprising herself.

"Ah, your brother, right?" Mel smiled.

"More of a close friend than anything," Shya replied, being careful not to sound defensive. "Our parents got married when we were teenagers and have been divorced for a while, now."

Mel nodded, saying, "Ah," and Dawn laughed.

Shya reached for her purse, ready to head to work and get things sorted there. And desperately needing to stop the conversation in its tracks.

Big Ed, however, was curious. "What?" He frowned in Dawn's direction.

Shya tried to meet her eyes, but Dawn was peering intently at Ed. "Nothing, Eddie. I'm just glad Shya has someone who cares about her to head to Québec with, is all."

Dawn's eyes flicked to Shya's and Shya smiled, grateful. The woman knew; she could feel everything, of course she knew! But she'd known enough to smooth it over instead of dig, too. Shya got up and hugged her, too, whispering "Thank you" in the woman's ear, and earning a squeeze back.

"You call us, OK?" Dawn held her at arm's length until Shya promised, and then the group made ready to leave, except for Mel, who seemed content to remain where he was while Dawn saw them out.

"Need a drive to work?" Ed asked, and she gladly accepted, and completely missed the sideways glances he gave her on the way there, as busy as her thoughts were with plans. She thought of being home with Rory again, how different it would be and how the same. She thought of her father, but only briefly. Mostly, though, she thought of the wooded path to the park, of the houses that backed into it, and of how it would feel to knock at the door of one in particular, knowing it would be Connor to answer.

CHAPTER 34 – CONVERSATION

Calm down

Speak more softly

But use much less words

And stop crying; it doesn't help, but know you've been heard

I'm so sorry

I ran

When I left our childhood home

Followed a man we'd both loved, who broke my heart and then some

Sorry to laugh

But are you saying

You followed Drake off to school

And learned too late he wasn't worth all you'd sacrificed?

I was a fool!

I can't deny that

But what does it have to do

With this boy and how he's haunted?

Why's it you who's reaching out to help the one being taunted?

I missed you, Shya

But was ashamed

And so reached out on my own

I gathered friends, we got a board, asked for guidance... it was a game!

Oh, Beth

I told you never

Don't ever use such a thing

How could you forget my warnings of all the dark it could bring?

I can't say

Sorry enough

But it's too late now, you see?

I brought the monster back home. I resisted, but he couldn't, could he?

His mother's absence – it was her funeral I travelled home for

And it was so good to see Connor's face at the door!

Can you imagine, after all those years we all suffered for, that it was him all along that my heart yearned for?

My God, Bethie

You're selfish

I can't believe what you say

And now I know it's your fault the demon has him. For shame!

I hate myself

And Connor hates me

And you hate me more

For bringing something that clung long to me to their door!

But you can help

That's why I'm calling

I don't ask for myself

I ask for Jordan who's too weak to get hold of himself

Please, old friend

Put aside

All our tensions and past

Please, for Connor, come quickly. It's not for me that I ask

I'll come

Not for you

I know now I was right

To swear you off, to drop our friendship, to face alone my dark night

I come for Jordan

For his father

And I'll bring all my friends

But know this: you're not forgiven, not now or after this ends

CHAPTER 35 – CONFRONTATION

"Wow."

Shya gazed expectantly at Rory.

He glanced sideways at her, then back to the road. "I mean, I don't know much about poetry, but as far as *your* poems are concerned, forgive me, but that -" he gave her another sideways glance, "- wasn't awesome."

She stared at him, incredulous, for a moment, then punched his arm. "You're an asshole."

He laughed. "An asshole who loves you."

She looked out the window so he wouldn't see her smile.

"I get that you didn't want to rehash the conversation," he continued, but she cut him off.

"Right! I didn't want to have to remember every word and feel how I felt, etcetera, etcetera! Reading the summary is easier."

"I get it!" He patted her knee.

"It's not like I was planning on entering it into contests or anything."

He laughed as she sulked.

"Poetry is just a way for me to put things down… to get them out of my head!"

"I *know!*" he laughed again. "That was just a bad poem,

that's all." He roared with laughter when she punched him again.

"See if I ever read anything to *you* again," she muttered as she put her notebook into her bag and retrieved her phone. She was kidding; she'd always shared her writing with Rory. Though he could be harsh, his honesty was refreshing, and usually echoed her own thoughts, though she'd never admit it aloud.

She scrolled through her messages.

"I can't believe she followed that twit to university," Rory said, shaking his head.

"I can't believe I was jealous of them," she replied, but absently, having spotted a new text.

He made a noise of disapproval.

She opened a text from Bethie herself, laying a hand on Rory's arm.

"What is it?"

"Connor and Jordan's address," she said quietly as the reality of the situation overcame her again.

"And now *they're* together?"

She shook her head, her eyes still on the screen. "They were, I think, for a while, but not anymore."

"Can't say I blame him," Rory mumbled. There was no trace of humour in his voice.

"You alright?"

"Why does it want you? How did it know to want you?"

She sighed. "You're the one who said I was 'bright' in the darkness, remember? Maybe when Bethie and her friends were using the Ouija board and it came through, knowing her mind was enough to let it know about me."

Rory watched the road, his jaw flexing rhythmically.

"Mom always said the dark spirits were more dangerous for people like us, that we were easier to latch onto if we didn't know how to protect ourselves. Easier to control." She shuddered involuntarily.

"I wish I could've met her."

She smiled. "But if she was still around, you never would have."

"Huh," he raised his eyebrows, "that's sort of crazy."

She watched the tall grasses whiz by. "It is."

"Do you think she'd approve?"

She laughed lightly. "Of you?"

He nodded, and she was surprised by his sincerity yet again. "You really are sweet, aren't you, Rory?"

He rolled his eyes. "Took you long enough to notice."

They both laughed.

"I think she would've liked you," she said, finally, and leaned over to kiss his cheek.

"Let's hope Dad does," he winked impishly.

She made a sound of frustration and turned the radio up when he laughed. She turned back to the window and let her gaze soften so the scenery could flow together as it flew by. She reached absently for his hand. *If only he knew how grateful I am for the distraction of "us,"* she thought, at once comforted and afraid. She closed her eyes, the colours of the world beyond the car window still whizzing by inside her mind, and focused on comfort as she willed herself to sleep.

CHAPTER 36 –
PREAMBLE

Shya's anxiety nearly tipped over into panic when Rory turned into their old neighborhood. He squeezed her hand, which he'd taken when they'd crossed the border and hadn't released since.

"You alright?"

She clenched her teeth. The brief conversation she'd had with her father hadn't comforted, nor discouraged her. As it had been since her mother's death, apathy seemed to rule his actions and reactions when Shya was concerned. "Maybe we should just stay at a hotel," she voiced as sweat beaded on her upper lip.

Rory shook his head. "The house is better; closer. Don't let your dad make this harder than it already is."

She knew he was right, but her reply was swallowed up as they rounded the corner and her childhood home came into view.

Rory squinted toward it. "Is that...?"

Shya's heart fell into her stomach. Bethie was sitting on the front steps, her eyes on them. "Shit," was all she seemed able to say.

"How'd she know when we'd be here?" He pulled into the driveway and Bethie stood.

Shya eyed her old friend critically. She was a little taller, but lighter, somehow – her shorts ballooned around thin legs, and were contradicted by the unlikely match of a calf-length brown cardigan, which draped over her shoulders as though it hung from the bones. Shya found herself getting out of the passenger seat in a daze, eyes on Bethie's face, which had changed, too. Her friend seemed to have traded in delicate, pretty features for a face lined with worry. Above anything else, the absence of Bethie's youthful bounce and cheerful - if not a bit impish – smile, was the biggest change of all.

It was Bethie, but Shya barely recognized her.

"Oh, Shya," Bethie cried as Shya closed the car door, and surprised her by running to her, arms outstretched and regret deepening her look of misery. "I'm so sorry. Oh, thank God you've come," the woman murmured beside Shya's ear and Shya's heart immediately lowered it's walls toward her, surprising Shya all over again.

Bethie's hair had been pulled back into a ponytail, and it tickled Shya's nose. It smelled oddly stale, as though it hadn't been washed in days.

"How'd you know when to come?" she asked, but Bethie didn't let her go right away; her thin arms held Shya captive.

"Interesting to see you, Bethie," Rory spoke in his smooth baritone from behind Shya, making both women jump. Bethie released Shya, saying, *oh!*

Rory draped an arm around Shya's shoulders. Shya realized in that moment that she hadn't a clue how well the two knew each other – they'd been introduced by Shya herself, but she and Bethie's friendship had ended not too long after Rory and his mother had moved in. They would have seen each other at school – and Rory was apprised of what had happened between the two girls – but beyond that, they hadn't spoken much about her.

"Rory," Bethie gave him a curt nod.

Shya gazed up at him questioningly, but he was already plowing ahead, reaching for Bethie's hand and muttering something about how the past belonged in the past and that they needed to focus on the "task at hand." Shya was baffled when he kissed her cheek and carried their suitcases to the door, giving it a light knock and then letting himself in, yelling, "We're home, Dad!"

Shya rubbed absently at a temple.

Bethie turned back to her after having watched Rory disappear into the house. She appeared mildly entertained. "He's a good guy," she smiled.

Shya frowned. What did Bethie know about Rory at all?

Bethie went on as though she'd heard Shya's thoughts. "He talked to me once, after we – and after he moved in with you guys. Let me know how shitty he thought I'd been to you."

Shya found herself looking at the door, which Rory had left ajar – something he knew aggravated her father.

"He was right," Bethie added, and Shya met her eyes again. "There's no excuse for how I betrayed you – first with Drake and then telling them about what you could do. I told myself for years it was raging hormones," she laughed weakly, but her smile faded quickly. "But I think I was just jealous, you know? And Drake really did have me under his spell…" she made a sound of frustration and rubbed at her eyes. "Like I said, there's no excuse, and once I realized everything I'd done, I felt terrible."

"When was that?" Shya remembered their conversation, how Bethie had confessed that Drake had dropped her before they'd even discussed whether they'd live together in a serious way.

"At university. Took me a while – even after Drake broke up with me, he sort of kept me in his back pocket, you know?"

Shya frowned.

"Someone he could call if he was lonely, visit late after drinking with his friends..." Bethie lowered her eyes.

"Someone he could string along so *he* never had to be sad and lonely," Shya finished, and Bethie nodded.

"When it finally clicked," Bethie touched her head with a roll of her eyes, "I realized I was where I'd started before he came along – sort of adrift in a world that didn't seem to have a spot for me. Only there was no *you* to make it alright."

Shya only shook her head, mixed emotions tumbling through her. Rory distracted her from the sorrow in Bethie's eyes, though, reappearing on the steps, then winking at her subtly as he went back to the trunk. Her father's head emerged shortly thereafter, and seemed to freeze when he met Shya's eyes. Shya was momentarily frozen, too, the reality of missing him for so long hitting her in the gut unexpectedly. He broke the spell by lowering his gaze and she tried to remember the last time he'd really looked at her... and failed.

He stepped outside, looking between the three younger people in his yard and then nodding toward Shya. "Good to see you, Shy. You going straight over to Connor's, or you coming in for a bit, first?"

Shya sent a questioning look to Bethie, who jumped to explain.

"I told him you and I plan to go over and see Connor." Her eyes were hard, begging Shya not to elaborate.

Shya nodded, slowly, then looked back at her father. "I wanted to pay my respects."

"He's had a rough go of it," her father folded his arms over his chest. "He did some work for me, putting up the new subdivision." He nodded in the direction of the park and the woods beyond, and Shya recalled the hew houses edging on the woods in her dream.

She took a deep breath, seeing Bethie's lingering tension. *Don't tell him,* her eyes seemed to say, and it was easy enough to comply, she and her father hadn't gone beyond pleasantries in many years. "How's city planning going?" she referenced the work he'd taken up shortly after her mother's death. It was a comfortable topic for the man, and true to form, he appeared instantly relieved.

Rory squeezed past him with another bag and Shya's purse, but sent her a smile before disappearing inside again. She was inwardly grateful for his presence, though she couldn't help but wonder if the precedent of secrecy Bethie had set would carry into all topics that followed, including her relationship with her father's ex-wife's son. She felt her fists clench at the thought.

"Shy?" her father was frowning at her when she snapped out of her thoughts.

"Huh?"

"I asked if you knew about Connor's son. He's been sick since... well, since his mother died, but worse lately."

Bethie grabbed her hand and squeezed, making Shya want to flee altogether, but she squeezed back before replying, "Bethie was telling me about it," and stopping there.

"It's like the poor kid's heart just broke, and the rest of his body seems to want to follow," her father noted, his face grim.

"I had no idea you were so close with Connor," Shya said, frowning slightly. Truthfully, she had no idea her father *cared* like his face reflected, then.

Her father looked put out. "Known him since you were a kid, haven't I? And then he did all that work for me... we're practically neighbors, now!"

Shya nodded, shoving her confusion down.

"We – uh, do you want to go over now, Shy?"

Shya shook her head. "I want to get settled first." Her agenda whirled through her head. She looked back at her father, who appeared somewhat lost on his own front step. "I'm going to talk with Bethie a bit more, then come in," she said, pasting a smile on before he nodded and went back inside. She looked back at Bethie. "What is going on?"

"Everybody knows about Jordan," Bethie's eyes filled with tears as she spoke, "and because of the exorcisms, there are rumours. The exorcists were professional, but tongues will wag when so much activity happens at one house."

Shya nodded. "Have you been here the whole time?"

She shook her head and pressed her lips together. A tear escaped and she wiped it away, as though angry it had fallen. "Like I said, I came back when I learned Connor's wife – her name was Lauren – died. I knew her a little from visits back home. She and Connor met in university..." she trailed off when she caught the look in Shya's eye again. "Sorry, but I think it's important that you understand what happened."

Shya had been unaware she'd been displaying anything but curiosity. "Go on," she urged, wondering at her sense of annoyance.

"Connor and I always stayed in touch," she went on, "in fact, he was a great friend after Drake dropped me."

"Hm," Shya muttered. But that was it; she was aggravated because she'd been suspicious that Bethie had used Connor, too, for her own purposes.

"We were good friends," Bethie said, defensive.

"What does that even mean to you?" Shya spat, then shut her mouth, trying to pull back a reaction she hadn't predicted. Bethie looked as though Shya had slapped her. "I – I'm sorry. I guess I haven't dealt with everything as fully as I'd assumed I had," Shya apologized.

"You coming in, hon?" Rory's head appeared around the door.

Bethie's eyes cleared, and then she smiled. "I always thought you two were meant for something more than what your parents' marriage made you."

Shya sought evidence of teasing, or even disapproval, in the face of her old friend, but found none.

"It's OK," Bethie added. "I just – I'm happy for you."

She'd always been able to read Shya like a book. She realized she'd missed that as a blow to her chest, and found herself unable to say anything, to either of them.

"Shy?" Rory's face revealed his concern.

"It's OK; I'll be right in," she gave a little wave and he nodded before he was gone again. She inhaled. "It's sort of... new," she said, peeking through her eyelashes at Bethie and feeling angry that she automatically sought her approval. She sucked in a breath and straightened. "I mean, admitting it is, at least." She met Bethie's eyes: a challenge.

"I think it's wonderful," Bethie replied, some of the old light back in her eyes.

"I should go in soon," Shya said quickly, wanting to get past the conversation about Rory and feeling the need to hurry for the boy who was now just down the street, too.

Bethie seemed to regroup, her face turning serious. "I didn't mean it when I asked if you wanted to go over to Connor's. I'm lucky he's talking to me at all, and besides that, we should prepare a bit first."

"Does he know I'm here?"

Bethie nodded. "That's *why* he's talking to me. He's always been amazed by what you could do, Shy. He believes in you."

"OK..."

"But he's scared. He's reluctant to take Jordan through another experience like the exorcisms." She shook her head. "It's so sad..."

"Bethie, I think you'd better tell me exactly what happened." Shya regarded her plaintively.

Bethie nodded, then glanced back at the door. "Can we take a walk?"

The park at the end of the street flashed into Shya's thoughts. She nodded and they started off, Shya only pausing when she thought of Rory alone with her father. But when she looked back, he gave her a thumbs-up from the bay window and she had no excuse not to carry on with Bethie. Resolved, she matched her somewhat halting pace and they walked, wordlessly, both lost in their own thoughts. And as hesitant as Shya had always been to leap into the fire, her thoughts were not of fear, or plans, or of the days ahead, but on serendipity instead. Fate. And how it made sense, somehow, that she'd learn the harrowing details of the demon that possessed Connor's son in a place that had been the focal point of her past, where Bethie was the center of everything and her betrayals had played themselves out. The place where things had changed so much... and she was certain in that moment that they would again.

CHAPTER 37 – CALM BEFORE THE STORM

I'd heard the words before
Without grasping their full meaning
How one's path in quiet lull
On the precipice is leaning

Unaware in grace or fall
That a breath could tip it sideways
And the choice is made for all
Forks dissolve, path crystallizes

Then step and kindred step
Into chaos manifested
And gentle slips behind
Past and present drawn and tested

Pray, heed my words and warning
In heavy apathy's seduction
Poised, alert and wary of
The beast that waits, bent on destruction

CHAPTER 38 –
INCEPTION (BETHIE)

They sat at a picnic table, likely one of the same they'd sat at before, judging by its state of wear. But Shya didn't recognize the most prominent inscriptions, and felt no urge to seek her own carvings out. Reminders of the past were present enough in the woman who sat across from her now, pulling her bulky cardigan around bony shoulders despite the warm air around them.

"You look... thin." Shya settled on the descriptor with a sense of hesitation. The words *old* and *haunted* had surged forward as she'd spoken, and "thin" was the only replacement that rang with any sort of honesty. Still, she had the feeling Bethie would draw into her sweater and disappear completely rather than address her appearance.

Indeed, she smoothed flyaway hairs behind her ears self-consciously, then hugged her arms to herself before replying. "Things haven't been easy," she said, her hollow eyes flicking to Shya's briefly. "But that doesn't matter... all I care about now is Jordan and Connor." She met Shya's gaze more solidly, now, and reached for her hands even as Shya reflexively pulled away, at first. When Shya did allow her to grasp them, they were cold and thin, like steel. "You were right; I have been selfish. Trust me, I've paid! But now I'm afraid I can't undo what I've started." She pulled her hands back into her sleeves, her face crumpling as she began to cry. "I've snarled everything good in my life into a giant mess. Even my Mom acts like I'm a stranger, always asking why I don't go to a specialist for my insomnia or why

I don't take something for the panic attacks..." she trailed off, meeting Shya's eyes with a look of something like regret. "It doesn't matter," she continued, chewing a chapped lip as she paused, "I know now that nothing will get better – for me or Connor or Jordan, or even for you! – until that *thing* is gone." Her skin pinked with apparent anger, and the appearance of colour in her pale cheeks was a strange relief, but only lasted a moment.

"You said 'Mom'. What about your Dad?"

A tear streaked down her cheek. "He's gone."

Shya blew out a breath, trying to recenter herself. She'd never been close with Bethie's folks – even Bethie hadn't seemed to be when they were kids – but it seemed loss after loss had been piled on top of the friend whose existence she'd denied for many years. She let out a low whistle, shaking her head. "I'm sorry, Bethie. I'll be honest; I never imagined feeling compassion for you if we ever saw each other again, so I'm having a hard time knowing where we stand right now."

Bethie nodded and sniffled.

"But I am sorry about your father."

They were quiet for a few moments.

Shya straightened as a sense of urgency surged through her again. "Look, I can see you've been through a lot, and don't worry; I know I have a part to play in this, but I feel like time for catching up isn't a luxury we have right now. I need to know the details... anything you already know. Anything can help."

Bethie sniffed and gave herself a shake, then nodded. "Sorry."

Shya leaned forward, reaching for Bethie's hands, that time, which she squeezed and then patted, hoping to comfort but still at odds with this new version of her old friend, and then released. "What happened?"

Bethie inhaled and looked toward the trees as if her past hid in the branches. Then she started talking.

"I told you I followed Drake to university... honestly I knew it was a dumb idea before we even left, but my options here didn't exactly spell out success, either." She wiped her nose on the dowdy cardigan's sleeve, and Shya fought against cringing at the slug-slime path it left.

"Anyway, it took less time than *anyone* could have predicted for Drake to cheat. He was exactly what frosh girls were looking for: charming, funny, and with so much confidence it spilled over and calmed the nerves of anyone he was around!"

Shya nodded. "Sounds like Drake."

"Not to mention his looks," Bethie seemed to catch herself and had the decency to blush. "I *am* sorry, Shya. You know, if I'd had any clue that being with him would mean losing you, I would never have..."

Shya held a hand up, then motioned for Bethie to continue. It wasn't that apologies weren't needed; it was that the words didn't ring true.

"I was stupid."

That was more like it. "OK, Bethie. What next?"

"Right." She sniffled loudly. "I'm not proud of what happened next, but I'll be honest. I spun out of control." She toyed restlessly with one of the buttons on her sweater. "I guess that's not surprising, considering I was on my own in a new place and had lost the boy I'd ruined my relationship with you over."

Shya waited quietly as Bethie seemed to struggle for words.

"It was so easy to find a new group of friends. I moved into one of the dorms and my roommate instantly adopted me into her group. I was so desperate for connection that I didn't care that they weren't people I'd have gravitated to in any other situation – you know the type: black lipstick, permanently gloomy?"

Shya had had friends like that. She nodded, smiling. "I like those ones."

Bethie laughed. "Me, too! I never, ever had to be anyone but myself with them. Thing was, I *wasn't* myself, then."

Shya made a face. "So... sorry, but I have no idea where this is going."

"I was lost," she gestured helplessly, hands rising and falling in frustration. "And those guys were my home for a while. We hung out in big groups, wandering the town or the dorms. We drank... a *lot*... but it was all fun, you know? And they were strangely dedicated to their classes; we studied as much as we partied. And when they started getting into para-normal stuff, it was like proof I belonged with them."

Shya became oddly uncomfortable, as though her phys-ical self knew what was coming before her mental self could catch up.

"They were so excited when I told them about you! They asked so many questions, wanted to know how it started, when it started, whether you had asked for your gift or..."

Shya barked out a laugh. "Everyone's curious until the reality of it hits."

Bethie shut her mouth, which had frozen open when Shya interrupted. Her shoulders slumped, the previous anima-tion she'd spoken with dissolving. "You're right. It was all fun and games to them, and they *begged* me to invite you to visit. I couldn't tell them we weren't friends anymore; I needed them, or I thought I did..." she trailed off, her eyes going to the trees again and her tears suddenly renewed. "I felt like a walking, talking lie." Bethie met her eyes again. "You know I was always jealous of you. Not even in a bad way! I was amazed by what you saw, and naively sure I'd be able to handle it better than you seemed to." She shook her head. "I'm sorry."

Shya's skin tightened as the breeze blew cooler with the slow fall of the sun toward the horizon. And her heart felt cold, too. "Keep going."

"I thought about calling you. I imagined us making up and being close again... it became a fantasy! A scenario I held on to, playing our conversations over and over in my head just to get through a tough day. But I couldn't do it. Despite the happy reunion I had conjured in my mind, I knew you'd still hate me."

Shya shrugged. "Maybe not."

Bethie's eyes widened.

"What? Let's just say I've come to realize some things about myself in the last while."

"Like that you're stubborn as a mule?" Bethie smiled, then bit her lip, but Shya was quick to smile, too.

"Yes. Like that," she admitted, and it felt like... relief.

"I should've called you," Bethie said, quietly. Her tears hadn't fully halted since her last bout, and there was something about the way they shimmered on her lashes that made Shya's stomach ache.

She looks like a remorseful puppy, she thought, but what she said was, "What's done is done. We're here now." It felt like less than what Bethie needed, but she found it was all she could offer.

Bethie smiled gratefully.

Maybe it's enough.

"When my friends realized I was never going to produce this amazing medium friend of mine, they started talking about other ways to learn more about contacting the dead."

Shya frowned. "I don't like where this is going."

Bethie shook her head. "You wouldn't, and I didn't, either. I *did* remember what you'd told me about Ouija boards and the like, about how they can act as portals, but they didn't want to hear anything else about you unless it came from your mouth."

"They didn't even believe I existed, did they?"

Bethie shrugged. "Some of them said as much, but others still really wanted to meet you."

"You know any object can act as a portal if enough energy is focused on it with intent. With all the reputation the Ouija board has, though, it's that much easier for the right kind of atmosphere to be set."

"I remember. I said all of that, but they were deaf to it! I tried... I felt somehow like I was being loyal to you by warning them, but I failed. They came up with a plan to get a board, light a bunch of candles and do, like, an open séance."

"Shit."

Bethie nodded. "Once the plan was in motion, it was like a freight train barrelling down on us. I didn't know what to do! The date loomed closer and closer, and whenever I considered just skipping out on it, I'd feel guilty. I *did* know more about that stuff, maybe even some safeguards to take, you know? From knowing you. I thought maybe I could protect them."

Shya clenched her jaw against the words that wanted release. Instead, she waited for Bethie to continue.

"In the end, I went, because if anything happened to them, I'd never forgive myself! And I'd already fucked up so many relationships..."

"What happened?"

Bethie seemed shaken by the question. "Huh?"

"You don't need to convince me of the whys or hows, Bethie. I just want to know what happened."

She nodded. "Right. Sorry."

"We don't have time."

"I know." She dried her cheeks and went on. "The night before it happened, I was freaking out. I went to bed feeling sick to my stomach, just overwhelmed that I'd sort of encouraged the whole thing by talking about you and your experiences, and had already failed at protecting them."

"People are going to do what they want to do. If not then, later. They were already interested in the paranormal, right?"

Bethie nodded.

"Then it was probably more a question of *when* than *if.*"

She paused, thinking, then smiled weakly. "Thank you for saying that."

Shya squirmed a bit on the hard bench. "I don't remember these being so uncomfortable."

Bethie laughed. "I have, like, no cushioning," she said, gesturing toward her backside.

Shya didn't laugh; her friend's acknowledgement of her nearly emaciated state made it that much more real. "What happened to you?"

Her smile faded. "It's got Jordan now, but I still can't sleep or eat or... anything!"

Shya saw the tears threatening again and struggled to get back on track. "What has him?"

"It was the first séance – oh yes, there were many – but it was the first where it made itself known." Bethie's eyes widened, which intensified the dark hollows of the sockets they sat in. "The demon. The... evil... *thing*."

Shya shuddered. "Tell me more."

"I wasn't even at the table. I didn't want to be directly involved. But it didn't matter. They asked for spirits to come through and communicate, said it didn't matter who or why, and the room felt different right away. Heavy." Bethie's eyes were far off, remembering. "The guy next to me grabbed my hand when the – thing – what's it called?"

"Planchette?"

"Yes. It started to move and one of the girls with her fingers on it let out a squeal. Nobody said a word as it spelled out the word which I now know to be a representation of its name."

"What was it?"

She shook her head, pressing her lips together. "I don't want to say it."

"You have to. Don't let it have power over you, Bethie."

She looked doubtful. Scared. "But – Jordan!"

"It already knows I'm here. It knows I'm coming and that it's not to make friends. Saying its name gives *us* power."

Bethie nodded quickly, but her breath came in hitching fits and starts.

"What did it spell that first night?"

She glanced at the trees, eyes darting in all directions and making Shya's skin crawl. Her eyes were wide when she met Shya's gaze again. But despite her apparent terror, she inhaled and whispered, "*Four*".

Shya said nothing. Not because it was a shock or because it was ridiculous, but because it gave her that feeling again – the one that convinced her she was missing something. The one that had accompanied the sudden quiet, if not complete departure, of her mother's ghost.

"What is it?"

Shya frowned as old memories tried to resurface, but sank down again as if stricken by thrown stones. Her efforts to grasp them made her head ache. "I don't know."

"It says it in other languages, too," Bethie was whispering again.

"But it's always a version of 'Four?'"

Bethie gasped at the sound of the word, though it was only spoken in Shya's indoor voice, then nodded. "What does it mean?"

Shya shook her head. "You know I don't even think about that side of things if I don't have to. You've never tried to figure it out?"

"I did, and I have theories, but even the exorcists couldn't confirm them. It's like the thing refuses to acknowledge anyone unless they could lead it to..." she regarded Shya with sorrowful eyes, then finished, "you."

Shya plowed on. "What happened after that first night?"

"Wait, I didn't tell you all the details... candles were flickering or blown out, shadows were accused of being more than shadows..."

"OK...?"

"But it was much more disturbing for me. Like it was a weight on my shoulders that never left, even after we left the room. Left the house, even."

"What else? Did it say anything to you? Come into your dreams? Make you see things? Things that shouldn't... *be*?"

Bethie visibly shivered, "No. Not then."

"Not then? So, later?"

There were more tears in Bethie's eyes. "Yes."

Shya looked to the sky. Wished for her mother. Wished the sun was higher and that the sunset wasn't quite so extravagant. Just for that night.

"Do you want to know about the other seances?"

Shya looked at Bethie again. "Not tonight. Skip to why I'm here."

Bethie looked genuinely confused for a moment, then seemed to shake it off. "As it's hold on me grew, it was like it knew my mind. Things I wasn't even consciously thinking. And I think it got frustrated with me; I resisted the whole time, Shya. I remembered everything you'd said."

Shya scoffed. "I only told you what my mother taught me."

Bethie's face went blank except for something in her eyes – fear? Regret? *Both*, Shya thought.

"What is it?"

"I – this is what I've been so scared to tell you. I wouldn't blame you for never speaking to me again after all this is over. I hate myself for doing it!"

Shya leaned forward, somehow needing the hard edge of the table sharp against her ribs. "Tell me."

"I... oh, God. I couldn't talk to you, but I needed help! I was so scared. I didn't know what to do, who to go to. And I did remember that much of what you told me when we were kids was just a regurgitation of the lessons your mother gave you and I thought... I couldn't imagine a scenario where it would turn out like it has."

Shya's blood ran cold. "You called for my mother?"

Bethie's face crumpled as the tears flowed afresh. "I asked her to protect me – and my friends! Before the second séance, I – it was like praying! I just talked to her, told her every-thing... asked her to help!"

"So, it knew me *and* my mother through you."

Bethie nodded, bits of hair sticking to her cheeks, which were looking irritated and red.

What must the composition of tears be to visibly etch their pain on the skin? Shya wondered absently, and realized she was caught in that automatic web of denial she was so good at weaving... an unconscious distancing of herself from a reality too hard to face.

"I never saw her like you see... *them*, but Shya, I swear I felt lighter after the first time I talked to her. I felt *her!*"

Shya bit the sides of her cheeks so she wouldn't scream.

"I'd always felt closer to your mom than to my own," Bethie was blabbering through her tears, now, and Shya felt, despite recognizing her go-to coping mechanism, as if she was watching the scene on a movie screen.

"I don't want to talk about this anymore."

Bethie reached across the table, fumbling in the air when there was nothing for her to grasp. Shya didn't reach back. Not that time.

"Will you ever forgive me? I can't tell you how sorry I am!"

"It has her, too," Shya heard the words as if she were an eavesdropper on her own conversation.

Bethie's features contorted into a new expression of mortification. "What do you mean?"

"I don't see her anymore. Haven't in months."

Bethie's hand flew to her mouth. "Oh, no."

Shya gave herself a hard shake, then brought her palms

down on the table as if to end that part of the conversation. She wanted to forget it. To move forward. "I want to see Connor. I want to see the boy."

Bethie nodded, her head jerking up and down and her hand still covering her mouth.

"I won't do anything yet – I won't engage the demon without my friends, but I want to talk to Connor and see the boy in person. I've only seen him in dreams and I feel like I need to rectify that version of him with reality."

Bethie let her hand fall. "He's – not well, Shy. And he's terrified of the hospital, because of how his mother died, you know? But Connor tried taking him in, more than once... but Jordan got worse every time, as though his fears took over completely and let that *thing* have control. And now... if you think I've changed, the state of Jordan will render me newly beautiful," she finished on a high, wavering note, then buried her face in her hands as she burst into a new torrent of tears.

Shya stood robotically and went to Bethie's side of the table. She put a hand on one of her forearms, gently, and said, "Come on. It's getting dark."

Bethie peeked up at her over her fingertips, questions spilling from her eyes and pooling between her fingers and her red, raw cheeks.

"I need time to process all this," Shya said, and it struck her as the kindest thing she could've said, and she was proud of herself. She thought of Rory, then, and telling him about her conversation with Bethie, and of filling The Seers in, too. "I have to go back." She let her hand drop.

Bethie stood and used her sleeve to dry her tears. Shya cringed at the state the sleeve must be in. "Thank you for listening, Shya," Bethie muttered, but she was unable to meet Shya's eyes.

"Can I go to Connor's tomorrow?"

She nodded. Looked a bit hopeful under the mess of her misery. "Yes. Thank you. Your Dad knows exactly where it is."

"Will you meet me there tomorrow morning?"

Bethie smiled and nodded again.

"Are you staying at the old house?"

She shook her head. "Mom moved into an assisted living place – the one downtown?"

Shya recalled the building of the place – a ten-storey complex with a grocery store on the main floor and the shopping mall attached. Convenience for the elderly was the touted intention, but Shya'd heard the prices were borderline criminal for something little more than glorified condos. "Does she like it?"

Bethie shrugged. "Seems to."

"So... where *are* you staying, then?"

Her eyes brightened, just a bit. "Connor's."

Shya's internal response was mixed. Connor had always loved Bethie; she'd seen it in his eyes when they'd watched Drake and Bethie wrestling playfully in the park half a lifetime ago. Half of her feared she'd take advantage of Connor, too. But the other half – and this surprised her greatly – was happy for a flash of something that could be good in the whole mess of circumstances they were all in. Love, in the midst of terror and uncertainty. *Maybe it'll conquer all, like in the movies,* she thought. Hoped.

"Don't worry," Bethie said as though she could read her thoughts, "I'll never do anything to hurt him again. Or Jordan," she added, her eyes brimming with tears, then spilling over.

Shya wiped a tear from her old friend's sore-looking skin without thinking, her heart lurching at the memories that surfaced the moment she touched the woman's cheek. She drew her hand back awkwardly, then forced a laugh. "You're going to get dehydrated if you don't stop."

Bethie smiled through her tears. "You always surprise me, Shy."

CHAPTER 39 –
BURST DAM

Shya and Rory lay in her bed, awake. Rory half-sat, as if on alert. His hand was loosely wrapped around hers. They'd lain like that countless times before, when they were younger, usually after a nightmare of Shya's or an especially disturbing ghostly visitor. Or after Rory had come in late and wanted to share details of his excursions as she tried not to doze off.

She was drained in all ways by the events of the evening. Recounting her conversation with Bethie to Rory had been the last of it, and in her depleted state she found herself confronted with the memories of younger days without her usual determination to frame them in a way that was less shocking – less, in her mind, *wrong.* But rather than an inundation of guilt or shame, she found what followed to be more positive than she could have expected. Relief. Lightness. And mostly, gratitude.

But she knew something else in those moments, too. She thought of Rory's barely-contained jealousy when Big Ed had shown up to comfort her, and understood it. He'd always been that for her, even though she'd failed to see it for so long. She peered up at him, her heart lurching in her chest. He was awake, still, and looking troubled. "Rory?"

He wrapped her in his arms. "Hm?"

"I'm so sorry."

He frowned. "Huh?"

"I was so stupid," she whispered, the words fighting to stay where they'd always belonged. Shoved down. Forgotten. But then he smiled down at her and dissolved her lingering angst.

"Yeah, you were," he said, smiling even bigger.

She laughed. "Why did you keep trying?"

He ran a finger down the line of her jaw. "Let's just say it's a damn good thing you're cute."

She couldn't laugh again; the lump in her chest was too big and hurt too much. She stretched upward to kiss him, then threw her arms around his neck as she climbed onto his lap. Images of the boy and the dark spirit that held him captive filled her mind. Twisted black fingers in gnarled bark, a desolate shoreline that oozed crimson at every line and curve, and the tortured face of the friend she'd been so close to when her mother's gift was showing up. Taking hold.

She knew what was to come. She'd managed to shove it into oblivion, like she'd shoved aside her love for Rory, but now it was staring her down. The next day, she'd see Connor... a man changed by the death of his wife, then torn apart by the possession of his only child. And Shya would see him, too: the boy of her dreams, in the flesh. And she knew she'd come face to face with the demon that called itself *Four*, even if only through Jordan.

She knew, too, that it was only a matter of time until that thing tried to take her for itself, and she didn't know if she could stop it.

She pulled back, taking Rory's face in her hands. "I love you, Rory."

He chuckled. Joy sparked in his eyes. But then, his face fell and he held her gaze, moving his hands to her face, too. "Why do I feel like you just said goodbye?"

That was all it took; the dam burst and she let her hands drop as she crumpled under the full weight of her sorrow.

"Baby," he muttered, taking her into his arms again. She pressed into his chest and sobbed, unwilling or unable to hold back any longer.

"I miss my mother," she found herself saying. Sobbing.

"I know," he said into her hair, making her scalp tingle.

Something new rose in her, then. She sat up, confused and unselfconsciously wiping her tears away.

"What?" Rory's expression mirrored hers.

"That thing's got her," she said, her voice finding some of its strength again. "And I've been pretending not to know it, just so I wouldn't have to... *feel* this way again!" she hit her chest with her fingertips, right where her heart pounded frantically against her sternum.

He took one hand into his own and ran the other down her arm.

"What is *wrong* with me?" she cried, angry all of a sudden. "Why am I still trying to run from anything that feels hard? Feels like work?"

Rory shook his head, his expression clearing. "No, Shya... don't say that."

She let her hands fall, palms-up on his blanketed thighs and stared at them, self-hatred coursing through her. "Everybody calls it a gift, and what have I done with it? Tried to ignore it! Sometimes successfully, even!" She looked back at him through her tears. "I've never been thankful for it, Rory. Not once. I never wanted it. Even when I helped the ghosts, it was only to make them go away! They never stopped scaring me," she lowered her head again, sobbing. "I don't deserve this gift," she said, shaking her head, and then she buried her face in her hands, helpless.

He put his hands on her knees, but said nothing. Just let her cry until she was too tired to cry any more, and then he gathered her close again. And she learned he was only quiet because he wanted to let her cry. It wasn't because he had nothing to say.

He ran a hand along the back of her head and down her neck, gentle with her curls. "You are amazing, Shya." She started to protest, but he wouldn't let her. "This *gift* – you didn't ask for it. You had no choice. And while your mother and her mother and her mother's mother had the benefit of having half a lifetime of experience and training, your own teacher, mentor, not to mention the only person in the world who could understand what you'd be going through, *died* when you were ten years old. And even without considering the ghosts that *immediately* started showing up, losing your mother at so vulnerable an age had to have been devastating."

She breathed against the damp material of his shirt, his words flowing strangely through her resistant mind. It had always been her failure, her own flaws and careless actions solely to blame for the misgivings of her life. She'd never seen it any other way.

"I don't know how you've done it," Rory said, and she heard the force of the emotion that pushed the words out. "I don't know how you're still *sane*. All I've ever wanted to do was help... to take care of you! Because you tried to be so strong and I could see what it did to you. It's not fair, Shya, that you've been saddled with a massive otherworldly responsibility, not to mention the loss of the one soul who could help you."

She strained to look up to him, but had to sit up to do so. "You really do see me, don't you?"

A tear escaped, finally, and she realized she'd never seen Rory cry. She watched it traverse the stubble at his jawline with an ache in her heart.

"And your father – I don't know what he was like before your mom died, but he wasn't a father to you, Shya, not while I lived here and not after, that's sure." He wiped absently at his nose. "And after Bethie... you never really had close friends. I mean, maybe the people in your Seers group understand you, but would I be wrong in assuming you haven't let any of them get too close?"

She nodded dumbly.

He touched her cheek. "And that Gary guy," he whispered, shaking his head. "You deserve so much, Shya. I'm *glad* you have The Seers. But you deserve friends, close friends, too! And you deserve a partner. You deserve to be happy. Supported! Loved. You deserve someone who will share your burden, even if it's just to listen when you need an ear or hold you when you need to be held," he smiled, a hopeful look in his eyes.

"You wanna be that person," she stated rather than asked, the full realization of his love hitting her.

"It's all I've ever wanted," he said with a hiccough, more tears escaping.

"Oh," she breathed, and fell into his arms again.

They held each other for a long time. Shya was dozing when he gently shook her.

"Huh?" she sat up and realized the stiffness of her hips and knees. "Oh, I need to move," she laughed quietly and rolled to stretch out beside him.

"Shy," he sunk to his side, resting his head in his hand. Waited for her to give him her undivided attention.

"What?"

"I've been thinking. Can't you get your friends to help find your mom?"

She frowned. "What do you mean?"

"They have gifts too, right? You've told me about the fortune teller... and the twin psychics. Can't they help?"

She smiled at his description of her friends. "Sheila," she said with a trace of humour. "Sheila's the 'fortune teller.'"

He rolled his eyes. "You know what I'm saying, right?"

She felt her smile fall. She'd never needed help seeing her mother, so hadn't considered it, even when her mother seemed lost. "I hadn't thought about it," she frowned.

"You should."

She shook her head. "I'm meeting Jordan tomorrow. Helping him is more important."

He sat up, impatient, now. "I know, but helping him would be easier, not to mention safer, if you had your mother by your side."

She knitted her eyebrows.

"Figuratively speaking."

He was right.

"And you shouldn't do this without all the help you can gather, Shya," he added. "I love you. And I'm worried."

The rare vulnerability on his face struck her more than any words could have. She thought about the fact that the group would be joining her shortly. As soon as she called, probably. She fixed her gaze on Rory's and nodded. "You're right."

He let out a long breath. "That's right!" he lay down, knitting his fingers behind his head and looking self-satisfied.

Shya laughed. "Thank you," she said, and kissed his cheek before getting out of bed.

"What? Where you going?" he asked, bewildered.

"No time like the present," Shya smiled, thinking about the twins' instructions to call them.

"You're going to call them?" He reached for his phone and peered incredulously at the screen. "It's almost one AM!"

"The twins are probably already up and sitting by the phone," she muttered, then ducked into a pullover. "I don't want to piss Dad off, though, so I'll go outside." She shook her head as she looked pointedly at Rory, who was stretched out on her bed. "God knows he's not happy you're not in your old room, alone!"

Rory sat up, leaning forward conspiratorially. "Your Dad's changed, Shya."

She stepped into a worn pair of slippers that were her mother's, once. "Sure," she rolled her eyes.

"No, really! And yes, he knows I'm in here with you, because I told him we're together."

She froze. *"What?"*

He held both hands up in surrender. "He asked, Shy! He said he always knew we should be together!"

Her jaw dropped.

"What's more, he *approves.*" Rory's eyebrows seemed permanently fixed in the surprised position.

"Are you joking?" she asked, half sure he was.

He shook his head. "You should talk to him, Shya."

She laughed. "OK."

He stood, then manoeuvred himself between her and the door. "You really should. Like I said, you need all the support and love you can get."

She eyed him skeptically. "Tell you what, I'll talk to him if you get out of my way."

He moved aside. "Hurry back," he called after her as she slipped into the hallway, "so I can show you some extra special support and love... naked!"

She closed the door quickly, and made a frustrated sound when she heard him laughing. But as she started down the stairs, phone in hand, she was smiling.

CHAPTER 40 – VEIL

There was the sound of the phone being manipulated and then set down at the other end, and then the perfectly synchronized answer from Jane and Anna.

"Shya?"

"Hi guys."

"We're glad you called." Shya had long ago given up trying to decipher which twin was speaking when she didn't have the benefit of seeing them in person.

"It's not too late?" She rolled her eyes at herself, noticing the stars as she did and fixing her gaze there, on the clear black of the sky dotted extravagantly with winking stars. She thought of laying in the grass in the graveyard with Bethie, feeling like the whole world was theirs for the taking. She shook her head. *Had* she ever felt like that? It seemed impossible, now.

"We've been waiting."

Of course, they have. "My old friend Bethie was waiting for me when we arrived, and she gave me the details on how this all started. The demon latched on to her at an amateur séance with university friends."

"Ouija board?"

"Yep."

"And she resisted?"

"Yes, but it made demands. She said it wanted me all along."

"Does she know its name?"

"She said it calls itself different versions of the number 'four' – any idea what that means?"

There was a brief pause, during which Shya could practically see them exchanging a pointed look. "It depends," one of them said.

"On...?"

"You should call Mel; he's the historian of the group, and he's quite knowledgeable about biblical references to demons and possessors."

Shya nodded, resolving to call Mel in the morning.

"Don't wait, Shya," the twins chorused.

She rolled her eyes. "Stop that!"

"Don't waste time; call him tonight."

Shya made a non-committal noise, but inwardly added another call to her list of things to do before she could get some sleep.

"What else?" one of the twins brought her back to herself.

"What I'm really calling about is my mother."

The women at the other end were silent.

"I still haven't had any sort of contact with her, and Bethie told me tonight that *she* contacted her for protection when she was going through all the séance stuff at school."

There was a sharp intake of breath at the other end, quickly overlapped by an identical intimation of surprise. "We didn't see this."

The other twin added, "Of course it would use her mother!" which was followed by a half-whispered conversation between the sisters while Shya studied the stars, waiting.

"Shya, we think trying to connect with your mother might be helpful, but of course it comes with risks."

"Like coming up against the thing that stands between she and I?"

"Exactly," came both voices in reply.

Shya shivered.

"Why don't we try it on our own, without Shya?" One of the twins spoke solely to the other again, and Shya – unwilling to be a spectator to her own conversation any longer – broke in.

"Go ahead."

"Really?" Both voices, again.

Shya closed her eyes and pinched the top of her nose. "Yes. I need her and she's being blocked… who knows how. And I'm worried about her. Anything you guys could do without putting her… or I… in danger would be… appreciated."

There was a shuffling movement at the other end, and then the awaited commiseration. "You're right."

"Thank you. Do you know her energy well enough?"

"Of course."

How could I have doubted? Shya chuckled quietly. Her mother had been at least a passive presence for so long; of course Jane and Anna had gotten to know her, too. "I'm lucky to know you two."

They laughed quietly. "We feel the same. We'll do it tonight."

"OK. I'll sign off and call Mel."

"Are you OK, Shya?"

"Yeah, just very, very tired all of a sudden."

"Get some sleep; you'll need it."

She nodded. "Yep."

"The whole group is coming tomorrow night."

Shya snapped to fully awake. "Really?"

They laughed. "We're all chomping at the bit, Shy. We love you."

Tears pricked in her eyes and she laughed wryly.

"What?"

"I thought I was cried out."

"Aw," the twins said in unison.

"I love you guys, too. Thank you."

"We'll talk tomorrow morning."

"OK. And, guys?"

"Yeah?"

"Be careful."

CHAPTER 41 – FOUR

Shya stared at her phone, contemplating her call with Mel, but not for long. *Better do it now,* she thought as her muscles begged for rest.

She dialled Dawn's number without thinking, but realized it too late and Dawn answered, sounding rather awake for such a dark hour.

"Is everything OK?" The edge of urgency to her voice made Shya nervous rather than amused, as it would on any other day.

"Yes; I'm sorry, Dawn. I actually meant to dial Mel."

"Oh," the woman sounded a touch hesitant. "Well, it turns out you did."

Shya surprised herself by whooping in surprise, the elevated pitch echoing off the houses on all sides of her. She slapped a hand to her mouth, then removed it and loudly whispered, "Sorry! Got way too excited, there."

Dawn made a disapproving noise, but there was humour in her reply. "I'm glad you ain't in too much trouble just yet. I'll hand the phone to Mel, but first: are things OK? I'm thinking you haven't met him, yet?"

Shya's elation fizzled. "Nope. I'll go over tomorrow, though. Just to talk to Connor and meet Jordan. And my friend Bethie is here, too."

"And you'll bring Rory with you?"

Shya frowned. She hadn't settled on that, but she'd

thought of it.

"You should," came Dawn's voice again, before Shya could form her own reply.

"I will," she found herself saying.

"We're coming tomorrow."

"I know; the twins told me. I'm so glad. Thank you, Dawn."

"You'd do the same for me," Dawn said. "Here's Mel."

"Hi, Shya."

"Hi, Mel."

"What can I do?"

"Little puzzle for you: the possessor calls itself 'Four'"

"Ooo," Mel sounded immediately intrigued. "Just a sec."

She heard a faint kissing noise and then a low grunt as he got – she imagined – out of bed. She smiled, glad for the glimpse into their newfound happiness. "You don't have to do this tonight, Mel."

"No, no worries. I love this stuff. I mean," he made a sound of disappointment, "I'm sorry. I don't love that any of this is happening, but..."

"I know, Mel," Shya stopped him.

"OK." Faint tapping at a keyboard sounded and she shook her head.

"You really are doing this now."

"Yep. Here it is. Listen to this: *"Asmodeus is said to be one of the seven princes of Hell; he was the fourth of them to exist, and the eventual King of all Demons."*

Shya realized her jaw was hung open. She mindfully closed it, then replied, "Holy shit."

Mel chuckled. "Yeah. Now, that was just the first thing I found, and only because I knew what I was looking for. What's important to realize is that *any* determined soul can possess a being if it has the power and intent."

"Uh," Shya shook her head in an effort to absorb the words, but it proved too difficult while images of her bed and snuggling up to the always-warm Rory filled her mind. "Sorry, Mel, but... *what?*"

More keyboard tapping. Mel was off and running. "Meaning it's most likely not the King of Demons possessing Jordan. Dark souls will often refer to more widely-known demons in order to intimidate those who fight against them. That said, they play tricks. It's hard to really know. I mean, that's part of what an exorcist seeks to do: to identify the beast in order to take its power."

A wave of nauseating overwhelm rolled over Shya.

"Shya? You still there?"

"Yeah," she swallowed, swaying on her feet. "I'm just exhausted, Mel. I need some sleep, or tomorrow's visit with Jordan won't go very well."

"Of course! Go! I'll keep digging and give everyone, you included, the summary tomorrow night."

"Sounds good." She perked up. "Oh! Where is everyone staying? I mean, my dad has a basement, but... "

He laughed, "Oh, no. We're at the British; no worries."

"Oh, good." The historic hotel was in Lower Aylmer, a five-minute drive.

"Huh."

"What?"

"The number four is considered unlucky in some Asian cultures. Even sounds like the word 'death' in Chinese."

Shya headed toward the door. "Huh. Interesting."

"I'm sorry, Shya. Go to bed. We'll talk tomorrow."

"Thank you, Mel."

"'Night."

She chuckled as he hung up. "At least I won't be the only tired one tomorrow," she whispered aloud. Then, frowning, she said the name as she considered Mel's words. *"Asmodeus."* She grimaced at the sour taste of the word in her mouth. As she reached for the door, something whispered back.

We shall burn together, it said, making her jump as adrenaline shot to her fingers and toes.

A sudden stench found her nose – that of burning. Something acrid. And then there was a weight, dark and heavy and reminiscent of the pressure at her back as she'd fled down the wooded trail just at the end of the road and in her dreams, and her temporarily-frozen arm shot out, turning the doorknob and then pulling the rest of her into the house, where she slammed the door and leaned against it, panting. Shoulders instantly lighter. Strange smells fading as the lingering scents of their spaghetti dinner took over. She pressed her forehead hard against the door. Dinner seemed like so long ago, now.

And she sunk down, crying. Giving herself another minute to feel the sadness and fear, and then the deep longing for her mother's presence before she went up to bed. Before she gathered all her strength the next day and went into the house where her pursuer waited.

CHAPTER 42 –
DYING MOTHER

Please don't say you're sorry anymore

You've taught me all you could, and then some more

Blanketed me with anecdotes and lore

You've been tossed on stormy seas, now come ashore

The fighting spark is dimming in your eyes

Though still you whisper, still you teach and try

You linger on intention, love and sighs

Protecting me from those whom in darkness lie

The worn and weary thread to which you cling

Runs down the time to linger, rope to string

And tattered dregs of fluid, flesh and all physical thing

Hold far less promise than release will ultimately bring

You've given me what I need most to know

Instructions to accompany the gift you will bestow

Let me lie beside you, match your breathing oh so scant and slow

Feel the essence of you change as you finally let go

Mother, death has changed you – and changed me!

I wonder if I manage to be all you hoped for me to be

The presence of your ghost, it carried and comforted me

It's all I had for so long, but now it eludes me

Come back I whisper as I lay my weary head

Upon the flattened fluff that was the pillow of my bed

I'll look for you in dreams, where living souls meet with the dead

Come to me there, lost mother; ease the looming sense of dread

I glimpse you there but only in the beating of my heart

A warmth about my shoulders, comforting me from the start

But quick I'm woken long before the sentiment imparts

A distant scream from one possessed does split the air and hark

Come back I cry into the empty stillness of the air

Come back, mother left too soon, a loss too hard to bear

Come back I say. *I took your soul for granted – how unfair!*

And without you I fear I lose my compass, lose my care

I'm here, a gentle pressure of your hand smoothing my hair

I'm here... lemongrass, rosemary, sweet orange in the air

But then it whips you back with the love you try to share

And roars inside my being, leaving searing pain to bear

Not again, little bright star

Do not tiptoe past again

Let this little headache serve to warn you

Do not dare to try again

CHAPTER 43 - SLIDING DOORS

The pain she awoke to wasn't like anything she'd ever experienced. Her skull felt as through it had shrunk two sizes, relentlessly compressing its contents while the flesh atop it sunk and burned. Her eyes flew open in panic, but with the sudden onslaught of sunlight streaming into the bedroom from the eastern window were immediately closed again, and covered with both arms in an instinctively protective move. She cried out, too, involuntarily assaulting her own ears with shock-based pitch and timbre.

Rory startled beside her and was hovering above her in a second, his beloved form blocking the wicked brightness of the sun and she found herself reaching for his shoulders, steadying his form in an effort to solidify his position.

"What is it? You're pale as a ghost," he touched her cheek, which made her whimper. Everything enhanced the pain.

"Head," she whimpered again as the single word throbbed inside her skull as if it had been shouted. She absently noted the tears that escaped and rolled over the bridge of her nose and down her temple.

"A migraine?" he spoke quietly, carefully. Rory had suffered with occasional migraines since before she'd met him. "No," he answered himself when Shya only moaned and pressed her face into the darkness of her pillow. "This isn't right."

She made a sound into the pillow, hunching her shoulders at the pain it caused. Rory attempted to roll her to her side, gently.

"Everything OK?" her father's voice made her clench herself into a ball. "Oh, my God!" she braced herself against the panic in his words, and moaned again as he hurried to the bed and sat heavily on it to place a hand on her back.

Rory was saying something as vertigo whirled inside her head and the overwhelming urge to be sick took hold. "Uh-oh," she muttered, bolting upright and swaying as the world tipped and danced around her. There was a flurry of movement and suddenly a hard-sided container was placed in her lap. She cracked her eyes to make sure it was intended for the purpose she required, and noticed everything in her vision was doubled and tilted as her insides clenched, then heaved, and the metal garbage can was put to use. She absently placed it as the can that had sat beneath the small desk in the corner. Registered, even as she was overtaken again by the force of her nausea, that it was her father who held the receptacle beneath her face.

Someone was patting her back. Saying soothing words. Her eyes were squeezed shut against the spinning world, but determined tears streamed down her cheeks, nonetheless. She whimpered weakly and the sound reverberated against the metal can. "Ugh," she mumbled, gently pushing it away. And then Rory was laying her down and the weight of her father lifted off the bed as he left the room with the contents of her stomach.

"I'm sorry," she cried, uncaring that the sound of it was sharp inside her head and hot against the backs of her eyes.

Rory kissed her forehead and wiped at her mouth with something soft. "We need to get you to the hospital," he said, his voice low, and she instantly shook her head. "Don't do that," he muttered as she grimaced at the new onslaught of pain.

"I'll get her purse and wait in the car," her father's edge-of-panic tone cut through the air between the door and the bed and renewed her nausea.

"No," she cried, the word dragging on into a moan as the pain intensified. She couldn't go to any hospital. She needed to go to Connor's. She needed to see the boy. Something inside her lurched... a determination. The demon had done this to her. Wanted her to stay away. If she did, it would win. "No," she said again as she found Rory's hand. She squeezed, desperate for him to feel her need. "It's trying to stop me," she said, her head pulsating with each syllable. Bright white light flashed behind her eyelids with the crash and fall of every word.

She felt both men's attentions on her, then. Waiting for her to convince them. Almost unwilling to let her. They were scared for her, and right to be.

"It wants me to stay away," she whispered. She rested back against the pillow. Moved an arm to shade her eyes. Slowly. Focused on breathing.

"What? *What* wants you to stay away?" Her father's voice again, then a pause as Rory made some motion beside her. The bed moved ever-so-slightly with it, and she moaned again as the vertigo surged forth.

She put a hand up. "Don't move, Rory. Please."

"You said the boy was possessed," her father spoke again, but straining against the quieter tone he'd adopted.

"He is," Rory whispered.

"Then why is it hurting *her*?"

Another motion, but quickly stymied as Shya's hand shot into the air against it.

"Sorry."

"Pills," she muttered.

Her father's footsteps immediately headed for the stairs, then faded as he went, she imagined, to the downstairs bathroom. She breathed deeply, picturing the medicine cabinet there as her salvation.

"Why would it try to keep you away?" Rory whispered. He ran a finger over her cheek and she held her breath, wanting stillness. Silence. "Doesn't it want you?"

Her brain tangled around the question. She pressed against her eyes and the top of her nose with the arm that lay across her face.

"I can't believe it would try and keep you away, Shya. Something's wrong and I'm worried. I want to take you to the..."

She gasped as pieces of her dream came back to her. She remembered her mother, apologizing from her sickbed, but not just for dying too soon... she apologized for everything since her death, too. Mostly, for not being there to help her now. She remembered the feeling of her mother's presence, the brief confirmation of her being there... and then how it was torn away so easily by the beast that held her prisoner. "It doesn't want me to stay away," she whispered, steeling herself against the pain talking caused her. "It just wants me to stop trying to contact my mother. It doesn't want to have to fight both of us, together."

She felt the air move against the back of her protective arm as Rory sighed. "I hate this, Shy."

Her heart swelled in her chest. "I know."

"What are we supposed to do?"

She could think of only one thing, and she said it in a single word: "*Resist.*"

He let out another sigh, then lowered his forehead to her

shoulder, making the arm on her face heavy. The pressure felt good.

She must've slept, for the next thing she registered was Rory sitting her up, just slightly, and her arm falling away from her face. But the sun was dimmer, then, and her father was placing two pills into her palm. He held a cool glass to her mouth after she'd put them at the back of her tongue and she gulped, swallowing them and the blessedly cold water with them. Feeling it rush down her throat and then pool in her stomach, where it warmed and disappeared into the workings of her body. "Thank you," she whispered, and Rory lay her down again.

She was only partially aware of the men going out into the hallway. Only able to catch the occasional, incomplete sentiment. "Pills're for the pain… to relax her… Xanax… let her rest a while or … trip to Connor's will be wasted." It was enough. She felt herself let go as the realization that her father and Rory meant to get her to where she needed to be washed over her in a wave of relief.

But she resurfaced as Rory lay back down beside her and took her in his arms. He whispered, "The twins called. Jane and Anna. They say your mom will be alright… said she's trapped by her own fears and that they can't see her very well. She's behind a veil… something about the levels of consciousness," he trailed off. Yawned. And held her tight to him; her back against his torso. Warm.

Safe.

CHAPTER 44 – INTRODUCTION

She'd planned on walking to Connor's hand-in-hand with Rory with time to contemplate the reunion before knocking on her old friend's door. But the headache was still splitting her in two when Rory and her father finally let her get up, and at that they only acquiesced because the afternoon was waning and Bethie had called twice to check on their estimated time of arrival.

Nothing – aside from sleep – helped. The pills her father had tipped into her palm had been good in that sense, but the pain remained untouched.

She rode in the back of her father's car as he drove – he'd insisted in a rare flash of concern, which would undoubtedly have puzzled Shya, had she been in her usual state of mind. Her head rested on Rory's lap and a sleep mask pressed gently against her eyes. Sunglasses hadn't sufficiently blocked the light, and the arms felt tight against her head and on her ears. *Everything* seemed painful. Loud. But she insisted on fulfilling her promise, shoving worries of worsening pain and how she'd sustain her determination in the face of the demon's relentless punishment down deep, as she was so skilled at doing.

Rory walked her to the door, but didn't knock. She felt the arm she clung to dig for something in his pocket, and imagined him texting Bethie - or Connor – to announce their arrival. Her love for him intensified to the point of stinging, but she resisted any burgeoning proclamations in the hopes of maintaining her current status: conscious, upright, and focused on the task.

The *snick* of a door opening came quickly, and then she was enveloped into wide arms, broad shoulders, and the scent of body odour badly masked by a sloppy effort with deodorant. Connor was taller and substantially more solid than he's been the last time she'd been in his presence, perhaps in part due to his construction work. And he was sadder; his heavy arms trembled at her back and despite his efforts to approach her quietly, he was crying into her hair. "I'm so glad you're here," he whispered, then sent a razor-sharp ribbon of fire through her brain with a sharp intake of breath beside her ear.

She couldn't help it; she cringed, and the sudden movement had her world spinning again. She was directed to the railing before Connor had fully released her, Rory's familiar hands steering her as she clutched her stomach and groaned. And then she was vomiting. The sound of it landing conjured visions of newly-sullied cedar hedges. "I'm sorry," she whispered when it was over.

"Maybe this has to wait," came her father's voice, shocking her. She'd assumed he'd go back home after dropping them off, but there he was, sounding low and a bit distant, as though he were calling out from the driver's seat, after all.

"No," she answered, low and firm.

A hand gripped her upper arm, and Connor's grief grew louder. "Thank you, Shya," he said quietly. "I don't think there's time to wait."

She wanted to nod, but her entire body resisted the movement. So, she patted his hand instead. "Let's go in."

"Shya... oh, God," Bethie muttered quietly when they stepped inside. And then there was the work of coat and shoe removal, which Connor vetoed halfway through, seeing how much it took for Shya to manage, even with Rory and Bethie's help.

She moved as if in a dream... or a nightmare: blind, relentlessly assaulted by pain, and dependant on the hands of others to guide her. It was easy, then, to recognize the dark energy that ran like an undercurrent through Connor's home. It oozed around her legs, pulling her forward. Weighing her down. "Oh," she heard herself utter, surprised by the force of that which was unseen but so very, very present.

"OK?" Rory's voice came. He was close; right behind her. She heard Connor and her father, too, and in some secondary level of awareness, she was simultaneously confused by and impressed with his ongoing presence.

But through it all she was moving, following her feet as they took her on that sludgy undercurrent, her arms outstretched.

"Oh – I thought we could talk in the kitchen, first," Connor called out.

Shya said nothing, but jumped when Bethie answered from just ahead of her. "Just wait, Connor."

She knows where I'm going, Shya realized. *But of course she would. Where else would the demon pull me but to Jordan? To itself?* Her heart tripped and tumbled in her chest. She'd thought they could talk first, too. She'd even been contemplating holding off on meeting Jordan... at least until she was feeling better. Or until The Seers showed up. But she moved mindlessly. The pull was too strong to stop.

Her hands found a corner, and then walls on either side of her in what must have been a hallway, so she walked that way, outstretched arms steadying her as the current flowed, then shifted to the right. That's when she did freeze to the spot, though, for she found not only a closed door, but something else; the wall of stench and heat that barred her way was just as solid as the door. Her gag reflex was instantly triggered, but she clenched her jaw, refusing to throw up in Connor's hallway.

I have to be strong now, she thought, *or how will I ever face this thing?*

"Are you ready?" Bethie's voice was a relief, that time.

Shya forced herself to nod, just once. But when Bethie's hand went to the doorknob between she and the door, she held a hand up. "Can you smell it?" she whispered, needing to know the assault on her senses wasn't solely to torture her, alone.

"Yes, I do," she answered, and her throat sounded tight.

Shya frowned. "Have you always?"

There was a pause and Shya wondered if she should have asked the overarching question, instead. The one that drove all the others: *have you smelled this, seen this, felt this for so many years, alone and without hope?*

When Bethie answered, the weight of the word confirmed her suspicions: "Always."

So much about her relationship with Bethie was healed in that moment when, despite the onslaught of stench and terror that bound her, she realized Bethie's sacrifice of keeping the demon to herself for years, just so she wouldn't have to drag anyone else into the new chaos of her life. Shya found Bethie's hand and patted it, but there was too much to say and no time. Speechless, she shook her head against insistent tears, and the pain ratcheted up again as the world spun. She braced herself on the frame of the door and said, "Open it."

She was glad for the sleep mask when they stepped inside, Rory's hand on her lower back to let her know he was there and Bethie beside her. She was glad for the company, too. The air hung putrid and damp in the room she assumed to be Jordan's. The smells of sick and sour and death itself intensified to something near a solid thing that smacked the senses again, again, and again with every breath. Bethie whimpered to her left and Rory tensed behind her and she knew they were reacting to the sight of the boy, which she was saved from by the mask. By the punishment of the demon itself. But in that moment her mask was ripped away, as if in answer to her silent relief, and she saw him, too: a wretched husk of a child, ruined by the thing that lived within him. A child that should not be alive... not with the withered shell he dwelt in, nor with the oozing sores or thundercloud bruises that marked his flesh. And yet his chest rose and fell. Not only that, but his head was slightly raised, and glittering black eyes were on her.

The pain inside her skull was incomparable to this: the sight of a tortured soul twisted by some evil thing until he was barely recognizable as human anymore. No longer recognizable as a *child*. His arms were tied to wooden bedposts, and trembling. It was a twin bed, yet too long for the diminutive boy that occupied it, and so his legs were given some slack with longer ropes at the bottom. He wore pyjama bottoms, but they were filthy and shredded. His pelvic bones stretched the waistband. Small and gaunt as he was, Connor or Bethie must have kept them on him in an effort to keep him warm. But it was clear that any effort at caring for the boy had sunk into the sucking pit of darkness that held him.

"Bright one," the demon said in a grating voice that didn't belong in the body from which it came.

It was too much. She collapsed, grateful for the pain that shot through her knees as she landed. Grateful to feel something other than outright misery for the child before her.

Encouraged, she cried out, wanting her headache to knock her senseless. Anything not to know the truth of the task before her. Rory squatted on one side of her, and soon Bethie was on the other, and she was apologizing, crying, voicing Shya's own distress. And there was Rory telling her she must resist, which confused her at first. But then she remembered that he'd spoken to the twins that morning, and that they would have warned him, would have told him to remind her not to let it in, no matter what.

And then it hit her: she could save the boy. It could all be over now! The demon wanted *her*, so why not give it what it wanted? She stood, shaking Rory and Bethie's hands off, and rounded the bed. The boy's head moved to follow her, but the eyes – those black eyes – were not his.

"Take me now!" she cried, her palms on her belly. "If I'm who you want, just do it! Leave him be!" She reached to touch him.

Rory's footsteps closed in at lightning speed, but before he whisked her away, out of the room and the house entire, she saw the creature smile. Black eyes glittering. Dark grime between its teeth. Oh, yes. It wanted her.

She screamed when Rory took her, kicked her feet as he stole her away, but then there was another voice to quiet her, though no one else could hear, for it came from inside her pounding head.

We shall burn together, little bright star. We will light the fires in the catacombs of Hell, and let the beasts surge forth again!

And then, there were images… piles of corpses, chambers of death, live bodies burning, fleeing, screaming. Different moments from history, some she even recognized – an unstoppable movie reel of horror inside her mind of the things people did to people, had done before and still did, and would do in the coming years and for as long as time permitted. And she screamed and balled her fists and punched her weak and tired head as images of blood and gore, suffering and torture filled her mind and Rory yelled as he ran and burst through the door and took her to the lawn and it all stopped, everything, just stopped in a split second the moment they left the house.

And she was light again, and free of pain, and she dissolved in Rory's arms as the others gathered 'round them.

But the images it had played inside her head; the knowledge of hate and lust for power and greed and sin and the terrible things that people did... that knowing would never leave. Not ever.

CHAPTER 45 – TOSSED
ON A WAVE

When Dawn called to let Shya know the group had all arrived and were settling in at the British, Shya nearly raced to the door to leave.

She'd been strangely energized since their trip to Connor's - practically the polar opposite of how she'd felt before they'd gone, and though the power the demon had proven to have over her well-being was intimidating, she felt so relieved to be herself again that she found herself eager to welcome her friends. And, of course, to fill them in.

But she was surprised when Rory appeared beside her, sliding into his shoes, too, and watching her in the sidelong glance sort of way he had been since they'd come back home. She straightened, hands going to her hips.

"What?" he grinned. "Did you think you were leaving me behind, just because I'm not one of the group?" His expression declared his disbelief as much as his words. He rolled his shoulders, then stretched casually, looking down at her with hooded eyelids. His demeanor had switched so quickly from incredulity to overblown self-confidence that she was thrown for a loop.

"You must be amazing in court," she laughed, but it was breathless. He had always had that effect on her.

He smiled. "Your friends are going to have to get used to having me around," he said as he ran a finger down her cheek. "And I *am* amazing in court. You should come see, sometime."

She was mesmerized, lost in the gaze that was so obviously borne of love. The same way he'd always looked at her, but different now, because she chose to see it.

He let his hand drop, a look of satisfaction mingling with his smile.

She shook herself as if to slough off his charm. "Actually, I *had* thought I was going alone," she said, a bit loudly in her effort to sound as confident as Rory looked. "After all, I always do... besides, there's an understanding in the group that it's just us. Makes everyone feel safer, you know?"

He smirked. "This isn't *any* meeting, Shy. And until this thing is over, I go where you go." There was no humour in his eyes. They stood, studying each other's features, until her father appeared at the top of the stairs.

"You two off to your psychics meeting?" he called, gripping the railing and looking down at them soberly.

Shya giggled, then gave Rory a questioning look. "What'd you tell him?"

Rory shrugged. "Exactly that!" he gestured toward her father, who'd been strangely awkward since the three of them had left Connor's. Shya thought it must be the witnessing of how her mother's gift affected her... he'd always known it was there, of course. He'd known it because of her mother, but he acted as though he existed around it rather than within it. That day, though, he'd probably seen more in ten minutes than he had during Shya's lifetime.

"When can I expect you back?"

Shya frowned, looking to Rory again. He'd never cared to keep track of her whereabouts – nor Rory's! – either.

But Rory handled it smoothly. "Likely late. There's a lot to discuss."

Her father nodded, lips pursed. "Wanted to ask if you

two were planning on seeing Lou while you were here? I know she'd like to see you."

Surprised again, Shya kept her eyes on Rory. She couldn't remember the last time she'd been so flummoxed as the result of such seemingly innocuous questions, but there she was. And, perhaps stranger still, she hadn't even given her ex-step-mother a thought, though she lived just fifteen minutes from them, in Hull. To her relief, Rory seemed similarly affected, that time.

"I hadn't really thought about it," he replied, his eyes on her father, and then on her. "This trip is really about helping Jordan, and I want to focus on supporting Shya." His eyes were soft.

She smiled.

"You two're lucky to have each other," her father said quietly.

She realized the distracting effect of her father's presence as she and Rory got into the car. She hadn't agreed on him coming, but it seemed suddenly less important.

And the group seemed unsurprised.

Big Ed and Mel were standing outside, lit by the festive lights of the courtyard between the hotel and its counterpart, the British Café. Shya was stricken at how surreal it felt to see her friends in one of her favorite hometown hangouts, but any strangeness of the moment dissolved as the men greeted her and Rory with hugs and handshakes all around.

Big Ed held her gently back when Mel and Rory headed for the entrance. "I'm just going to spend a couple minutes with Shya," he called, and then Rory met her eyes before the men went in with a little wave. Ed turned to her, looking nervous, and Shya frowned.

"Everything OK?"

He looked back at the door, and then up to the windows. "We're meeting in Dawn and Mel's room," he said, then shook his head. "Funny, but them being together feels like... I don't know..."

"Like, *finally!*" Shya laughed, and Ed pointed at her, nodding.

"Yes! Like it was always an eventuality, and now that it's happened, it feels right."

She nodded, wondering if that was the reason he'd wanted to keep her outside, or if there was something more.

He cleared his throat. "The twins have a room, and Sheila and I have a double Queen," he shrugged. "Just made sense."

Shya nodded. "You're not going to tell me you and Sheila are a thing now, are you?" she teased, but she could see his cheeks colour, even in the imperfect courtyard lighting.

"Nah," he said, his eyes on the gravel as he shuffled his feet.

"What is it, Ed?"

"I – it took me a while to clue in that you and Rory's relationship had... evolved," he said, and she could see that it pained him a bit.

"I would have told you, but I don't think I even let myself see it until it was right in front of my face, you know?"

He nodded.

"Are you..." she floundered, unsure of what he needed from her. "I mean... I'm sorry if you were caught off-guard."

He shook his head, waving the sentiment away. "You don't have to say anything. You don't owe me any explanation or... I just wanted to say I was happy for you."

She released a held breath. "Oh! That's really nice, Ed. Thank you."

"And that I hoped we could still be good friends."

She frowned again. "Of course, we are. My relationship with Rory doesn't affect my friendship with you in any way."

Something flickered in his eyes, but he let it go, smiling and clapping his hands together. "Good! I think you're a special person, is all, and I'm glad you're happy."

"Aw." She hugged him, and it gave her an ache in her chest, because he was trembling, just a little.

His arm around her shoulder, they headed for the door, and as he ushered her in ahead of him, she let herself realize another love she'd refused to see. One she could have kindly staved off if she'd been more present, but instead she'd let it linger hopefully in a man she cared for deeply.

She wanted to apologize as they stepped into the elevator, but she thought it might do more damage than good to acknowledge her folly too late, when she could have - *should* have – done it in the time he'd borrowed outside for both of them.

And she internalized the guilt that followed, without knowing how it added to the mountain of denied emotion she collected, blindly saving it for later when, inevitably, it would all come crashing down.

CHAPTER 46 – SITREP

It was strange to join the rest of the group in Dawn's room, where Rory appeared to be holding court, her friends all smiling and rapt with attention on him, and then laughing as he delivered what Shya could only assume was a punch line. Then they saw her and rushed over, all happy greetings and exclamations about her healthy appearance.

Has he told them everything, already? Shya's eyes were on Rory as she exchanged hugs with everyone. But Jane and Anna manoeuvred their way between them, and Shya knew it was news from the twins that accounted for the group's reaction.

"You're better," Jane stated, her eyes somehow intently on her and vibrating somewhat disconcertingly at the same time.

She nodded. "I feel better than I have in a while," she smiled, hoping to reassure everyone, but inwardly cringing at the sound of her words, and how they clashed with the events of the day. She noted Big Ed gravitating to Dawn, who met his gaze pointedly, then embraced him, her head just reaching his sternum. *There are no secrets in a group of psychics,* she thought wryly.

"We were able to contact your mother; did Rory fill you in?" Anna pulled Shya's attention back to she and her sister. Both were casually dressed, but still stylish. Their fashion sense was not limited to interior design, but it often struck Shya as contradictory to their preference of keeping to their own shared and mysterious world. Then again, their coloring was enough to elicit stares of fascination and confusion. Perhaps they presented themselves so carefully in order to render them a spectacle both strange and beautiful, rather than just strange. Like crocuses that burst forth with cheery colours as the dirt and slushy dregs of winter faded, or fireworks that twinkled even more prettily when set off in the rain.

"Thank you," Shya gripped their hands fiercely, which caused the twins to exchange a look of concern. "I'm fine," she said, and managed a laugh. The entire group turned to her, then.

"I've never seen you so... expressive," Mel remarked, and she felt her cheeks burn with the sudden attention on her.

"She's been like this since we left Connor's," Rory announced, and she frowned at him. "It's weird, Shy," he gestured helplessly in her direction and added, "I'm worried."

She let out a sound of surprise and frustration. "I can't win!" she exclaimed. "I thought I had to be dying this morning, which had everyone tense and hovering, and now that I feel really good, everyone seems... what? Even more worried?"

Sheila was the only one who responded, and it was to nod her head, her eyes large, but she stopped, self-conscious, as soon as she noticed she was the only one admitting her concern.

"Look, it all stopped – the headache, the nausea... even the fear! – as soon as we left that house today, and if that visit was any indication, we have some rough days ahead of us. I'm just happy to feel good right now. And happy you're all here. Thank you for coming."

The tension fizzled as the group relaxed a bit.

"Can you tell us everything that happened?" Dawn patted a spot at the head of the bed, then sat with Mel at the foot of it, and as Shya got comfortable, everyone else found spots around the room to sit, facing her. Expectant.

She found herself seeking Rory's eyes alone. Wishing he'd sat beside her but knowing he was purposefully letting her have the floor to herself. He gave her a small nod from his spot between the twins, which was strange, but somehow right, too... the women never sat apart, unless someone was in distress or needed comfort, at which point they'd sandwich their target between themselves without a word.

"Where do I start?" Shya muttered. She studied the bed-spread momentarily, then started talking, beginning with the dream she only half recalled from the night before, and ending with Rory's mad sprint from Jordan's room with her in his arms, to Connor's front yard.

Everyone was silent for a brief moment, and then they were all asking questions.

"What's next?" Dawn wanted to know.

"Did you feel your mother's presence at all when you were in the house?" came the question that was foremost on the twins' mind.

And "Did you feel threatened by it?" was from Big Ed.

But Shya answered the final question first. It had come from Sheila.

"Is Jordan alright?"

Shya shook her head. "He's not." She eyed all members of the group in turn. "I don't know how he's still with us, guys. And it makes me nervous about any sort of exorcism; I don't know if he'd survive it."

"Well, that's why we do it carefully," Dawn leaned forward to pat Shya's knee. "We have an advantage over most exorcists in that we can contact the demon *without* going through the boy. We just need to use everything we've got to protect him while we do," she eyed Sheila pointedly, and then the twins.

"We can do something similar to the night we went looking for the boy," Jane said, and Anna nodded on the other side of Rory. "Except we won't contact the boy at all if we don't have to. We'll deal directly with the demon," Jane finished.

"And I can shield Jordan," Sheila piped up, voice high and trembling. She looked from the twins to Dawn. "But, I'm worried. This – thing – is strong. How do we hope to exorcise it without involving the boy?"

Dawn shook her head. "Our focus is on sending it back to where it belongs; not whose body it inhabits. If we focus on that, we can hopefully free Jordan and keep Shya safe at the same time."

Sheila lowered her eyes, but said nothing. Shya knew that if Bethie was there, she'd voice the follow-up question Sheila seemed so determined to deny, but voicing it herself felt wrong. Felt dangerous, when she was so light and free.

But Rory voiced it, instead. "What makes you think there's anything you can do to lead it away from Jordan *or* Shya? Bethie says it clung to her all those years with one goal in mind." His eyes flickered to Shya's and she looked away, bent on reserving her terror until tomorrow. Or for as long as she could, without hindering the process, anyway.

But it was difficult to maintain her strangely buoyed outlook when Dawn floundered to find a response.

Mel piped up, and Dawn exhaled. "It might help to know more about it; it claims to be the King of Demons; Asmodeus."

They all jumped at a sudden clap of thunder, so loud they all peered at the ceiling, mouths open. Someone started to voice what they were all thinking: *What the fu* – but then the rain started. It pounded so fiercely against the windows that Big Ed jumped up from the windowsill he'd been leaning against and backed away, his face a mask of shock. They all sat, frozen, for seconds that seemed to stretch into eternity, until

Dawn exclaimed, "Holy *shit!*" and they all burst into laughter.

But Shya quieted quickly when she met Rory's gaze and saw he shared none of their mirth. She frowned. "It's just a thunderstorm, Rory." And as if to answer her, thunder crashed again, directly overhead, making them cringe and duck their heads.

"Then where's the lightning?" Rory asked.

They all looked to each other for the answer. All hoping someone had seen the flashes that must've come before the answering thunderclaps. All absolutely certain they hadn't seen it themselves.

"Maybe we don't say that name right now," Ed muttered, and Mel's face cleared as he nodded.

"Right." He watched the rain hit the windows for a moment, then turned back to the group. "All I wanted to say was that the possessor could be *any* demon... any *energy,* in fact! Just because it calls itself one thing doesn't mean it's the truth."

"They lie," the twins agreed in unison, making Rory look from one to the other, confused.

"It's just raining, now," Sheila noted as she walked to a window, arms folded across her chest. She looked back at Shya darkly. "Whatever this is, I think we can all agree it's powerful." She looked around, challenging the group to disagree. Shya thought she even looked a little hopeful someone would. She landed on Shya last. "I think we have to be very careful. And I think Dawn's got the right idea: we need to work together to confront it without involving Jordan, if we can. But we need to protect Shya, too." She looked to Dawn. "I don't think any of us fully comprehends just how determined this thing is to have her."

A heavy silence met her words, save the rain, which had already quieted to a dull backdrop of white noise.

Rory stood, and all present seemed quite willing, if not relieved, to give him their attention. "What Sheila just said is what's most important to me." He met Shya's eyes, but she couldn't read his expression, which was a rare thing, indeed. "I've only just gotten her to see how much I love her." He smiled, his eyes shining with tears, and a jolt of sorrow formed a ball in Shya's chest. "And by some miracle, it seems she loves me, too. Either way, I won't lose her."

Dawn leaned her head to rest on Mel's shoulder, and Shya caught a wistful look from Big Ed.

"I have no intention of letting it have me," Shya replied, but her words were weak by the time they surfaced, as they'd had to work their way around the ache of emotion in her throat.

Rory shook his head, and a tear escaped and ran down his cheek. She felt some part of herself wanting to chalk it up to drama, as "typical" for Rory, as she'd done so easily before. But there was no denying things were different now, and backtracking felt next to impossible.

"No, Shya," he said, his voice husky. "There's something you didn't tell everyone; a part of the visit to Connor's you seem to have forgotten entirely! I've watched you since then, wondering how you could be so carefree after everything that happened, and now I think I have the answer: either you truly do forget, or you're purposefully remembering it differently."

Shya scoffed without thinking, then laughed as everyone turned toward her. "I may be the queen of denial, bro, but I don't think I portrayed today's events unfairly."

Rory looked stung. She focused on keeping her own tears at bay, the word "bro" tasting terrible on her tongue. "I'm sorry," she found herself saying. "I didn't mean to call you that."

Rory laughed sardonically, then, and threw his hands in

the air. "It doesn't matter what we call each other, Shy. We're interwoven. Always have been, and whether you're still having trouble admitting it or not, you know it."

In the face of his vulnerability, she could do nothing but nod in agreement.

Dawn put a hand up. "Wait. What happened today that Shya skipped?" She looked between Shya and Rory.

Rory pointed at Shya, making her feel immediately defensive, but she froze, needing to hear what he had to say as much as everyone else did.

"When we talk about protecting Shya, I seem to be the only one who grasps the seriousness of that priority, and that's because Shya skipped the whole bit about her offering herself to the... *beast,* today!"

Shya gasped, because she hadn't forgotten, but Rory was right; she'd omitted it. It had been there, the whole time, masked only by the false sense of well-being she'd been shielded with all day. "Oh, no," she said, seeing the shock in all their faces. Seeing Rory's finger, still jabbed in her direction as if to pin the truth to her. As if in fear of her denial. "He's right!" she exclaimed, half-whispering, and the cursed finger dropped. She fixed him with her gaze. "I'm so sorry! I haven't forgotten; it just felt so unimportant..." she frowned down at the bedspread as she trailed off, her puzzlement all-encompassing. "But how could it?" She looked at her friends. Asked the twins directly, "What's happening?"

"Isn't it obvious?" Sheila stepped forward, arms still folded over her chest, lips trembling. "If it can make you sick as it did this morning, why shouldn't it be able to make you feel good, too?"

Dawn whirled, her face a mask of fear. "To make sure you go back! It wants you to forget how terrible it was... how willing you may have been to give yourself up to it! Did you really?" Dawn reached for Shya's hands, and Shya gave them up, but she moved as if in slow motion.

She nodded, finally, recalling in some distant way how obvious it had been - the need to save the boy by giving herself up. And even then, she felt it: the undeniable urge to run right back to Connor's and do the thing that so needed to be done in order to save his son. She met Dawn's eyes, from which tears flowed freely, and realized she was crying, too. "He's just a little boy," she sobbed, and then Dawn was pulling her forward and taking her in her arms.

"It already has a part of you," she cried into Shya's hair, and though she knew it to be true, she found herself unable to be shocked or scared. "Why shouldn't it?" she cried, and Dawn pulled back to meet her eyes in disbelief. "Why not me instead of him? Why should a tiny child have to suffer when I could handle it in his place?"

"No, Shya," Dawn whispered, and Shya became aware that the group was drawing in around her.

She looked at Rory, who'd reached between Mel and Dawn to grasp her shoulder. "I could handle it better!" she cried, uncomprehending of the desperation in his eyes. "Besides, my mother is there... neither of us would be alone, anymore!" She ended with a sob, having plucked at the little bit of truth at the heart of her willingness to be lost to oblivion in Jordan's place. The need of her mother. Her own emptiness without her.

"Shya, it could be worse, don't you see?" Mel was talking, but Shya only half heard him. She was thinking of Connor's. She could run up the hill, could get to the house in twenty minutes. Fifteen, if she was fast. She could end this all tonight, before any of her friends had to be involved.

"It could use your gifts for itself! Travel more easily between realms!" Mel sat back, frustrated at Shya's lack of response.

Big Ed broke in to stand over her, then knelt. A gigantic finger pressed her cheek to look at him, and she let her eyes be turned as her mind whirled.

"He's right, you know," Ed said, his eyes intense. "Taking you could mean we'd all be in trouble."

Somehow, the words got through, and she saw a flash of it, of what could be if the beast not only possessed her, but used her. Controlled her to do its bidding. She felt her eyes widen. "Oh, my God!"

Ed nodded. "You see?"

She peered, panicked, at the friends and loved ones who looked upon her. "Of course! Oh, God, what's happening?" She reached with both hands and they were taken immediately, one by Rory and the other by both Mel and Dawn.

"It's inside your head," the twins lamented from just outside the circle.

Shya trembled, a violent spasm of understanding working through her. "What do I do?"

"You fight," Dawn squeezed her hand.

"You let us help you," Ed murmured.

"And there's no time to waste," Rory cut in, then added, "right?"

Everyone nodded.

"We do this first thing tomorrow," Dawn said firmly, her eyes on Shya's.

"I'll call Connor," Rory said as he left the small circle, already pulling out his phone.

"But he's not ready!" Shya protested, remembering Connor's tears when they all sat on his front lawn while Shya was recuperating. "He wants – Connor, I mean – he insisted that we try it one more time with the priest! He trusts him."

"But he must know it's more dangerous that way?" Sheila's high voice had everyone turning to her. "Traditional exorcisms deal directly with the possessed! And the priest can't see what we can! Can't do what we hope to do!"

Dawn nodded in agreement, then faced Shya again and took up the hand Rory had dropped. "Surely, we can make him see."

Shya shrugged helplessly. "I can talk to him. He trusts me, too."

"But is it smart for Shya to return tomorrow?" Big Ed's question had everyone frowning. "She's already been so affected. If the priest is to lead the next attempt, we'll be at a disadvantage."

"He's right," Mel murmured, his mouth near Dawn's ear.

The group contemplated silently as the rain pattered ever more quietly against the windows.

Rory stepped back into the room, his phone dark in his hand. "Connor knows we're coming tomorrow, but he's still insisting on the priest."

Nobody replied.

Rory sent Shya a questioning look.

She shook her head. "I know my being there is dangerous, but do we have a choice?"

"You're not going," Rory answered immediately.

"What?" the group asked in chorus, which made them all titter a bit in response.

Rory shook his head. "I'm staying with Shya at the house while you all go and take part in the final attempt with the priest."

"This can't work," Dawn said, defeated.

"I don't know if Jordan will make it!" Shya protested.

Rory made a calming motion with both hands. "It's the only way Connor will consider any other option. The way I look at it is that you guys can be there to prevent any further injury to Jordan."

Slowly, the members' faces lit up.

"We can protect him," Sheila smiled, her voice finally sounding solid.

They began to nod and talk quietly as Shya shot Rory a look of gratitude.

"If nothing else, we'll set the stage for doing it our way," Mel's voice penetrated all the others, and a hush fell over them again. "And Shya will be safe."

"I doubt it'll even respond without her there," Dawn muttered, and as well-intentioned as she'd been, another vein of uncertainty went through them all.

"Let's hope it's the most uneventful exorcism ever attempted," Rory said lightly as he crawled to sit by Shya. He hugged her sideways, kissing her temple. Shya noted the effect his presence had on the others as their faces changed. Relaxed.

"Should we talk more about how to approach this when we do it our way?" Mel asked.

The group was eager to do just that, and so they did, with Shya mostly listening as she allowed her body to be warmed by Rory's. And thought about going back home, of being alone with him, and making sure he knew in no uncertain terms just how much he meant to her before the next day – and whatever it would bring - dawned.

CHAPTER 47 – EFFORT

She'd stepped directly into a dream after she and Rory had made love; they'd both fallen away from each other, heads crashing on their respective pillows and then reaching for each other as they drifted, exhausted but elated, too. And the next thing she knew, she was ten years old and standing at the foot of her mother's sickbed, childish fear gnawing at her heart while she tried to comprehend the helpless sense of doom that encompassed her.

She was vaguely aware that aside from the bed, the diminished form in the bed and herself, the entirety of her surroundings were empty and black, but regardless of that strange fact, her eyes were glued to that form beneath the blankets. She'd been transported so swiftly that she'd lost her knowledge of her dream state and became singly aware that she'd somehow gone back in time to when her mother was sick and Shya was at her side, witnessing her decline in panicked solitude.

But then she became aware of something else... something that felt dangerous. She realized that, sick or not, her mother's presence was a near excruciating relief. She frowned, recognizing a feeling of missing her already, but couldn't fathom *why.* Regardless, the gift of her presence overwhelmed all else.

"Mommy?" The single word echoed around them, and it occurred to her that there should be walls in her mother's room, and suddenly there were. She turned on the spot as furniture followed, magicking into existence – the bureau with the broad mirror above it, the tallboy with her mother's jewellery displayed so tantalizingly – to Shya, anyway - on top. Then, the antique chaise by the bay window with a book lying open, spine bent, to where her mother had stopped reading for the last time.

Remembering, she whirled back to the bed, and the scene was complete. The room where Mom had both lived and died. The distant whistling of Shya's father from downstairs in the kitchen, and the sounds of her mother's shallow breath. She stepped around the foot of the bed, feeling suddenly too small in body, as though she might be forced right out of it, but then she halted just as soon as she'd started, because something was still off.

Her mother's wrists were wrapped in heavy chains, wound around the posts on either side of the headboard. Shya's fingers flew on their own to her mouth to catch the sound of mortification that escaped her. Such weight upon the woman's frail and bruised arms, and for what? Was she not trapped already by the stage of her disease? Held down by sheer lack of strength to move? A sudden need to free her surged through Shya, and she moved instinctively, determined to remove the chains, if not the disease itself.

But as she rattled them impotently against the wood, careful as she wrenched at the metal links not to further damage the beloved soul whose arms were already so bent and withering, another oddity dawned on her. Her mother's face was covered by her thin quilt. The only indication it was her at all was evidenced in wisps of what hair she had left after her last round of chemo, delicately framed against the pillow where it stuck out of the blanket.

Shya let her hands drop as fear stole her breath and, with her eyes on those scant strands, reached to pull the blanket back. She gasped, then cried out when she did, for what she saw was not the motherly body of her memory. Instead, the body from whence Shya herself had come was in a state of decomposition far past that of the early days of death. And yet her mother's eyes stared back at her from decaying sockets. Somehow, she was inhabiting her dead and rotten body – chained back into that which had failed her so completely in the end.

Shya reached for her, but froze when she could see her own hand. The hand of an adult, of herself long after her mother's death. She shook her head as she tried to grasp it all.

Her mother tried to speak, but couldn't, for the prison of her corpse was far past working... what remained of her voice was dragged over the gravel of a ravaged gullet, then drowned in the gargling fluids that had pooled in the recesses of a long-defunct voice box.

Shya cringed as she witnessed the efforts of the pitiful creature. Unthinking, with only her instinct to comfort driving her, she reached for her mother's captive hand and grasped it, only to have it fall apart in her own, stinking flesh draping in ribbons over pockmarked bones, which crumbled, too, when Shya backed away, taking bits of her mother with her in an unintentional reactive move.

She helplessly watched the remnants fall, crying aloud and falling to her knees, then found her mother's eyes again, which rested to the side of a skull that had turned to watch her back away, the whites not white, but brown and black and oozing something putrid. Shya wailed as the chained arms collapsed at the elbows and fell, leaving the dangling bits of flesh they parted from to wither in the chains.

And then, something changed, and her mother's eyes darted grotesquely to a spot just over Shya's shoulder, and yes, there was a heat there. A heavy weight that Shya recognized. And everything else was gone: the recalled fragments of the room, the walls, the very notion that this – any of it – was anything but a dream.

"Wake up!" the corpse screamed, a disembodied, curdled cry that knocked the last sinew of her body's jaw asunder. When it sunk off of its hinges, ripping remnants of paper-thin skin to shreds, Shya screamed, too, and let her eyes shut so she couldn't see it anymore: the imprisonment of her mother's soul in the pile of bones that had been her physical self. In her sickbed, perpetually dying, yet not, doomed to go in circles in the worst pain of her life.

And thankfully she burst out of it, bolting upright with a shrill cry. Back in her childhood bed, to her own realm of existence, with the love of her life swiftly rising to comfort her. But she carried new knowledge of where her mother was and how *it* held her prisoner. Knowledge that shook her to the core, but served her well, too. She started to smile into the darkness, realizing fully that, just as it used the fears and sadness of the boy to build that rocky shore where he was trapped, it was using her mother's most painful terrors to trap her. Like the twins had said, it used her fears, and so it would try using Shya's, too.

"Alright?" Rory whispered.

"My mother came to warn me," she said, and Rory was silent for a moment, not even breathing.

"Really?"

She nodded. "I know how it has her, and how it'll try to get me, too." She laughed, and the sound was eerie in the chill dark of the night. "I thought it was a nightmare until just now; one created by the demon to torture me, but no... she was able to get through to me, Rory, despite everything, and she was – terrible! But she did it anyway, trapped as she is, and the demon hated it!"

Rory's stubble scratched her shoulder as he shook his head. "This isn't fair."

She straddled him and took his face into her hands. "No.

It's terrible. It was awful. But she got through to me."

He started to cry.

"She got through," she whispered, and pressed her forehead against his, holding his hands and breathing slow and sure while he cried.

When he quieted, she got off the bed, pressing his shoulder gently back so he'd lie down. He did, and she kissed his cheek. His hand darted out to grasp her arm. "Where are you going?"

"Just to get some chocolate milk. Want some?"

"No." He yawned and let her arm drop after a moment. "Hurry back."

CHAPTER 48 – AMENDS

She left the room feeling a mixture of emotions that was entirely new. She knew she should be trembling in fear, if not entirely repulsed at what she'd seen inside her dream. But instead, she managed to rise above all that with the knowledge that her mother could get past her captor, if only for a few moments.

She opened the fridge in the dark, then bent to grab the carton of chocolate milk, almost smiling, and then cried out as she rose, the carton falling as she backed away from the figure that stood behind the refrigerator door.

"It's just me!" he said, palms outstretched in surrender in the dark. And then he flicked the switch and the light came on, and Shya exhaled loudly, her hand on her heart.

"Dad!"

"Oh!" Her father spotted the carton of milk, which was dribbling freely onto the tile from its landing spot.

Shya grabbed some paper towels as her father retrieved the carton and inspected it for leaks. He winced when he found one at the middle of a side seam, and moved quickly to get two glasses from the cupboard. Shya let out another breath of relief. "What are you doing up?"

He poured the tall glasses of chocolate milk, effectively lowering the remaining liquid beneath the leak, then held one out for her. She rose and took it, then disposed of the paper towels she clutched into the compost container. "I woke up when you screamed," her father said, shaking his head as he looked resolutely into his glass. "Just like when you lived here." He met her eyes with some difficulty. "You always suffered from nightmares. And it always woke me up. I'm just sorry it was never me to comfort you."

She eyed him, dubious.

"I truly am, Shya." He put his glass on the counter. "Sorry, I mean. For everything."

"Why now?"

"I miss you. You're my daughter, though I know I only did the minimum to care for you," he rubbed his stubble roughly with one hand. "I want to make it up to you. I've just been too scared to reach out. Your being here now... I know it's not ideal, but I'm hoping it's the start of us seeing more of each other."

Shya was frozen, even more confused by the new twist the assault of her emotions had taken on.

"You don't have to agree," he went on, "but if there's any chance you'll let me make up for all those years I..." his cheeks reddened as he struggled.

"Ignored me?" she finished for him. Her voice sounded so small she nearly flinched, but managed to hold strong.

He nodded, his face crumbling as he begun to cry.

"Jesus," Shya muttered. She took a swig from the glass in her hand. "Lots of crying tonight."

Her father smiled.

"Was it because of Mom dying?"

His smiled melted. "What?"

"You were always distant... but after Mom died, it was like you wished I'd died with her."

He sobbed, covering his eyes. Shya felt awkward, like she

should want to go to him, arms open, but also like she didn't want that at all. It was like it had always been: she watched her father from behind what felt like an invisible shield. One he'd erected and maintained for all the years of her life. Until now.

"I can't handle this right now." Her words were quiet, but sure. Her father looked up from behind his hands and she saw it clearly – how much he'd aged. How the lines around his eyes had multiplied. How tired he seemed. And there was something else there, too. Hope, maybe.

He wiped his tears away. "I understand. I know it's too little, too late, but trust me when I say I'm willing to do anything I have to until the day I die to show you how sorry I am."

She looked down at her milk.

"I mean it. And you were right; it was always hard for me to relate to either of you. I felt like I was on the outside of this big secret the two of you shared. And when she died -" he balled a fist, "- I made up my mind to try harder, and I did for a while! But you were so like her, Shya. Still are." He stepped toward her. Reached out to touch her curls and tears did well in her eyes, then. "You're the spitting image of her." He let his hand drop heavily to his side. "I was scared. You grew so fast and I couldn't give you anything you needed. I was scared of what you needed at all, truth be told."

"I just needed you to love me," she said, a little more coldly than intended, but loudly ringing of truth.

His face crumpled again. "Can you ever forgive me?"

She nodded. "I think so."

They eyed each other, both unsure. Both feeling a modicum of hope where before, there had been none.

He put a hand on her shoulder and she fell into his arms, and they stood locked in an embrace for a long time, both barely breathing, but unwilling to let go.

"I need you to be careful when you deal with whatever's hurting Connor's boy," he said into her hair.

She pulled away, nodding. "I will."

He nodded, then picked up his glass. "You'll get some sleep?"

She nodded again, and he shuffled off into the hallway, leaving her to deal with the chaos of her thoughts. And something happened, as it tended to when she had the time to reflect without distraction: something germinated in her mind, like a tickling feeling in her brain. A poem, the words rising from the mire of her day and coalescing as if in happy reunion.

She fished in the junk drawer beneath the counter for a pen and found a notebook, too, for good measure, and then she sat at the table, sipping at her drink while the passages organized themselves in pleasing rhythm, then put pen to paper and reorganized for rhyme and reason.

Then, satisfied but suddenly not satiated, she went back to bed to wake Rory.

CHAPTER 49 – DISCOVERY

Rory fell instantly asleep afterword, muttering about how she was wearing him out, but Shya was wired. She lay quietly for some time, wishing for dawn but fearing the dark would go on forever. She avoided thinking about the dream that had woken her in the first place, and figured her poem was complete, though she couldn't remember exactly what she'd written... but that wasn't entirely unheard of, so why ruminate on it?

A little voice kept piping up, wondering about her sudden unslakable lust, but that was easy to explain; dark times were upon her. She was making the most of the present. It didn't completely quiet the voice, but she was able to shove it aside and rose from bed again, feeling antsy, bordering on anxious.

The house was dead quiet. She opened the fridge again, but nothing appealed. Her chocolate milk, in fact, still sloshed inside her stomach. Sighing, she wandered. Looked out into the fenced back yard, contemplating the season. Autumn, yet unaccompanied by the usual anticipation of cozy evenings, pumpkin spice and the like. Autumn had always felt like change, but she couldn't shake the fact that now, it felt like the end.

She went to the stairs, wanting the TV in the basement. Wanting distraction. But when she flicked the light on, the photos on the walls were what caught her eye. Her as a little girl, dark hair flying as she ran, laughing and looking back over her shoulder. She wondered what chased her, then. A school photo for each year until her mother wasn't there to keep up. There was the only family photo they'd ever gotten, her mother already showing signs she wasn't well, though she hadn't been diagnosed, just yet. Shya leaned in to see the dark circles beneath her eyes, and the dream flashed inside her mind. How her mother's eyes had rested in the sockets of her skull, rotting. Watching.

She shuddered as she backed away, already seeking something different, and finding photos of her father and Louise, then the perfunctory school shots of she and Rory. She smiled, then, at how she was awkward in all of hers... pimples, frizzy hair and shiny skin, as was expected during those years. But Rory was beautiful in all of his, seemingly traversing the teenage years with ease. Even with braces, his smile was easy. Confident. His chestnut hair differed in style and length, but always shone. Gratitude filled her again. She frowned at the few shots of her father and stepmother, pondering their relatively short time together.

Maybe they only came together so that Rory and I could, too?

That felt right.

It's not fair.

That voice again.

We deserve to be happy.

She took the stairs back up, fueled by anger, that time.

What if I don't survive?

She stood at the top of the stairs, fists balled so her fingernails bit into her palms.

What if I do, but he doesn't? What if I do, but one of The Seers is hurt?

She crossed to the bay window that looked onto the street. The neighborhood slept.

I could just end it all right now. Save the boy and prevent anyone else from getting hurt.

It sounded right, and that scared her for reasons she couldn't make materialize. She shook her head. Her heart raced. "No," she said, quietly. It wasn't right. Her gaze snapped to the light pole at the corner of the street where something moved. There was something there. A silhouette, only, too tall and with arms too long to be human, separating into long fingers with points of claws at the ends. She grimaced as a flash of snake-like fingers moving within the grooves of bark hit her.

"No," she said again, and was headed down the stairs and toward the door before knowing she'd decided to.

Get out of my head.

She knew that was what was happening, but was having trouble separating her own thoughts from those of the beast that stalked her. She slipped her shoes on. *What do I hope to gain by going out there?* Her jacket, next. It was as if her body was obeying a set of instructions she didn't know she was giving it.

Go to it.

She gasped as her hand shot out to open the door.

"Oh, God," she whimpered aloud, just to hear her own voice, and a dark laughter resonated in her head, growing to fill her with the sound until she found herself wanting to let go, just to fall and let herself land where she may, as long as she could go to sleep. As long as she could not be there, listening to that horrid sound. And as if in response, her body slipped outside.

Her eyes went to that spot beneath the streetlight, but it was empty, now.

I'll have to find it, then.

A burst of adrenaline surged through her and she started to run, and she was picturing Connor's. Thinking of Jordan's room with the damp and heavy air. Of freeing her mother.

She screamed when she turned onto the driveway and someone stepped out to grab her. Someone *big*. She ducked and turned toward the road, to the dismay of the figure, who grunted in surprise, then started after her. She glanced back, but her pursuer was in shadow, and something pressed her on, made her fleet of foot. *Is it the demon?* She made a sound like a frightened animal, her feet pounding the road, never questioning why she would run from the demon in the direction of the boy it possessed. The duality that existed within her prevented it.

"Shya!" From behind her, the breathless cry of her name. And she noted how the footfalls slowed and fell behind, then cried in frustration at the effort it took for her to slow, herself.

"Stop!" Came the voice again, and she realized she knew it, and made a wide turn when she found herself unable to stop, so she was running, still, when she saw that indeed, it was Ed, and he was stopping, hands going to his knees.

"What the – Ed?" she called, and he straightened, and it was a good thing, because she couldn't stop. "Help!" she cried, reaching for him, reminded of ice skating as a child, unable to stop and readying to brace herself against the boards.

He planted his feet and held his massive hands, spread like starfish, in front of himself and then she crashed into him and he stepped back to absorb the blow, crying, "Whoa!" as her feet were swept off of the ground and she pressed against his chest. Feeling the anger of the demon... the rage at her success. Became aware of its exhaustion just as she sunk a little too far into Big Ed's arms and, in the blink of an eye, was transported to that room, her mother's sickbed with its chains and reinhabited corpse. Just a flash, but sure enough to make her scream again, and then she was back and Ed was falling to his knees, so she landed in his lap, still in the vise of his arms but solidly *there* instead of the other place.

She peered up at his face, crying, confused at what had happened, start to finish, and saw his grimace of pain. "What happened?" she managed, her voice like a child's.

He looked down at her. The streetlight stretched the shadows of his features, drew his pain and sadness in long, dark lines on his face.

"Why were you at my house?" she asked, the words falling from her mouth in tandem with the realization as it formulated.

"Did you feel that?" he loosened his grip on her and placed a hand to his heart.

"Are you alright?" Shya scrambled off his lap and studied his face. Tears rolled down his cheeks, like diamonds in the streetlight.

"I don't know." He looked at her. "What happened?"

She shook her head. "I went back to a place I saw in my dream. The place my mother's trapped." She took the hand that clutched at his heart and squeezed it in both of her own. "When I crashed into you, it was like I sunk into you, and that was where I landed."

He wiped at his cheeks with his free hand, then touched his chest again. "It hurt."

"Are you alright?"

He gazed, confused, at her. "I saw it, too. The bed. The... chains?"

Shya was wracked with an unexpected sob. Like his saying it aloud confirmed it. His seeing it, too, made it not a dream at all. His seeing it made it real. She bent forward as every-thing she'd held back and balled up hit her full force. Without the manipulation of the demon – who'd seemed to have faded when she broke free of the run it had her on – everything was raw.

Big Ed caressed her hands with his thumbs, and bent for-ward to rest his head on the top of hers, and they sat like that, in the street as the neighborhood slept on around them, until Shya was cried out.

She straightened, then laughed through lingering tears at the sight of her friend, who'd never looked quite so dis-traught.

"You're making fun of me," he said, so straight-faced it made her laugh some more, and to her relief he joined her, then helped her stand. And she was overjoyed to find she was cap-able of walking beside him, back toward the house.

"The portal thing," she said softly, then looked up at him.

He nodded. "Guess it's time I start trying to figure it out rather than pretend it's not there."

"It's like you see both sides... you're the door between two places, somehow."

He rubbed at his chest again. "Only you're crashing through it rather than opening it, first."

"I'm sorry."

He shook his head. "Maybe *I* need to open it?"

They walked in silence until they reached the driveway again.

She remembered another of her questions, as yet un-answered. "Why were you here?"

He hung his head. "It's not as creepy as it seems, I prom-ise."

She watched him, waiting.

"The group thought it best if someone stood watch to-night, seeing as how that – thing – has some hold over you."

She peered in the direction she'd been running, the ten-drils of her fear gripping her again.

"And it seems like it's a damn good thing I insisted on being the one to be here."

"I couldn't stop," she started, and then she was crying again, and he was gingerly taking her into his arms. "I won't go through," she muttered, patting his chest lightly as he patted her back.

"I need to let the rest of the group know what happened."

She pulled away. "Does that mean you're leaving?"

He took out his phone. "No way."

She nodded, sniffling. "Thank you, Ed."

He nodded, but he was already dialling. "Try to get some sleep. I'm not going anywhere."

She turned, but then looked back. "Did Rory know you'd be here?"

He shook his head, then said something into the phone before looking back at her. Covering it, he said, "He's so loyal to you. We thought he'd either insist on keeping watch himself, or tell you what was going on."

Shya smirked. Sounded about right. "Say hi to Dawn," she gestured toward the phone, then went inside, Ed's "Shya says hi," following her in and making her smile.

When she climbed into bed, sleep was her one and only desire. She wondered again at her sexual appetite earlier that night, and was still trying to figure out a way to ask Mel about it without sounding like a fool when she dropped into a deep and dreamless sleep.

CHAPTER 50 – EXORCISM

Rory was anxious. They sat on the front step and his foot bounced relentlessly on one of the paving stones of the front walkway, effectively jiggling Shya in a most unpleasant way, given that he also clutched her right forearm between his side and the arm closest to her.

Shya's jaw ached from being clenched. She knew she and Rory were only outside at all because he loved her – hell, it had taken all the persuasive power she had to convince him they didn't need to stay inside the house – but she wasn't sure how much more of the haphazard jiggling she could take.

"Rory?"

He peered sideways at her, and she could see that his jaw was clenched, too.

"Remember that wicked headache I had yesterday?"

He frowned.

"Well, the one that's building up today won't be the work of a demon."

His foot paused mid-bounce. "Sorry," he muttered, eyes going again to the road in the direction of Connor's house, where The Seers were joining the family in a last-ditch attempt at an exorcism.

"Do you think it's already happening?" she wondered aloud.

He shrugged. "You're the one with the link to the demon." He caught himself and shook his head. "That wasn't meant to sound so accusatory."

She squeezed his arm gently. His foot was ramping up again, though, until he realized it and stood, a growl struggling in his throat.

"It's alright, Ror." She watched him pace the walkway, arms swinging clenched fists. "You know," she called out, "I haven't felt it today. Not like yesterday." It was true, but she still found it difficult to separate what happened the day before into the things she'd initiated, and the things pushed on her by the possessor. She said none of that to Rory, though.

"It's a damn good thing Ed was here," Rory had paused in his pacing and faced her, hands on his hips.

She forced a laugh. "You're very handsome when you're stressed," she teased, and he threw his hands up in defeat.

"That's another thing!" His pacing resumed.

She stood and went to him, reaching for his hands when he paced in her direction. "What is it?" she asked when he'd stopped. His eyes were dark reflections of his inner turmoil.

"Shya, I don't even know what was you yesterday and what was that monster."

It was hard to keep her face clear of emotion when he said exactly the thing she'd been anxious about. Lost for words of comfort, she only found herself nodding a brief acknowledgement. "I know."

He lowered his head, leaning close as if to share a secret. "I hate the thought that it was that fucking demon in bed with us last night."

She inhaled sharply. He'd taken her fears one step further, to a place she, as yet, hadn't voiced aloud.

"I know you like sex, Shy, but that – I mean, you were like fire last night. And it felt like there was no amount of water that could dampen the flames."

Teasing words tried to surface – it would have been so easy to make light of his concerns – but seeing as how they echoed her own, all she could do was nod, again.

"I talked to Mel a bit before we left the British last night," he said, still conspiratorially, the scents of toothpaste and coffee reaching her nose, "and he said this demon… this 'Four', is also known as the demon of lust."

She smiled, but it was only a reflex and it disappeared as quickly as she became aware of it. "Oh, God," she muttered. It was exactly the thing she'd suspected Mel would tell her, if she dug deeper.

"Just how much control *can* it have over you without you realizing it?"

Their gazes locked, and they stayed there, saying nothing more for the impossible mountain of angst it could bring down on them.

"You two have some breakfast?" her father's voice made them both jump. "Didn't mean to interrupt." he stepped back, seemingly ready to shut the door, but Shya rushed to him instead, and threw her arms around him for only the second time since she'd left for university. And it had been awkward then, but now Shya squeezed him tight, eyes closed, until he relaxed into it, and she heard him make a noise of mingling surprise and relief beside her ear. "Good girl," he muttered then, patting her back, and she couldn't help but laugh. And then he was laughing, too, a little. When they pulled away, both were still smiling through happy tears. And then something happened – a distant rumble, first, but not like thunder, for it stretched on and gained in volume, and then they were feeling it, and Shya knew: it was an earthquake.

Her father held tight to one of her hands, but reached with the other to brace against the door frame as the earth trembled beneath them. His expression struck a sick knot of fear in her belly, and she looked to Rory, who was using the car to brace himself, his eyes on Shya with something like suspicion behind them. And it occurred to her as a massive *crack* split the air, that just as the thunderstorm had seemed influenced by something otherworldly the night before, it could be the demon causing the earth to shake, too.

One of the giant branches of the oak in the yard across the street toppled with another spectacular cracking sound, and the rumbling intensified, eliciting a scream from Shya before the street in front of the house seemed to break, then split, and then yawn open with the darkness of the underground exposed for all to see.

"Shya!" she heard Rory call her name, but another call was greater, and before Rory could react, she was running again, the ground still shivering beneath her, but her footing strong and sure, toward the epicenter, where an exorcism had no doubt been forced to pause.

Fuelled by terror and by something else that wasn't borne within herself, she ran. She leapt over fallen branches and cringed at the sounds of glass rattling, then exploding all around her. But her eyes were on the road ahead. She should have paused at the end of it, where turning right would lead her to the park and then the wooded trail, and turning left would take her to Wilfrid-Lavigne and then to Connor's, quickly. But her feet took her left before she even thought to slow, and she saw the road had cracked in other places, and that people had stopped their cars on the main street haphazardly, and some ran now, toward home, maybe, or someplace safe, or just *away*.

But she was just an observer; she knew another entity steered her, now, and she did not fight it, so needful as she was to find her group of friends safe, to stop the earthquake that had torn a swath in the road beside her house when it only cracked in other places... to find the boy and take his pain away.

But then as she reached Wilfrid-Lavigne and kept right, up the slope of the hill, someone was running toward her and it was Bethie, skirt flying and hair unpinned, but her expression said it best: there had been trouble, and she needed to get to Shya. But Bethie slowed as Shya approached, her eyes widening and arms outstretched. "No! Don't!" she screamed as Shya passed her by, but Shya had no time to stop and talk; she was needed just ahead.

She nearly screamed in frustration when she was almost there and someone else came out to block her way. It was Ed, and she knew his size alone would cause her trouble, but even then she didn't slow. Even when Rory called out from somewhere behind her, even as the screams of strangers faded into the deafening sound of the quaking earth, even as Big Ed stopped, planting his feet, and closed his eyes, his face a mask of focussed intent...

And suddenly, she was on that rocky shoreline; the one that reminded her of Port Williams in Nova Scotia, where amethyst treasures hid between the rocks for those who cared to risk the tide to look. But here the sky was navy rimmed with red, all edges doubled over with that crimson tide, blood tide, and rocks were bones, each little lump a dying creature or one long dead, and there was Jordan, on his knees and sifting through the little bodies, crying, screaming, because there were none to be saved.

There was more, but Shya kept it all in her periphery, the lone, gnarled monster of a tree at the shoreline that wound around itself with vine-like limbs and further on the water, a bed with a wasted lump of a body beneath the covers and chains stretching taut from the bedposts. But no, she went to

Jordan only, and he didn't even see her coming, so consumed was he with his task, and stayed that way until she reached out and touched him, and suddenly they were both transported.

Shya looked around to get her bearings, on a journey that was not her own, and realized it was the back yard she'd seen before. Jordan's house, where a featherless baby bird floundered in the blades of grass beneath its nest. But this time, there was a picnic. Checkered blanket, plates of cookies and a pitcher full of lemonade, and there was a boy in her lap – *the* boy - hair smelling of dirt and sweat and sun and soap, and he was hers. She knew it in her core: she was somehow his mother. The mother that had died was alive, here, and perhaps what he'd been looking for all along, for he seemed to realize her presence and he looked up into her face and she knew it wasn't hers he saw; it was his mother's and that was OK. It was good, because his face was plump, still round with the last of his baby fat, and his hair was shining in the sun, and his eyes, dark brown like his father's, were filled to overflowing with his love for her. Shya felt the mother's arm rise up, touched the boy's sweet cheek as her heart swelled, too, and felt the dichotomy of the love of a mother for her child – like being more than whole, like perfection, and at the same time like a part of you was ripped out of your body to walk the world as separate, and you will never be whole again outside his presence.

It hurt. It was a twisted, sweet pain like Shya hadn't ever known, but she knew it with certainty then: nothing she had seen or felt or even comprehended could compare to the depth of feeling she had here, inside this mother's body as she held her struggling son. Her son who could flourish here, but lay dying just outside the dream.

The boy's face changed, then. It darkened as the sky began to, and he held out cupped hands for her to see. She locked her gaze on his, wanting to prolong that swift, sweet moment of before, but knowing it was fading as surely as the sun did in the sky, and the mother's eyes did turn to see a tiny bird, pink and frail, eyes still shut, never to open, and then, thank God, Shya suddenly awoke.

CHAPTER 51 – THE PRIEST'S WAY

She was surrounded, sitting amongst the frenzied greetings of her friends, but looking for the one who'd transported her to stop her from making it inside the house. And there he was, twenty feet away: Big Ed laid out on the grass with Mel and Bethie bent over him. Mel was performing chest compressions. And there was another: a man in black with a bit of white at his neck. The priest. And he was praying. Shya crawled to them, vaguely aware that Rory was at her side, crawling, too, and that the earth no longer shook, but car alarms still blared in overlapping states of warning. Rory took her up as soon as they reached Big Ed and slowed, holding her tight and murmuring "You're alright; I can't believe it. You went right through him, Shya."

She peered over his shoulder at the unconscious Ed, searching for signs of life and finding none, then meeting Bethie's eyes and knowing he was gone.

"No!" she cried, squirming out of Rory's arms and going to her friend. Instinctively getting between Mel and Ed, making Mel fall backward, breathing hard, then leaning over Ed, her portal, and touching chest to chest, where the break had happened, wanting to heal it there with no idea whether she could or not. Then suddenly, Ed was coughing and gasping and everyone was leaning in to see and to exclaim *Oh my God! He's alive!* And, *how'd you do that, Shya?* But Shya only looked pointedly at the man in black who knelt across from her, and he was looking blankly back. She saying "He's not going anywhere" with her eyes and he in no position to do anything but stare. "How?" he finally said, but then there was a voice next to her ear.

It was Connor's; he had crawled with her, too. "Next, we do it your way," he said, and Shya nodded.

"Is he -?"

"Jordan's alright, but only because we stopped when we did. I'm so sorry I didn't listen." Connor sunk down behind her, his face in his hands, and soon Bethie was there, too, holding him as he wept.

Shya turned to Rory. "Where is Sheila? The twins?"

"Inside with Jordan."

She collapsed into his arms. Saw her father just down the sidewalk, looking entirely flabbergasted.

Sirens blared in the distance, but one grew more intense as an ambulance approached. She looked to Dawn, who was waving it down, then pointing to Ed. Ed, who sat now, hand on his chest and eyes on Shya, saying something about not being able to open up first, about being too scared. About needing guidance, next time.

And she knew, if nothing else, that next time would have to be the last.

CHAPTER 52 – DEBRIEF

They sat, still reeling with shock, as a group in Shya's childhood home while her father made strong coffee in the next room. Dawn had gone with Ed to the hospital. She'd already called to say they'd found internal bleeding, but couldn't find the source, or *sources*, and Shya knew it had been she who'd hurt him, she who had been the source. She who'd crashed through a door that had refused to open.

"I'm sorry," she muttered, and the group dutifully waved her off, as they had countless times already, but Mel didn't meet her eyes. He'd seen what Rory had, and though she'd experienced it, she hadn't seen it herself, so Shya found it hard to fathom, too.

The twins were muttering in the dining room, just off the living room where the rest of them sat, but Sheila was squished up close to Mel in a chair meant for one, obviously grateful for his calming gifts. And Rory, of course, was at Shya's side, quiet but steady, his fingers interwoven with hers.

Her father came in with a tray, then, laden with mugs and a full carafe, and a plate with cookies, too. Shya recognized them as the gingersnaps Louise used to bake, more to feed her own obsession with them than to placate hungry teenagers, and sent him a questioning look. He smiled. "She likes to stock my freezer, now and then."

Rory shook his head. "Still taking care of him," he whispered when her father left to get milk and sugar.

There was a knock at the door and the group collectively jumped. Sheila parted reluctantly with Mel to peer out the bay window, then looked back at them. "It's Father Marion!"

Shya's father hastily put a little pitcher of milk and some packets of sugar on the coffee table, then whisked off toward the door saying, "I'll get it."

The twins came back into the room. Shya eyed them. "Connor said we'd try again, but our way."

They nodded.

"And Jordan – is he really alright?"

The twins looked at each other, saying nothing. Sheila answered, instead. "Where he is – it's both a prison and a refuge to him."

Shya thought about the shoreline, and then the grassy back yard where she'd held him, safe and healthy in the arms that were his mother's. "That makes sense, given what I've seen."

"The thing is, he thinks it's better than being here," Sheila finished, her face looking pained.

"At least he finds her there, sometimes," Jane said. Her eyes were sad.

"Are you saying that, no matter what we do or how we do it, we might not get him back?"

Anna stepped forward. "The demon is smart. And you saw today what it can do. It's more powerful than we ever expected."

Shya looked to Mel. "Could it actually *be* Asmodeus?"

Sheila lurched, then bent over double and vomited violently onto the ugly, oatmeal-coloured carpet Shya had always hated. There was a flurry of activity, then, but Shya only watched, overwhelmed, as her father came back in, then rushed to get something to clean up with. The priest stepped in behind him, looking forlorn. The twins, meanwhile, were leading Sheila to the bathroom.

Mel caught Shya's gaze again. "You probably shouldn't say its name."

Her eyes widened. "It *is* the King of Demons, then?"

Mel shrugged resolutely. "If not, I'd hate to see what the actual fourth demon of Hell could do."

Shya sat back on the couch, feeling helpless.

Mel leaned forward. "What do you see when you go there? Is it still the shoreline you talked about before?"

Shya nodded dumbly.

"Has anything changed?"

"Yes," she glanced at Rory, then back to Mel. "When I went this time, my mother was there in her sickbed, floating way out in the water, and there was a tree, just like the one it – the demon – disappeared behind when I was a teenager and in my dreams."

Mel frowned. "Wait. You saw it as a teenager? Before Bethie ever had?"

Shya opened her mouth to counter him, but shut it again as she frowned.

"You might want to let Bethie know," Rory mumbled, and Shya peered at him, disbelieving.

"It doesn't excuse what she did – how she involved my mother!"

He rubbed at his eyes. "She's been destroyed by this, Shy. She deserves to know if that thing was eyeing you before she had anything to do with it."

Something tweaked inside her and she ducked her head, the full realization of the situation hitting her full force. "My God," she whispered. "This is all my fault. Everything, right from the start!"

Rory hugged her while Mel protested, and then her father was back to attend to the mess of the carpet.

The priest spoke from the spot at the top of the stairs where he'd frozen, jarring them all again. "You can't take the blame for the actions of the evil spirit," he said, his eyes on Shya.

"Then I can't let Bethie, either," Shya replied.

The priest stepped forward. "I'd like to participate in whatever else your group does to free Jordan," he said, but as though it were a plea. "I've known Connor since he was a child, and Lauren since she came into his life. Jordan was their treasure... I was there at his birth, and I care very much what happens to him."

Mel nodded. "I think it would be good for you to be near. Seems we have to remind the boy just how much he is loved on this side." He looked at Shya. "The more, the merrier."

The twins returned from the hallway. "Sheila's in your bed," Jane said, looking at Shya.

Shya's father looked up from his work. "Is she alright?"

Shya frowned, watching her father's face as the twins reassured him. *Who is this man?* "Why are you cleaning up?" she asked instead, and her father looked at her, bewildered.

"What else can I do?"

Her cheeks burned. He was helping in any way he could, and she was still on the attack.

Little else was accomplished as the group waited to hear more from Dawn, aside from the successful filling of their bellies with coffee and cookies. Father Marion eventually left to pick up a smoothie for Jordan – apparently it was the only thing they could get him to consume – and Rory was snoring softly by the time the phone rang again.

It was Jane who spoke to Dawn, but Anna's grim expression mirrored her twin's as though she could hear the entire conversation. "Whatever the source of the bleeding was, it seems to have resolved on its own," Jane announced once she'd hung up. "But he needs to stay in hospital until the hematomas are improving, or at least stagnant."

"Hematomas... blood clots?" Sheila voiced from the hallway. She still looked frail.

Anna nodded.

"But he'll be alright?" Shya asked.

"They think he'll recover fully, yes," Jane said, a bit hesitant, "but they're concerned about what caused it, of course. I can see them holding on to him for a few more days."

Shya shook her head. "I might need him before then."

The twins nodded, but Sheila stepped forward. She glanced briefly at the wet spot on the floor, then turned her attention to Shya. "You really want to try that again? On *purpose?*"

Jane touched Sheila's shoulder. "There might be a way we can help them control it, so he doesn't get hurt."

Sheila looked doubtful. "Then I think we need to figure that out, first."

"Practice," Anna nodded.

"There was something else," Jane gestured Sheila toward the couch and Sheila sat, sending a remorseful look to Shya.

"It's not that I don't trust you, Shya. But I'm scared for Ed."

Shya grasped her friend's hand. "I know. And I'm sorry I made you puke."

She made a face. "That was weird."

Jane sat cross-legged on the floor, and Anna perched herself on the arm of the chair Mel was in. "Dawn said Ed is talking. He's a bit loopy with pain meds, but he had one message loud and clear." She fixed her gaze on Shya. "If there was any time you might be able to speak with Jordan without compromising your safety, Shya, this is it."

Shya frowned. "Now?"

Jane nodded. "Come on... the demon's been harassing you for days. Do you feel it at all?"

Shya shook her head.

Sheila gasped. "It's tired."

Jane and Anna nodded.

"As powerful as it is, it's still a monumental task for it to interact like it's been doing without the benefit of a physical body for a physical plane," Jane explained.

Mel held a hand up. "Are you suggesting Shya go over there now?" He sat forward. Anna rested a hand on his shoulder, just as Mel had done so many times for everyone in the group.

Rory perked up beside Shya. "Not alone, that's for sure," he said, his voice gravelly from having drifted off while they waited.

Jane turned back to Shya. "You're the only one that can cross to where he is, and Sheila's right; the demon caused the worst earthquake this town has ever seen. It's tired. Even evil needs time to recuperate."

Shya was standing before Jane had finished. "Let's go."

Everyone was up in seconds, but Mel and Rory still looked unsure.

"What are we waiting for?" Shya looked to the twins and then to Sheila, who seemed to understand.

"At the first sign that thing is waking up, get out of there," Jane took Shya's hand as she spoke.

Shya shook her head. "I don't even know if I can reach him – Jordan," she said quietly. "I've only done it in dreams, or through Ed."

"Literally," Rory chuckled, and received dark looks from the group for it. "Sorry."

"Or when the demon's there," Shya added, remembering the first and only time she'd been in Jordan's room. She sunk back down to the couch as it came flooding back to her: the heaviness of the air, the pungent odours, the sad state of the child himself. And then that feeling, that *need* to go to the boy.

To take his place.

"What if I can't do it?" she cried. She looked between the faces of her trusted friends. "What if I only cause more trouble, like I seem to be so good at doing these days?"

"We'll be right beside you," Jane squatted in front of Shya, beseeching her with her strange eyes.

Then Rory's hand was on her shoulder. "I don't want you at risk, but after what I saw today, I believe what the big guy says. There's no way he can survive that and not be able to see through to the other side. And Shya," he squatted beside Jane and Shya found a welcome refuge in his eyes. "I know you. If you don't try to talk to Jordan now, and none of this works, it won't leave you. It'll follow you – follow *us* – for the rest of our days."

It was true. She knew it. But there was still that niggling little voice inside her, telling her Rory was just saying that because he was selfish and wanted her all to himself. But for once, she shoved that down rather than heed her own, often misguided, instincts. She stood again.

"OK?" Sheila said from beside her.

"OK," Shya said, and they filed to the door.

CHAPTER 53 – CONTACT

The room was palpably lighter when they entered: Sheila first, then Shya, who clung to Rory, and then the twins immediately behind. Mel stayed in the kitchen where Connor sat with dark eyes and in the general atmosphere of pain and loss.

Bethie had helped Father Marion with the smoothie, and then had gone for a nap. The Father sat beside Jordan's bed, now, Bible clutched in his hand and snoring gently.

But Shya only had eyes for the tiny figure that laid on the bed. Someone had covered him up, but his arms and legs were still tethered, as frail as they were, reminding Shya of how she'd seen her mother in her own sick bed. Death bed.

She went to him quickly, though Rory seemed hesitant to let her go. The draw was too strong; even without the demon, she was still as tethered to the boy as he was to the bed, and it relieved her. Let her know she wasn't just there because she had to be. She wanted in her heart and soul to help.

He looked like he was gone already, closed eyes sunken in darkened sockets, cheekbones jutting out above the sallow-skinned hollows of his cheeks. But he was breathing, shallow gasps of air that would go undetected, had they been silent... but as it was, there was a rasp with every draw and every following sigh. Shya knew it was the rattle of the dying.

She fell to her knees beside the bed, held her breath when the sour smell of him hit her, then put her elbows on the mattress in order to hold a bound hand in both of her own. He didn't stir. "Jordan," she whispered. She closed her eyes.

Breathed him in slowly. Controlled. "I'm here. Where are you?"

And she was there in a sudden vacuum-sucked *pop!*: the shore, her mother's sickbed just a dot on the horizon and the tree just a tree, still and standing oddly where the water lapped at the would-be rocks. But they weren't rocks. Shya lifted her gaze, unwilling to be pulled into the misery that was the ground beneath her, and sought the boy.

He was there, just a shadow against a dark sky dripping crimson, and she kept her eyes on him as she traversed the unstable path beneath her. Sometimes she slipped, sending showers of splintered bone into the air, sharp, but only annoying when they should have been dangerous. Just another layer of sadness on an already tragic landscape with its little creatures, dead and dying, but worst of all, uncared for... except by Jordan.

She approached the little boy and saw he had sores on the back of his head. His hair had thinned and wisped between the scabs, too long since his last haircut, and no doubt too difficult when even sponge baths were fought off by something too filthy to be touched by warm, soapy bubbles.

"Jordan?" her voice was lost among the pulsing din of the waves, so she tried again, but firmer. "Jordan? It's Shya," she was nearly to him, then. Could tell that he could hear her but felt no urge to turn. "I just want to talk to you," she said, stopping just behind him and seeing he was cupping something in his hands. "What do you have there?" she asked, knowing it was the baby bird he'd found in the grass. The one that made his heart swell with longing to love it better, then taught him that sometimes love can't solve a problem. Taught him about death.

He opened his hands, just a little, and a pale-yellow beak poked out of its own accord. "Oh!" Shya exclaimed.

The boy looked up at her, then, and she bent low as she

struggled not to cry out a second time, for his face was just as it was in life, hollow, sallow, tired beyond belief. And he was smiling, his sunken eyes still dull, but crinkled in a rare moment of joy. "It's alive," he said, and his breath was rancid. Rotten.

Shya remembered what Sheila had said about Jordan's prison being both a torment and a refuge and understood. *Sometimes, the things that had died are alive, here.* She looked toward the tree and saw that her mother's bed was closer, nearing the shore. Her heart lurched. Every fibre of her being sung with the desire to run to her mother, who in this moment was surely better, too. She looked back to the tree. *Sometimes the demon sleeps,* she finished her original thought. Then she looked at Jordan again. He peered up at her in confusion.

"That's my mother," Shya explained, pointing to the bed, which now listed forward and backward at the shoreline, knocking bone-rocks to and fro.

"Is she alright?" The boy asked, his voice high and his eyes on the bed.

Shya sat so she could put her arm around his back and hold him when she told him the truth. "No," she said quietly. His hip bone was sickeningly solid in her hand, for there was no soft flesh to pad it.

He turned to look at her again, his expression sober. "My Mom isn't, either."

Tears welled in Shya's eyes when she saw his own. "I'm sorry," she said, her breath hitching.

"Don't cry," he said, patting one of her folded legs. "Sometimes, we can see them, and they're OK again!"

The light in his eyes was nearly compelling enough to make her want to stay, but she forced herself to shake her head. "This isn't where we belong, sweetheart."

He frowned. "I thought that at first, too, but then I gave up. I see her sometimes. We sit on the grass. That's the best."

Shya bit her lip. "Can we go there now?"

His eyes brightened as though he'd forgotten the possibility. "Yes!" he cried, then opened his hands and the bird, fully grown, flew into the sky as they watched, mesmerized. Then he grasped her arm and closed his eyes, and when she did, too, the air was suddenly sweet with freshly-mown grass, and she could feel sunlight on her face. And she hoped to be herself when she opened her eyes, hoped she could see his mother, too, but no. She had turned observer again, inside the mother's body only. There were pitfalls even in this happier place, she realized. It seemed that when the demon slept, things got messy.

"Mommy!" Jordan looked up at her again, but where he was plump and healthy at their last picnic, he hadn't changed at all this time from the state he'd been in on the shore. She found her fingers touching his face. A massive lump of emotion filled her... filled his mother.

"Darling," she cried, then he was in her arms, against her chest, barely breathing.

He pulled away and looked drunkenly up at her. "I don't feel very good."

She shook her head. "Shya was right, my love."

Jordan sat up suddenly, his pelvic bones digging painfully into her thighs. "Where'd she go?"

"This is your place, not hers."

He frowned, mirroring Shya's unseen reaction. "And yours, right?"

His mother shook her head. "No, baby. I don't belong here, either."

His face crumpled. "But I miss you," he cried and that ball of emotion surged in her chest again.

"I know," she breathed into his hair. "But I'm not far, and if you try, you can feel me in your heart."

He peered up at her. Scowled, more like. She laughed. "I know, you've heard that before, and it didn't feel true. But it is, love. I live in you *and* in another place, and I can see you living your life just as you can feel me carried through it in your heart.

He shook his head. "But I can't hug you there."

Shya wondered at his mother's capacity for pain. It engulfed her... the urge to scream, to pick her boy up and run was nearly overwhelming. But she took a steadying breath, instead. "I know it hurts," she said, and her chest nearly burst with her own pain, "but you aren't meant to leave, just yet. You have so much to do!"

He pouted, his eyes going to the overgrown grasses in the field behind them.

"And I will be so happy to watch you from my special place – better than this place!" She gestured around them. "I'll be so happy to see you and your Daddy... he needs a little saving, too."

Jordan looked up at her again, his eyes moist.

"And you'll go to school and ride your bike, and grow! You'll grow so big – bigger than Daddy!"

A smile twitched at the corners of his lips. Shya felt his mother's elation and basked in it, so healing as it was.

"And someday, you'll be a Daddy, too, and do you know what that makes me?"

He pressed his lips together and shook his head.

"I'll be a grandmother. Even from my special place."

"But I won't see you?" Jordan's chin trembled, though he tried to stop it. Shya wanted to cry out, but knew it would break the spell, so bit down. Tensed, and held tight so she could finish, because this was good. This was something Jordan needed.

She shook her head. "Not for a while. But I'll wait for you, and when the time is right, we can be together again." She smiled to mask her tears, and Shya wished that she could hug the woman she inhabited, this Lauren, wife of her old friend, who died too early, just as her own mother had. And there was something – a feeling of acknowledgement from within the woman, meant for Shya. Acknowledgement and gratitude. And, oh, God, love. There was that, too, unmistakable even amidst her pain.

Jordan looked up at her silently. Shya felt how easy it was for Lauren to get lost in his eyes. The eyes of her beloved baby. "What if I can't?" he whispered, finally, and there was fear behind his eyes.

"You *can*," she whispered back, but the sky was darkening, and Shya felt an alarm go off somewhere. Somewhere behind. Somewhere back.

"I'm just so tired, now," Jordan mumbled, and his eyes were drooping heavily.

She leaned in close, inhaling his scent, no matter that it was different, because he was still in there, and by God, he needed to *stay*. "All you have to do is want it, baby boy. Your friends will do the rest." She said it into his neck and for a moment, it seemed he didn't hear her, but then he nodded and she did cry, then, saying "I love you, darling boy. My Jordan. I won't be far!"

Thunder rumbled in the distance. Shya felt herself separating from Lauren. Could hear the voices of her friends calling her back, and so she closed her eyes and let herself be taken, but not before she said, "I'll be back for you, Jordan. Hold on!"

CHAPTER 54 – SETTLE

They had to drag her out. It was as though she'd left the easy part within the shadows and her place on the physical plane was more painful, now. The separation from the little boy who had warmed in the arms that were his mother's but Shya's, too, just for a few privileged moments. And when she emerged, crying and wanting back in immediately, the boy had opened his eyes and they weren't his; they were black and glittering and *angry* because she'd done it again: she'd snuck in while the beast wasn't looking.

And though she knew she needed to go, all she wanted was to protect Jordan, who felt like her own a little bit, now.

So, her friends took up her arms and legs and carried her out, wailing her pain but letting her body go limp in her undeniable exhaustion. When they let her down onto the grass outside, she collapsed in Rory's arms, crying, sobbing words about pain and separation, and about how she loved the boy and Lauren and Connor, too, and they needed to get him out right *now,* right *then,* because he would come, now. He was ready.

But they patted her back and whispered placating sentiments about how well she'd done, about waiting for Dawn for the next part, about getting some rest, first. About *Jordan* resting, too.

She looked up at Rory, pleading with her eyes, wanting him to say it was alright to wait if she was forced to. Wanting dreamless sleep so badly it hurt, and wanting, more than any of that, a big hamburger and some fries.

"We can't wait long," Father Marion was talking from behind her, and she was too weak to twist around, so Rory turned so they could face him.

"It'll kill them both *not* to wait," he voiced.

Shya saw the twins at the doorway, speaking to Connor. She wondered what magic they'd woven to make him look more eager, more awake. And Sheila was on the ground beside her and Rory, still rubbing Shya's back. But where was Mel? She scanned the yard as Rory and the priest went on, her eyes going to the back yard last, where the fence backed into the trees and a trail led to the path she used to wander so many years ago.

As if in answer, Mel appeared at the door with Bethie, who still looked sleepy. She saw Shya and rushed to her, falling to her knees when she reached her, and taking Shya's hands.

"Thank you for going again," she cried quietly. "I would have gone with you if I could have. I *always* would have come on your strange adventures... I'm so grateful for you, Shya."

Shya nodded weakly, then allowed Bethie to hug her and Rory at the same time. Sheila followed suit. Feeling rather safe and protected, she whispered into Bethie's ear, told her it wasn't all her fault. Told her she'd seen the monster first, on that Halloween night, that night when everything changed. Bethie pulled away just enough to meet Shya's eyes. Her face was a blank slate first, and then transformed by relief, and then she was holding her again, her tears running fresh. Shya looked up at the priest. "Tonight," she said, and he raised his bushy eyebrows.

It was Rory who met her eyes, that time. His were full of questions.

She nodded again. "It has to be tonight; he's dying."

He gently pried her out of her friends' arms, and Shya

watched in amusement as the two women simply held each other, instead. "Let's get you better, then," Rory said, his voice low. He carried her to the steps to the front door and said they'd return that night, regardless if the entire group was ready.

Connor searched Shya's face, then nodded. "It has to work."

Shya's thoughts whirled even as her eyes shut on their own and she started drifting in and out. At some point she felt Rory take her to a car, then heard her father's voice and knew he was driving. Through it all, though, there were relentless thoughts of Ed and Dawn, thoughts of Lauren and poor little Jordan, and the thought of her own mother, finally, and she couldn't help but wonder where *her* special place was, and if she'd be there waiting if Shya's efforts failed... or if she'd still be tied to that bed, floating on the sea of a tortured child's nightmares.

CHAPTER 55 – REPRIEVE

She awoke to feel her hand being clutched by the thin, cold fingers she'd come to reconcile as Bethie's. When she opened her eyes to confirm her suspicion, not only did she see she was right, but she was stricken with a sudden bolt of urgency, for the room had that grey, dull quality brought on by post-sunset twilight and the window reflected the same.

Bethie perked up, sitting straight in the chair by the bed and clutching Shya's hand with fervor. "She's awake!" she called toward the open door, then leaned in and kissed Shya's forehead. "Are you alright?"

Shya struggled to sit, giving in when Bethie stood to help, and though her head still swam a bit from exhaustion, she was better. "What time is it?"

Rory spilled in, and then Sheila and Mel, and Dawn wasn't far behind. Her father appeared in the doorway, too, but lingered there, worry etched in his features. Shya reached for Dawn, who sat on the edge of the bed.

"Ed, is he…?"

Dawn pressed her lips together. "It nearly tore him apart, Shy. I won't lie to you. His whole chest is a mess of bruises; dark and purple-blue like a sky brewin' up a storm. But he's healing, now. The doctors are baffled," she looked up at Mel, who stood with his hand on her shoulder, "but they all agree he'll make a full recovery."

Shya's emotions clashed: part elation, part confusion, and an overshadowing measure of guilt. Dawn touched her cheek lightly. "It was bound to happen one way or another, Shya. At least now, he can start to understand his gift."

Shya peered at her friends, who nodded in agreement.

Her father flicked the light on. "It's getting late."

Shya frowned. Was he trying to kick her friends out in some strange throwback move from her teens?

"Connor called while you were sleeping, kiddo," he continued. "He's on the edge of calling an ambulance. He's scared."

He's trying to hurry us over there. She gave him a half-smile, then looked at Dawn. "Are the twins there?" Dawn nodded.

Shya looked behind her at Rory, then reached for his hand with one of hers. "You're so handsome," she whispered, and Rory pulled her to him while her friends laughed.

"You did it again," he said quietly when they pulled apart.

"What?"

"You said it like you were saying goodbye."

All she could do was shake her head and swallow the lump of sorrow in her throat. She peered around at her friends, landing on Dawn. "Let's get this done."

Dawn hugged her tight, and then they were filing out. Sheila and Mel talked quietly about details Shya only caught bits and pieces of as they all dressed to leave. *Protect the boy... focus on freeing him rather than... have to watch Shya...* Rory supported her as she put her shoes on, his hand ever on her arm, his eyes ever watching.

When they all filed into Connor's, Bethie hung back, tugging on Shya's elbow. Rory stayed by default; Shya had proven to be shakier than even she had realized. He stood behind her so she could rest back against his chest. "I think we should go in," Shya frowned at her old friend, who seemed perpetually tearful in her older, thinner state.

"I know. I just... I had a dream today when you were in with Jordan, and it scared me."

Shya shook her head. "I'm no stranger to scary dreams, Bethie, but how can it even compare to the reality we find ourselves in?"

She reached out, grabbed Shya's forearm. "Connor told me not to say anything, but I love you. I – I have to."

Shya glanced through the screen door and saw Connor at the far end of the hallway, flanked on either side by Jane and Anna, but looking at her. She waved feebly. "We have to go in, Bethie."

"Just..." she pulled a bit on Shya's arms to regain her attention. Shya clenched her jaw against a protest. She looked hard at Bethie. "I'm sorry. But - just – don't give in, Shya. You might feel like you have to, but..."

"I'm not scared, Bethie." She said it quietly. Flashes of Jordan's rocky shore played on a reel in her head, but it was true. "Look," she straightened, squeezing Bethie's arms, now, "I know it wants me, and it's clever. It has my *mother*." Bethie winced. "But it doesn't know everything, Bethie. It doesn't know how much support I have." Her chest filled again, that little voice in her head whispering something new. Something about how loved Shya had found herself to be, and just in time. "I'm ready," she hugged Bethie, her heart as full as it had ever been, and perhaps more than it had been since her mother's death.

Rory kissed her neck, his arms around her waist. "Be careful, Shy."

There was a sound from inside. Connor cried out, and there was a crash – something falling and shattering – and then Bethie was gasping, her fingers flying to her mouth when she looked into the hallway.

And he was there, the tiny child so near death, standing just inside the entrance with torn fragments of linen hanging from his wrists and a grotesque smile stretching his gaunt features. And he started laughing, and it was a guttural sound no child could make, doubled over in an eerie chorus that no single human could accomplish. And then he started to teeter, his eyes rolling back in his head and his face going slack, and Rory and Connor were both running to him, the screen door slamming into the wall as Bethie supported Shya.

But then Shya was pulling away too, toward the boy, crawling on all fours when she crumbled, then taking his hands when Rory pulled him onto his lap, Connor getting there last and falling, crying, his forehead pressed against the bony shoulder of his boy as he sobbed his name. "Jordan. Baby. Please hold on."

And Shya saw the boy retreat into himself and knew it would have to be there, in the hallway. "Dawn!" she cried, and then reached for his hands, and as she was sucked into that other place, was aware of her friends gathering around, aware of the priest and the twins closing in to do a hallway exorcism, The Seer's way.

CHAPTER 56 – THE SEER'S WAY

The first part happened fast. She burst through storm clouds as though she were the rain itself, but by the time she landed in the thick emerald grass, it was no longer dark, and the sunshine was sweet on her face. There was a slight breeze and she turned on the spot as if to follow it, and recognized the place immediately: she was in Jordan's back yard again, where he'd found the featherless bird. Where she'd held him with arms that weren't her own, and had a picnic.

And in that moment, she realized they'd skipped the crimson shoreline entirely, and not only that, but she was herself. An observer, proven by the fact that there, in the middle of the lawn, were Jordan and Lauren on the checked picnic blanket, and she was tickling him, and he was laughing and it was music; there was nothing there but joy. But there was a pang in her chest, a wistful torrent that insisted on breaking through, a wish for the moment to stretch on into forever and the simultaneous knowledge that she was intruding. That reality waited. That it was time for Jordan to leave, lest he be trapped in this place that would mean his death.

The breeze changed, and Lauren looked up, suddenly, her smile faltering when she caught sight of Shya. Jordan saw her, too, but quickly turned back to his mother. Clung to her, clamoured onto her lap, began crying when Shya stepped forward.

Lauren spoke quietly into his ear and he shook his head, refusing to hear. He squeezed his eyes shut but his tears persevered, streaming down fat cheeks even as they hollowed out. Clung to his mother's hand even as it turned skeletal.

Shya neared them, bending to her knees at the edge of the blanket. Lauren peered at her sadly.

"Do you remember what we talked about, sweetheart?" she said as she dipped her mouth to Jordan's ear. "About all the life you have ahead of you? All the happy things you have to do?"

Jordan pressed his face into her chest, but quickly pulled away, for she was hard where she once was soft, all bones and sick and impending death. His eyes went to her face. "You're sick again!" he cried, his fingers shakily tracing a cheekbone.

"Not in my special place," she said, taking his hand and kissing the tips of his fingers.

"Then let's go there!" his face lit up and Shya's heart protested at the squeezing fist of emotion that gathered there.

Lauren laughed. "You're so clever, sweetheart. And someday, we will see each other there."

He peered up at her, his wasted chin trembling.

"But not until you've *lived*." She touched the end of his nose and he reached up for her. Lauren looked at Shya again as they embraced. Begging with her eyes, for just as Jordan had realized his mother's state, she could see his. It was now or never.

Shya crawled to them, the grass poking through the blanket to tickle her palms. She touched Jordan's shoulder. "It's time to go," she said, and it happened, as if on cue: the darkening sky, the distant threat of thunder. Jordan peered over his shoulder at Shya, his eyes swimming with fear. She reached for him. "I'll take you back. Your Daddy's waiting." Something of a realized promise flashed in his eyes.

Thunder split the air above them and they all cringed,

ducking away from the crack. And then there was another noise, barely there, but unmistakable. A baby bird chirped from the grass by the house. Jordan's face transfixed as he gazed in that direction, and when Shya looked, too, she saw it floundering, drowning in a sea of grass, its naked wings fluttering weakly as it cried.

"He's OK too," Lauren said, loudly, because the rain had started, and it was fierce, assaulting them, it seemed, from all directions. Sharp. Cold.

Shya held her arms out for the boy, feeling desperately like grabbing him up regardless of his willingness to go, but managing to hold back as he peered up at his mother, crying, "*He is?*"

Lauren nodded. "He has a special place, too. He visits me sometimes. He loves you very much, you know, for trying to save him!"

The thunder roared with the strength of more than just nature. There was a demon in the storm, and all of them knew it.

"Don't stop loving, Jordy!" Lauren held her son's face in her hands. "But *live,* son! Live the best life you can have!"

Jordan nodded, but still clutched at her wrists.

"I'll be watching... I'll be so proud of you! I already am," she cried, her tears competing with the rain for purchase on thin-skinned cheeks. She kissed his forehead, then nodded toward Shya, whose arms were still reaching, pelted with rain and trembling as the demon roared behind the thunder again, but then Jordan came to her, turning and leaping into her arms in one, swift movement that nearly toppled her. And then indeed they were falling, and Shya was patting his back and pointing to his mother as they fell away from her and she was standing, waving, healthy in the renewed sun. Jordan giggled as he waved, and clung excitedly to Shya as they fell, his face rapt with love as he watched his mother fade.

And then that place was gone, blinking out and taking Lauren with it, and Shya and Jordan gazed into each other's faces as they fell through endless space, each wondering at the presence of the other.

"Hi," he said, and she laughed, and then there was a pull at her back and they were being separated. He clutched at her and then at the air as they parted and she saw there was something in the distance pulling him. To her great relief, it was the scene she'd left just a short time ago, in Connor's hallway. She saw Jordan in Rory's lap, saw him fluttering his eyes and looking up at Rory, confused, and then finding his father and saying something. And Connor pulling him to his chest, crying, laughing, celebrating.

But Rory was looking toward her. Scowling. He said something, but she couldn't hear him. He was so far away. Shya twisted to search for her own destination, her heart racing. Something was wrong. And there it was: the darkened shoreline built of Jordan's fears, but different, now. Changed, for her.

"No!" she cried, and it took everything she had to turn back to Rory again, but she did it, muscles singing with effort and lungs straining to give strength to her words and panic taking hold when they came up short.

I'm dying, she thought, and in an instant, she was pulsing with adrenaline. She kicked her feet in the nothing and reached for that faraway place where Rory was... where Jordan had finally gone, too. She thought of what she'd seen in the place down below and willed herself away from it: a reflection of her own terrors, where her mother dwelt in never-ending sickness and Shya, in all ways, lost the sense of home she'd only just realized in her friends and in Rory... and maybe in her own father, too, for the first time in her life. And a dark soul who sought her own bright energy to grow strong on. To use as its own. She screamed and pushed away from it, reaching, reaching, and something happened; suddenly, there were hands reaching back, closer and closer as she kicked and swam up in an ocean of quicksand just trying to pull her down.

And then the hands had her and they were pulling her out, pulling her up, pulling her back to where there were friends and there were sounds of joy and exaltation and where Jordan smiled lazily as his father kissed his face over and over again.

CHAPTER 57 – POST-MORTEM

The atmosphere at Connor's was surreal after it all happened. Bethie and Connor were singly focussed on Jordan, who gladly accepted spoonfuls of Froot Loops and milk from Bethie as his father encouraged him to let them bring him to the hospital, just to get him checked out. *Just to make sure you're OK.*

Jordan smiled whenever Shya caught his eye. Even gave her a thumbs-up now and then. She could see the precocious little boy he was, then, and it was enough to soothe her heart… if not her worried mind.

Her friends spoke eagerly of the events of the preceding days, revisiting each high point and low point repeatedly. They spoke to Ed on speaker, telling him everything. Ed was quiet.

Shya was, too.

Rory seemed to sense it. He stood beside her, hand gently rubbing her shoulder, hugging her to him as if he could sense that though she was present in body, she seemed disconnected in all other ways. And she was.

She couldn't deny that Jordan was back, all the way, and that in her heart of hearts she knew he'd be alright. And she was here, too, and she had the comfort of friends who'd risk their lives to ensure the safety of any of the others. And Rory. Finally, she had Rory. Not to mention her father, who'd shown up at some point and sat smiling in the living room, seemingly pleased just to be there in the aftermath and celebration.

But she couldn't deny the things she'd seen: the altered shoreline that was the Hell that awaited her. The power of sorrow when it overpowered love. The return and captivity of her mother to the most terrible part of her life.

And she was still there.

She looked around at her friends and family, feeling sick, because no matter what had happened, the fact still remained: her mother was missing. And what could she do? Could she ask The Seers to help her go back? To help her save a ghost from a demon? They'd already done so much.

She saw Jane and Anna eyeing her from the other side of the room, and knew without a doubt that nobody had forgotten. It was only a matter of time before they devised a plan to save her mother... but somehow, the knowledge didn't comfort her. Of them all, Jordan was the only one who'd tasted the vast power of what wanted Shya, still.

How could she ever hope to defeat it? How could any of them?

And that was what held her back from celebrating, kept her quiet in the corner. Yes, things were better for Jordan, and she could see the way Bethie and Connor locked promise-filled gazes over the recovering child. But the veil of her own peril was dark, and it stood between her and the others, unrelenting.

CHAPTER 58 –
SURRENDER

Dawn insisted on returning to Shya's childhood home with them instead of staying with the group. Connor had invited them all to stay and they'd happily accepted, sprawling on cushions and furniture in the living room as someone built a fire, all wanting to be together. All wanting to be close, because although they wouldn't say it, there was the fear of it's return, even when Jordan went to sleep in his father's bedroom, insisting on Bethie sleeping on the other side of him. A Jordan sandwich, Connor had said, eyes twinkling.

But Dawn had followed them out the door, and chatted happily to Shya's father as they drove. And when they got inside, she went with Shya to the bathroom, meeting Rory's eyes when he'd laughed. And Shya was fine with her presence. Relieved when Dawn took up her toothbrush and instructed her to open her mouth so she could do the work while singing the alphabet. She laughed when Dawn kissed her on the tip of her nose and told her she was a good girl, and held on to her while she led her to the bedroom.

She listened when Rory asked if everything was alright and Dawn told him to stay close all night. Told him that if he got too tired, to switch off with Shya's father to watch her, because she was vulnerable, and too tired to fight, *should there be a reason to.* Drifted as Dawn whispered to her. *Just don't fall, sweet girl, and don't let that fear take you down. We're all here, OK? And we're gonna get your Mama, don't you worry.* And she felt better, then, like she could go to sleep and it would be alright.

But Dawn had long departed, back to Mel and the group when she spiraled down again, and landed on that shoreline and found it wasn't changed entirely. It made sense, though, that the bones and little bodies were still the rocks; it was worthy of anyone's nightmares, after all, and after discovering that part of Jordan's terror, it was only natural that it became part of her own. But other things were different: with the desertion of Jordan came the solvency of many of his fears. The crimson edges had vanished, and she knew she wouldn't see his back yard again.

And then there were the things she'd introduced into the landscape: there was the smell of her mother's room as she lay dying, and there were spirits, hoards of them on the periphery, but never close enough to hear. Just trying, trying desperately to gain her attention. And there were trees bordering the edges of the shore rather than cliffs. And distant sounds of children laughing. It would be Halloween here, always. But despite the hints of others nearby, she knew they'd never present themselves, for the most important element she'd influenced here was that she was alone as the ghosts tried to bombard her. No friends, no love, no new sense of home, finally, in a world that had always felt foreign. Here, everything she'd worked to gain was lost to her, never to be found again.

Except, of course, for the tree, which she spotted with surprise. She'd forgotten... but how? How had it hidden from her, here? But soon she saw it wasn't just familiar, wasn't just a tree. It was *the* tree, gnarled and barren, completely out of place on the deserted shoreline bordering the water and the bone-rocks. *It's the demon, the fourth of Hell, the King. Asmodeus.* It reached for her as she thought its name, and suddenly she was there, wound up in its vine-like arms as it whispered garbled half-promises: a different sort of belonging, an equating of hate to love, of destruction and new horizons, and then it pointed with gnarled bark-fingers and she looked out to sea and it was there. The sickbed. The chains. The withered carcass of her dying mother. The demon made promises about her, too, and though none of them would bring her back, nor did any hint at release for Shya, they were all better than *this.*

She teetered on the brink of letting go, part of her desperate for another way, but none of her seeing it.

Then, it made a final offer. It beckoned the bed to the shore and as it neared, her mother was sitting, not chained, and looking at her, worried, but *alive* or alive *here* and that was OK. That was good. Her mother started to shake her head, the beginning of a warning, but Shya barely saw it because the demon whispered, still. *Only if you stay with me,* it said and reluctantly she brought her eyes back to the thing that had entwined itself around and through her, root and stem and branch and twig and teeth and darkness, too and knew that there was no other way. No way to refuse without being torn apart. No way to feel the presence of her mother without losing herself.

So, while Rory watched her sleep in some other place, she took a deep clean breath in and it soured in her lungs as she closed her eyes, accepting, knowing everything would sour, here. Everything would rot and die, but death wouldn't be the end of suffering, no, not in that place. But still she gave herself over, on the cresting wave of molten tar that flowed inside the veins of the thing she was a part of. Knew she grew with it, now, rooting deep into the earth, beneath the sand and sea to where there was heat and fire and dark and pain, but at least there would be her mother. And at least the boy was safe.

And, finding that new purpose to be meaningful, the shame that had plagued her since it all began shriveled up until it was diminished and she let go. Gave up.

Surrendered.

CHAPTER 59 – RAVEN

Overhead, in times of dark and lines of light

The raven travels through them all on lofty currents flight

It sees them all, the living and the dead to him are like

Just wandering souls making their way through realms of death and life

Through the mire he seeks a treasure, his great glittering eyes are shrewd

He knows light, though he from depths of fiery bowels was spewed

Long lost the knowing of forgiveness, lost to the battle that ensued

When light and dark were ripped asunder and sickness of warring brewed

It seeks out the bright things, counterpoints to balance a hollow heart

Brightness that fills the corners and empty spaces love did part

It reminds the winged creature it was different at the start

Thought it can't untwist the tortured soul, cannot

light the endless dark

All light dwindles, dear one, even brighter ones like you

Do not think you are immune to what time will doubtless do

But before then, let me pluck you from the life you suffer true

Let me make use of that light you hold, as only I can do

Do not tremble, do not contemplate

Don't refuse, wish or run

For I have you, little bright star

And have already begun

Watch for The Seers Series Volume 2:

Soul Seer

Spring, 2021

THE SEERS SERIES - ADDENDUM 1

The Dark Poetry of Shya,
Spirit Talker

Solace

A darkened night
An unlit stair
She left her bed
And found her there

Led by her whispers
Murmurs, fissures
Desperate tones
Spells and wishes

And the voice
That answered back
Was cold and dark
A filtered trap

She stops inside
The door, ajar
Her mother there
But her eyes far

Affixed on something
Left unseen
Frosting the air
Window glass a sheen

More careful mutters
From Mother's lips
Warm breath a cloud
A sinking ship

And then a gasp
Escapes her, lost
A whoosh of movement
Rough seas toss

A cry escapes
The tiny girl
Mother cries out
Shocked, she whirls

"Shya!" she gasps
Extends her arms
Soft, spirit fades
With threat of harm

The Absence of Rain

It should've rained that day
It would've been an expected presence
But like you, it stayed away

You – your body – that was there
The shell that had held your effervescence
All frigid skin and strange, dull hair

And then you were there, too
Shrunk to my size and drenched in heaven
The wispy, lighter shade of you

Ghost of my mother, eyes alight
An introduction to life's new lessons
A gentle transition to my towering plight

Full, softly then came your embrace
Impossible cocoon, singular impression
Full grown behind your childish face

What monumental task to come
To traverse the boundaries, get through the frission
For an embrace beneath unlikely sun

It should've rained that day
Sky black and pendulous to threaten
But the sun brought you, sweet relief, solid joy, in the most
magnificent of ways

Just

Breathing, just
And listen
Just mist gath'ring in air

Just waiting
To be christened
With my protector fair

Just breath
And fear and whispers
Will you stay? I ask, and tarry

Just love
Cover and glisten
Lavender, sweet orange, rosemary

Just a blast
Dark against light
Menacing, blows her away

Just death
Crossing the boundaries
Tortured with answers long unknown

Just passing
On the story
Of the thing that made him gone

Just embers
For his eyes
Flowing lava 'neath charred flesh

Just words
I burned - two words
To tell the story of his death

The Dark

Do you feel them creeping there?
Beyond the door, under the stair
Roiling belly, whisper, glare
Dark energy dwells there

You're right to shun the musty rooms
Forgotten casket, eternal tombs
Headache pulsing, thick dread looms
Heavy heart, impending doom

They reach with twisted fingers, limbs
Hot, bubbling beneath the skin
Incite the boiling fear within
Paint canvasses of chain-linked sin

Once tethered, they will grasp and hold
With frost-lined tendrils, veins of cold
Infused with thoughts and dreams so bold
To terrify, sicken and drain when told

So do not let them hang from you
Dripping menace, sticky dew
Hell's honey clinging endless to
The secret danker spots in you

Turn body and mind's eye away
Tward lighter thoughts, dwell in the day
Let paths of good lead you and sway
Your tendency to joyful play

Turn, child, be safe! Build solid home
Between sinew and blood and bone
Hold strength and comfort, lessons shown
Your beating heart is not alone

Creep

There are those nights when darkness comes and eats up
daylight without pause
When sunlight dips and fades the day and brilliant sunset
fades to grey
When creatures slow, forget their work, hide in their homes
while spirits lurk
They're always there, but in the dark, they need not hide
neath ruse and hark
Silence pulls the mindless hoards, lost energies from times of
lords
And ladies lost to tragedy, ne'er satisfied nor drawn to flee
Untethered souls with forgotten purpose seek out the living
and entreat us
To connect with warmth and kindness, learn the tales of how
they left us
And sometimes they delight to find those gifted few who
cannot hide
Who hear them, see them and abide the unreal tales from
unseen sides
And if they've found one of the sought out few who have some
skill in what they do
There is a path revealed to them to end their torturous
suffering and
They can let go, ungrounded, soar where earthy sorrows are
no more

Shameful

Summer sixteen
And you're new in my life
Friend, boy and brother
Your mom my dad's wife

Gaping hollows, you teach me
When all my friends fly
Fill the gaps with attention
Feed my courage – or try

Summer sixteen
I ponder your caterpillar lip
Rough stubble at your chin
Your hand at my hip

Clouds above
Listless, sailing through oceans of sky
You are not what you seem
What's that light in your eye?

Summer sixteen
You teach me that touch has been missed
But you shouldn't have been
The first boy that I kissed

Summer twenty
I found a replacement for you
Rather, less shameful options
To incite the feelings you do

But I never could look
At your face without feeling
Your lips moving on mine
In that summer of healing

Missed

The silence of your signals
Or my choice not to hear
Or see them flashing brightly
Or feel them through my fear

The weight of my assumptions
My heavy wall to bear
Knocks all your efforts back
Regardless if it's fair

The ease to misinterpret
Has roots deep in my past
My mother's early gift
Through her own death did pass

And at the same time managing
My sudden empty home
The ghost of my live father
Who, quiet, long atoned

And normal life confused me
Each day past my home's door
My timely hopes and teenaged dreams
Fall flat onto the floor

Resentment built within me
Not only for my fate
But for other's hands in it
Too sad, too strange, too late

So, you were disadvantaged
You entered at the break
Your mother took the last
Of my dad there was to take

A precedent was set, then
With you inside its core
My confusion only mounting
Do you want less, or more?

So, crossed, mixed or warning
With humour, play or dark
Your signals try and fail
To reach their intended mark

I see you struggle onward
As life so fast unfolds
Frustrated in your own right
As I fail to crack the code

Conversation

Calm down
Speak more softly
But use much less words
And stop crying; it doesn't help, but know you've been heard

I'm so sorry
I ran
When I left our childhood home
Followed a man we'd both loved, who broke my heart and then
some

Sorry to laugh
But are you saying
You followed Drake off to school
And learned too late he wasn't worth all you'd sacrificed?

I was a fool!

I can't deny that
But what does it have to do
With this boy and how he's haunted?
Why's it you who's reaching out to help the one being taunted?

I missed you, Shya
But was ashamed
And so reached out on my own
I gathered friends, we got a board, asked for guidance... it was a game!

Oh, Beth
I told you never
Don't ever use such a thing
How could you forget my warnings of all the dark it could bring?

I can't say
Sorry enough
But it's too late now, you see?
I brought the monster back home. I resisted, but he couldn't, could he?

His mother's absence – it was her funeral I travelled home for
And it was so good to see Connor's face at the door!
Can you imagine, after all those years we all suffered for, that it was
him all along that my heart yearned for?

My God, Bethie
You're selfish
I can't believe what you say
And now I know it's your fault the demon has him. For shame!

I hate myself
And Connor hates me
And you hate me more
For bringing something that clung long to me to their door!

But you can help
That's why I'm calling
I don't ask for myself
I ask for Jordan who's too weak to get hold of himself

Please, old friend
Put aside
All our tensions and past
Please, for Connor, come quickly. It's not for me that I ask

I'll come
Not for you
I know now I was right
To swear you off, to drop our friendship, to face alone my dark night

I come for Jordan
For his father
And I'll bring all my friends
But know this: you're not forgiven, not now or after this ends

Calm Before the Storm

I'd heard the words before
Without grasping their full meaning
How one's path in quiet lull
On the precipice is leaning

Unaware in grace or fall
That a breath could tip it sideways
And the choice is made for all
Forks dissolve, path crystallizes

Then step and kindred step
Into chaos manifested
And gentle slips behind
Past and present drawn and tested

Pray, heed my words and warning
In heavy apathy's seduction
Poised, alert and wary of
The beast that waits, bent on destruction

Dying Mother

Please don't say you're sorry anymore
You've taught me all you could, and then some more
Blanketed me with anecdotes and lore
You've been tossed on stormy seas, now come ashore

The fighting spark is dimming in your eyes
Though still you whisper, still you teach and try
You linger on intention, love and sighs
Protecting me from those whom in darkness lie

The worn and weary thread to which you cling
Runs down the time to linger, rope to string
And tattered dregs of fluid, flesh and all physical thing
Hold far less promise than release will ultimately bring

You've given me what I need most to know
Instructions to accompany the gift you will bestow
Let me lie beside you, match your breathing oh so scant and slow
Feel the essence of you change as you finally let go

Mother, death has changed you – and changed me!
I wonder if I manage to be all you hoped for me to be
The presence of your ghost, it carried and comforted me
It's all I had for so long, but now it eludes me

Come back I whisper as I lay my weary head
Upon the flattened fluff that was the pillow of my bed
I'll look for you in dreams, where living souls meet with the dead
Come to me there, lost mother; ease the looming sense of dread

I glimpse you there but only in the beating of my heart
A warmth about my shoulders, comforting me from the start
But quick I'm woken long before the sentiment imparts
A distant scream from one possessed does split the air and hark

Come back I cry into the empty stillness of the air
Come back, mother left too soon, a loss too hard to bear
Come back I say. I took your soul for granted – how unfair!
And without you I fear I lose my compass, lose my care

I'm here, a gentle pressure of your hand smoothing my hair
I'm here... lemongrass, rosemary, sweet orange in the air
But then it whips you back with the love you tried to share
And roars inside my being, leaving searing pain to bear

Not again, little bright star
Do not tiptoe past again
Let this little headache serve to warn you
Do not dare to try again

Raven

Overhead, in times of dark and lines of light
The raven travels through them all on lofty currents flight
It sees them all, the living and the dead to him are like
Just wandering souls making their way through realms of death and life

Through the mire he seeks a treasure, his great glittering eyes are shrewd
He knows light, though he from depths of fiery bowels was spewed
Long lost the knowing of forgiveness, lost to the battle that ensued
When light and dark were ripped asunder and sickness of warring brewed

It seeks out the bright things, counterpoints to balance a hollow heart
Brightness that fills the corners and empty spaces love did part
It reminds the winged creature it was different at the start
Thought it can't untwist the tortured soul, cannot light the endless dark

All light dwindles, dear one, even brighter ones like you
Do not think you are immune to what time will doubtless do
But before then, let me pluck you from the life you suffer true
Let me make use of that light you hold, as only I can do

Do not tremble, do not contemplate
Don't refuse, wish or run
For I have you, little bright star
And have already begun

BOOKS BY THIS AUTHOR

Rose's Ghost - The Trilogy

When the dead seek justice for tragedies unsolved, the living will be called to piece the puzzle together.

Viktor and Rose Maplestone built their house in the woods as a hideaway, but their safe haven became a prison when those left behind failed to join them, proving to be lost or killed. When Rose and Viktor join those who've gone before, there is one left to solve the puzzle of his ancestors. But Greyson isn't alone; he has help from living friends and the ghosts of family.

In this complete collection:

Follow Rose in a quest to find her lost baby.

Join in on the search for an unmarked grave.

And finally, solve the riddle of Greyson's past.

Rose's Ghost

She just wanted her baby back. Rose's Ghost is the first book in a series of three about a family's connection with a tormented ghost, still desperate to gain back the child she lost.Rose remains tethered to her family's property, beseeching those who reside upon or around it to help in her quest. But somewhere between her death and the haunting of Maggie Ridgewood's family, Rose's reality has become darkly skewed, and her efforts to find her child threaten to alter the lives of those whose help she enlists – or end them.

Heather's Grave

Rose is at rest, but the haunting of the Ridgewood family continues in Heather's Grave: Book 2 of the Rose's Ghost series. Maggie is relieved to have found peace in the Ridgewood family home, having solved the mystery of Rose Maplestone. But with the onset of new adventures as she and Jack prepare for their new addition comes more ominous change. Max is forced to admit his anxiety stems from more than regret over his role in saving Alice Ridgewood from Rose's ghost. His body is sick, too. And the tragedies of the Maplestone family didn't end with Rose, for after all, the child she lost was a secret in life – her existence unrecorded and unacknowledged - except by those who'd witnessed it all. And as her desperation to honor her child grows, Rose determines to help Maggie in the strangest of ways – raising questions around her intent. Does Rose mean to help, as she's vowed, or do her methods force an ultimatum instead, wherein the life of Maggie's child depends on the finding of hers?

Dmitry's Shadow

Greyson is grateful for the peace he's found with the help of his friends, but all is not yet well; the questions of his ancestry remain. Why did Viktor Kotova flee his home country? Who was left behind? Amidst rumours of a family connection with the mafia and the suspicious circumstances surrounding his grandfather's death, there are ghosts that linger, insistent on the solving of the Kotova family puzzle. So, Greyson and the property of his family home - once abandoned and then demolished - remain haunted, and like his mother before him, he enlists the help of those who reside upon it.

But Max and Maggie are fighting demons of their own, and Charis finds her world rocked by the dark patches in her vision. Will they be able to pull together and face the truths of a buried past? And will the answers they find bring long-awaited closure to a man whose life is just beginning at the age of seventy-four?

Asylum

From the creator of the Rose's Ghost series comes another thrilling tale: Asylum proves to be a ghost story that stands on its own.

We follow Bailey O'Connor on an exciting urban exploration trip across the border to discover the secrets of a long-abandoned institution for mentally and physically handicapped children. But there's more than just mystery darkening the crumbling buildings they discover, and Bailey finds herself lost within them with the help of those who linger.

The search for her is mounted during the day while her own search takes place in the dark. Are the rumors true? The whisperings of experiments performed on the innocent and vulnerable? What secrets lurk within the few impenetrable buildings on the site? Most importantly, can the truth be uncovered before the property is leveled and its secrets are buried forever? Told in Dale's unique voice, readers both familiar and new will appreciate an engaging cast of characters and a compelling story that is hard to put down.

Constance & Enzo's Tea Time With Peyton

From the author of the Rose's Ghost Trilogy and Asylum comes a thrilling new tale featuring familiar characters...

Peyton's come a long way from the awkward twelve-year-old girl we met in That Summer, but her incredible gift is still wreaking havoc with her life. In her ongoing quest to find others like her, she's unknowingly left a trail of breadcrumbs to her front door – for commiserating friends and desperate souls, alike.

But she couldn't have predicted the lengths one visiting stranger would go to take advantage of her ability to talk to the dead. She's never been good at predicting the actions of people, dead or alive, But this time her weakness - combined with the all-encompassing need of her captor - results in her disappearance.

Her advantage? Those who love her will do everything they can to find her and bring her home, including the recruitment of two uniquely qualified women. Will Margot - a pioneer in the world of science and the supernatural, and Charis - a sometimes reluctant, but highly gifted psychic - succeed in using their own special talents to see clues the police simply can't?

Chrysalis

In Chrysalis, we explore the quiet underworld of an ultra-conservative Canadian city. Our unlikely hero, Trey, is an energy-seeing, cross-dressing sex worker on the precipice of a life or death decision, but when a friend goes missing, he finds himself distracted from the business of self-destruction.

Desperate to find his missing colleague, twenty-four-year-old Trey finds himself part of an unusual group, from a deranged kidnapper to a devoted cop, all focused on a missing girl. And when confronted with these Canadian people, dealing with both human and Canadian issues, we find ourselves suspending our judgement on characters we'd often prefer to look past.Through it all, we witness Trey's chance at transformation – will he be able to set himself on a new direction in life as he finally begins to understand that being different doesn't necessarily mean you don't belong?

Bird With A Broken Wing

A fourteen-year-old girl living in a rural community of Nova Scotia, a group of neighborhood kids, and hours spent exploring or just hanging out in the woods and on the train tracks along the river.

Bird With A Broken Wing brings us back to a time when the best thing about evenings and weekends was heading outside to find your friends - but there is nothing typical about Margot's new friend, Wren. And the new family at the bottom of the hill knows why.

Just as she tries to accept her feelings of being perpetually left behind, Margot discovers some of the different faces of love in the most unexpected way.

That Summer

Twelve-year-old Peyton is dealing with an Asperger's diagnosis and a summer spent away from her parents. Everything changes for her that summer, but it takes some new friends - live and ghosts alike - to get through it all. In the end, she not only learns that being herself is her best option, but that she can make a positive difference in the lives of others, too.

Soul Seer

Dawn prides herself on her strength as a leader, and her confidence hasn't let The Seers down... until Shya's possession, which every member of the group blames themselves for, Dawn included. But the confrontation of her own weaknesses uncovers more about her past – and the present! – than Dawn was prepared to face.

As they all travel to Shya's family home again, uncertainty seems to be the only constant they can rely on. Mel and Ed are absent, the twins have a terrible secret they've yet to share, Sheila is riddled with anxiety, Dawn seems to be the vessel through which Shya sends her cryptic messages in the form of poetry, and the world is suffering the effects of the portal ripped in the boundary between the living and the dead.

Can they close the portal and save Shya, too? As the group falls victim to the demon's trickery, their faith is badly rattled, and Dawn hasn't a clue how to make it all better.

www.ingramcontent.com/pod-product-compliance
Lightning Source LLC
Chambersburg PA
CBHW072125250626
47159CB00007B/2567